BOGEY'S ACE

A BOGEY MYSTERY

To Dorothy,
Thank you for your friendship and your valuable suggestions.
M

by
Marja McGraw

Marja McGraw

Oak Tree Press 🌳 Taylorville, IL

Oak Tree Press

Oak Tree Press books may be purchased for educational, business or sales promotional purposes. Contact Publisher for quantity discounts.

First Edition, February 2012

Cover by Suzanne Kelly

Interior Pages by Linda W. Rigsbee

Front Cover Art by Andy Kohut

ISBN 978-1-61009-047-6
LCCN 2012930603

DEDICATION

To the Church Ladies in my life. Thank you for being there and remaining true to your beliefs, and for your senses of humor.

ACKNOWLEDGEMENTS

Thank you to Dorothy Bodoin, my critique partner and close friend, whose gentle comments spur me on. My appreciation to Judy Lang, my sister, who has turned into a great critique partner. Thank you to all of the people who've taken the time to create lists of forties slang, and to all the writers of vintage mystery movies who supplied me with even more words and phrases. Al McGraw, I appreciate the patience you've shown when I disappear into my office and lose myself in the world of mysteries and computers.

And most of all, thank you to the voices of my characters who constantly ignore what I want to do and push me in directions I never expected to go.

CHAPTER ONE

"**P**amela, there are some women sitting at the bar and they're asking for you."

Someone was tapping on my shoulder and whispering in my ear. Turning around, I found Daniel, our bartender, looking at me with a question in his eyes. I raised my eyebrows at him with a question of my own. Who wanted to see me?

"They said it's a matter of life and death. I asked them if I could give you their names, and they said, 'Just tell her the Church Ladies are here.'"

"The Church Ladies are here? It's a matter of life or death? And they're in our cocktail lounge? *Drinking?*" I wanted to gulp, but my mouth had suddenly gone dry.

"Two are drinking iced tea and one is having wine."

"Wine?"

"Are you aware that you're repeating what I say to you?" he asked.

"I am?"

He shrugged his shoulders and left me standing there while he returned to his station.

The Church Ladies? The *Church Ladies!* Sitting in our cocktail lounge? A feeling of dread seeped into my heart. These were good women, but sometimes they were trouble. If they'd come into the restaurant for dinner, I wouldn't be worried. But they'd bypassed the restaurant and seated themselves at our bar. It seemed like these women usually had some kind of a crusade going. I wondered what it could be this time, and how I figured into it. I could hear 1940s music playing in the lounge. They'd like that, I was sure.

Glancing around at my surroundings, I stalled for time. My husband and I had opened our restaurant, *Bogey Nights*, in Los Angeles less than a year ago, after our original restaurant burned to the ground. It had been an old house, built in the 1920s, and we'd renovated and remodeled it into a restaurant and cocktail lounge with dancing. I couldn't help but feel some pride as I looked around at the tables, all full, and listened to the hum of voices. The smiling faces should have added to a feeling of well-being. They didn't.

I finally spotted Chris at the front door greeting some new customers. The restaurant had a forties theme – and so did my husband who was a dead ringer for Humphrey Bogart.

After waiting until the customers had been seated, I waved Chris over. On his way to meet me, he stopped and chatted with a few people.

I glanced at my watch impatiently. I'd already kept the Church Ladies waiting for about five minutes – probably not a good thing. I waved at Chris again, motioning for him to hurry up.

"What's the rush?" he asked, looking annoyed. "I can't just walk away from customers when they want to talk to me."

"*The Church Ladies are here*," I said, drama dripping from my every word.

"Who?"

"You know, the Church Ladies. I've talked about them before. The three ladies from my church who keep things stirred up all the time? Remember? Last time I mentioned them it was because they wanted everyone from the church to march on City Hall. They didn't like a remark the Mayor had made."

"Oh, *those* ladies."

"Yes, those ladies. They're here and they want something from me. They told Daniel that it was a matter of life or death. Of course, with them that could mean they haven't found any volunteers for their latest cause."

Chris sighed. "Pamela, why don't you go find out exactly what it is that they want? It may be nothing."

"Nothing? It's never nothing with these women. They're loveable little old ladies, but they very seldom take *no* for an answer. They wheedle and nag until we all do what they want us to just to keep them quiet. They're still seething because no one would join them on that City Hall march. That was practically a first."

"Just go talk to them. Find out what they want before you have a coronary. What could they possibly want from you anyway?"

Before I could respond, one of our waitresses approached to talk to Chris. Phyllis Sims looks like Marilyn Monroe, although she's a bit smaller than the original. Needless to say, we have a theme going at the restaurant.

"Mr. Cross, would you mind coming with me and talking to one of our customers? You were in the kitchen when they came in and they're intrigued by you and the restaurant. I think they might be from a magazine."

Phyllis always called Chris *Mr. Cross* when customers were within hearing distance. She and Myrna Loy, whose real name is Gloria Stark, had been with us since the beginning. They were loyal employees and friends, and we knew we'd be lost without them.

"I'll be right there, Phyllis. Which table?"

She pointed at a table by the window and went back to work.

Chris turned to me. "Okay, Pamela, find out what these women want. Don't worry until you find out what they need you to do – if anything."

"You're right. It's probably nothing. They came in here and went straight to the bar because they're closet lushes. Uh huh. If you see me waving at you again, come a'runnin', because… Well, just because."

All of us at the restaurant dressed in the styles of the forties, although occasionally I fudged and wore a thirties style, so I looked in the mirror before entering the bar, hoping I didn't look too weird because I'd be under the Church Ladies' scrutiny. What was I thinking? They probably grew up with the styles I wore to work.

I peeked around the corner of the doorway and studied the bar. Three elderly women sat there, heads together, quietly talking. Well, Jasmine Thorpe was doing the talking, and Lila James and May Martin were doing the listening. I wished for a moment that I could be the fly on the wall so I'd know ahead of time what was in store for me, but then I thought that with my luck that would be about the time the Health Department decided to do a check. No flies.

Jasmine took a deep breath and stopped talking to take a drink of her tea. Leaning in a bit farther, I checked to see who the wine drinker was. I could see tea in front of May, so that left Lila. Lila? I wouldn't have guessed it was her. I thought all three of them were teetotalers.

Although I didn't know their actual ages, I guessed that all three women were in their mid- to late seventies. Jasmine was still blonde. It suited her even at her age, and she was about my height, maybe five feet four or five. She was always impeccably dressed, and tonight was no exception. However, she was a… Hmm. She was what I'd call a solid woman. Not really overweight, but not small by any means – maybe somewhat buxom.

Lila had short gray hair and dressed like an old woman. She hadn't aged well, but when she smiled it always took about ten years off of her appearance. She had the most sincere, joyful smile I'd ever seen. I'd heard her friends, on more than one occasion, tell her she shouldn't age herself with her clothes and that she should have her hair styled and color it. On this night she wore a simple shapeless light blue dress and tennis shoes, and a large, floppy hat.

May seemed to be the most athletic of the group. She was tall and slender, and her salt and pepper hair was usually pulled back in a ponytail. She had on a flattering yellow dress, which surprised me. I'd never seen her in anything but slacks and a blouse or a jogging suit, except on Sundays at church services.

Taking a deep breath and steeling myself, I entered the cocktail lounge and sauntered over to the bar. "Good evening, ladies. I understand you wanted to see me?" I smiled broadly and hoped I didn't look nervous.

"Ah, Pamela," Jasmine said. "God bless you, and isn't that an adorable dress you're wearing? That shade of green goes so well with your auburn hair, and it really makes your eyes look even greener than they are naturally. Good selection on your part. Your forties theme here at the restaurant is commendable. Those were simpler times."

"I'm glad you like it. It's so nice to see all of you. Daniel said you have a matter of life or death to discuss with me. I can't imagine what anything like that might have to do with me."

The band started up another number and it became difficult for us to hear one another. I excused myself and asked them to take a short break when their song was over. It was only a four-piece band, but they sounded like there were ten of them. Occasionally the wife of one of the band members joined them and sang, but not tonight. Hiring The Sugar Daddies had been a good move on our part.

I returned my attention to the Church Ladies, stood at the bar, and explained that the band would be going on a break shortly. We all waited quietly for a few minutes and enjoyed the music. The band finally left for a break and I repeated my question. "So what does a life or death situation have to do with me?"

Jasmine glanced first at May, and then at Lila. Both women nodded their heads, and Lila said, "Go ahead. We need her help."

"Is this about the church bazaar?" I asked. "Because if it is, I've already signed up to work it on Saturday."

"No, it's not about the bazaar," Jasmine replied. "This is a very delicate matter and we believe you and your husband might be able to help us."

May and Lila were again nodding their heads.

"My husband?" This surprised me. Chris never got involved in church activities and the Church Ladies knew that. He always said he'd attend a service with me one day, but to date that hadn't happened. Once in a while he'd help with special projects, but that was the extent of his showing up at the church. I was getting a bad feeling now that they'd mentioned Chris.

"Yes, your husband. We need your help, but it doesn't have anything to do with the church, or even church activities. We read about the murders you solved before you opened this restaurant, and there's a situation that we believe you two are best suited to help us with. That's why we're here."

"Nothing to do with church? Murder? A situation?" I was beginning to sound like a parrot. These women seemed to bring out my dopey side.

"Yes, a situation. Would you like to ask your husband to join us before I tell you our story?" Jasmine took another swig of her tea, downing it as though it was liquor and would give her courage.

"No, I don't think so," I replied. "Why don't you tell me what's going on and then I'll decide if I should call him in?"

"If you think that's best," Lila said.

Jasmine glanced at May and Lila, and they nodded again. May fluttered her hands at Jasmine, as if to say, *Would you please get on with it*?

I sat down on the barstool next to Jasmine. I had a feeling that I might be glad I was sitting when I heard what they wanted.

"Okay, here's the deal," she said. "We have a friend named Addie. You don't know her because she goes to a different church. There are actually four of us Church Ladies, and yes, we know that's what everyone calls us. Addie is the fourth member of our little group. Addie is missing. We'd like you and your husband to find her."

"You'd like us to find her?"

"Dear, are you losing your hearing? You keep repeating what I say. Isn't that a sign of hearing loss?"

I took a moment to think over what she'd said before I replied. This wasn't at all what I'd been expecting. It wasn't church business. It was a missing person.

"No, I'm fine. I'm just surprised. How long has your friend been missing? And have you called the police yet?"

"She's been missing since this morning," Lila said.

"We did call the police," May added, "but they're not interested yet."

"She hasn't been missing long enough," Jasmine explained.

I was struggling with myself while I listened to the ladies. I was tempted to roll my eyes, a bad habit of mine, but my brain was telling me not to do it under any circumstances. These ladies wouldn't understand.

"How do you know she's missing if she's only been gone since this morning? Couldn't she be out shopping or something?" I willed my eyeballs to stay in place.

Jasmine had a very determined expression on her face. "No. We were supposed to go out to lunch together, and she never showed up. The three of us drove over to her house, and she wasn't there. She never misses one of our lunches."

"Never." Lila shook her head.

"Not ever." May shook her head in unison with Lila.

I almost shook my own head. "What makes you think she's actually missing? Couldn't something have come up that required her immediate attention? Did you at least ask the police to do a welfare check on her?"

"The police went to her home at our request. They didn't go in, but they looked through the windows and it didn't appear that anything was out of place. And like I said, she hasn't been missing for long, so they're not very interested. They said to get back to them if she doesn't turn up." Jasmine pressed her lips together after she spoke and folded her arms across her ample bosom. She made a formidable picture.

"Let me ask again. Why do you think she's missing?" I needed something more concrete than just the fact that she'd missed a lunch with her friends.

Jasmine unpressed her lips long enough to answer me. "We all have keys to each other's homes, in case of an accident or something. I mean, after all, we're not youngsters anymore. So we drove over to Addie's and went in to make sure she hadn't fallen or had some other accident. She wasn't there."

"But her purse and her bible were," May said, obviously thinking this would mean something to me.

It didn't. "And?" I asked.

"And Addie never goes anywhere without her purse and Bible. She says she'd feel naked without either one of them." Was it my imagination or did Lila blush just a little when she said the word naked?

"Is that all or is there more?"

"There's more," Jasmine said. "Addie's neighbor said there was a strange man at her door and Addie was arguing with him. The neighbor was going to go ask if she needed help, but the man left before she could unlock her front door. That was the last time she saw Addie."

"And her auto is still in the garage," May said. "Addie never walks anywhere. She says God gave the automakers their knowledge so that she wouldn't have to walk any more than necessary."

Lila giggled.

I had to admit to myself that it was highly unlikely that a woman would leave the house for an extended period of time without her purse. It just isn't done – at least, not by most women. And if she didn't like walking, why was her car still in the garage? Maybe there was a good reason for the Church Ladies to worry.

CHAPTER TWO

"**D**id the man leave alone or did your friend go with him?"

"He left alone, and the neighbor never saw her again. And when we checked her house, she wasn't there. Wouldn't you say that's a bit suspicious?" Jasmine was beginning to look at me as one might look at a small, unschooled child.

"You still haven't told me anything that makes me believe she's actually disappeared," I said, ignoring Jasmine's look.

"Her purse, bible and car aren't enough?" May asked, sounding like I might have left a few of my brain cells in the restaurant.

I gazed around the cocktail lounge, ran my tongue across my teeth and thought. Maybe there was a problem. I'd hate to do nothing and later find out that something had happened to Addie.

Glancing back at the Church Ladies, I could see an expectant expression on their faces.

"Let me find my husband and talk to him for a moment."

I waved Daniel over.

"Would you please bring each of these ladies another drink?" I glanced from face to face. "It's on the house."

The women smiled at me.

He nodded and turned to find clean glasses. "Sure thing, Mrs. Cross."

"I'll have iced tea this time," Lila said, taking a last sip of her wine.

I could feel the ladies' eyes boring into my back as I left the lounge in search of Chris. He was still talking to the people Phyllis had asked him to see, but it appeared that they were winding things up. I waited, none too patiently. The band was playing again and I tapped my foot in time to the music.

When he finally left the table, I waved him over.

"Phyllis was right. One of the men at that table is from a tourist magazine, and he wants to do a story on *Bogey Nights*."

I nodded distractedly at what should have been awesome news. "Okay, Bogey Man," I said, using my favorite nickname for him, "I know what the Church ladies want, and their request includes you."

Chris rolled his upper lip under in true Bogey fashion, and pushing back his jacket he stuck his hands in his pockets and rocked back on his heels. "Is this a good thing or a bad thing? Because your face says it's not a good thing."

"I'll let you be the judge."

I explained the situation to him and before I could even finish the story, he groaned. "Haven't we done enough detecting lately? First we solved a multiple murder, and then we found a missing relative for a friend of the sister of the dead guy. Now these women want us to find another missing person?"

"But this isn't just a lost relative. This is an actual missing woman."

"Listen, Angel, those dames –"

I cringed and glanced over my shoulder. "Please don't call the Church Ladies dames, Sweetie."

"Okay, I'll watch what I say for your sake. Why can't the coppers handle this?"

"The police aren't interested because Addie has only been missing since this morning," I said, feeling just a trifle sheepish.

"*This morning?* What makes them think something's happened to her if she's only been missing for a few hours?"

"Because her purse and her bible are still at the house, and her car is still parked in her garage."

"Oh, that explains it all."

"No need to be sarcastic, Chris." I narrowed my eyes at him. He'd been kind of snippy all day. I wasn't about to let whatever was bothering him be taken out on me.

He sighed. "Sorry, Doll, I'm just tired. I haven't slept well the last couple of nights."

"Something bothering you?" I asked.

"No, I just couldn't sleep. I'll have some Joe and that should perk me up."

"Come to the lounge with me to talk to the ladies and I'll ask Daniel to pour you some coffee."

I could see by his expression that he was debating whether or not to meet the women. I smiled at him and fluttered my eyelashes, hoping to make it more difficult to turn me down.

"Okay, I'll at least come hear what they have to say. But they'd better have a good story or I'm gonna take a powder, real fast. And quit batting your lashes at me."

"No taking a powder, Bogey Man." I knew that once Chris met these women he'd be an easy mark for them. I almost laughed out loud. Chris was no match for the Church Ladies. I knew it, and they knew it, but Chris was like a lamb being led to slaughter.

We walked into the cocktail lounge where the women waited for us.

"Oh, Mr. Cross," Lila said after the introductions. "You're such a good man to agree to help us."

"I haven't agreed –"

They cut him off at the knees.

"You're one of God's children," Jasmine said, "and He's going to use you to help us find our friend. I just know it."

May was nodding with way too much enthusiasm.

I caught myself nodding right along with her and forced myself to stop before I looked into Chris's eyes. When I did look, I could see that he was hooked. Or maybe trapped was a better description.

Daniel handed Chris a cup of coffee and my husband took a few sips before speaking to the women again.

"Does your friend have any relatives? Maybe she's taken off to visit someone," he said.

"She has a daughter," Jasmine said, "but we don't want to call and worry her. She thinks Addie should be in an old folks home, but she's dead wrong. Addie is as sharp as you and Pamela. Please don't call her daughter."

"This brings up another question. Could she have wandered off? I mean, she's not a young –"

May's face became a mask of stubbornness, not to mention annoyance. "None of us are young in appearance anymore, but believe you me, we're young at heart. Our minds are razor sharp and we use them all the time. None of us is going to seed."

"Okay, okay, but I had to ask," Chris said, almost apologetically.

"Did your friend's neighbor tell you anything about the man she was arguing with this morning?" Chris was on the case. I could tell. Something about these women had grabbed him and wasn't about to let go.

The band started up another number.

"Let's go to my office," I suggested. "Between the band and people starting to dance, it's not easy to talk business in here."

"Good idea," Chris said. "I'll go ask Phyllis to keep an eye on things."

Everyone followed me through the kitchen and back to my office, where we found Sherlock and Watson napping on the couch.

"Yikes," Lila said. "Dogs!"

"They're friendly," I assured her.

"How friendly?"

"Very."

"What are they?" Lila was intimidated by the dogs and backed up to the wall.

"Sherlock and Watson are yellow Labrador retrievers. Sherlock is a boy, and Watson is a girl. They're both about two years old. They saved someone's life once, if that makes you feel any better."

"They did?" Lila asked. "How?"

"They pulled a man out of a burning building."

"I read about that in the newspaper," Jasmine said. "Lila has a fear of dogs, as I'm sure you can see."

"Well, let's see what we can do about that," I suggested. "Come here, Sherlock. Come, Watson."

Tails flying like thick whips, both dogs came to me. There must have been something in my voice because instead of tearing up the rug to get to me, they both approached quietly and politely, the only sign of their excitement being their tails.

"Shake hands with Lila," I said, tapping her shoulder.

The dogs looked into her eyes and sat down in front of her, each lifting a paw as asked. Lila's eyes were large and round as she timidly reached out to the dogs. I held my breath, hoping they wouldn't lick her hand. She might think they were trying to bite her. She shook hands, or paws, with each dog in turn and stepped back quickly. Neither dog took a lick, although I could see Watson's nose twitching, and I let my breath out.

"Now let me show you something else."

I turned to the dogs.

"Slip me some skin," I said. I held out both hands and each dog lifted a paw and slid it down my hand. "Good babies," I said. "Now let's go outside." I opened the back door which led to a small fenced yard and the dogs meekly and quietly walked outside. It was a proud moment for me, but they shouldn't have been in the restaurant anyway. If the Health Department saw them in my office, I'd be in deep trouble. They were never allowed beyond my office though. I slipped them each a doggie cookie as they walked outside.

"What does *slip me some skin* mean?" May asked.

"It's like asking them to shake my hand, but more jazzy. Kind of like the modern version of a cool handshake, only the term is an old one. You know, instead of shaking hands, you slide your hand down the other person's hand."

"I've seen teenagers do that," Jasmine said. "I have a grandson."

May and Lila nodded. "We've learned a lot from Jasmine's grandson."

Chris returned from talking to Phyllis and sat down on the edge of my desk. "Alright, ladies, convince me your friend is really missing."

"I'm sorry, Mr. Cross, but you're just going to have to trust us. We know Addie like we know ourselves, and she wouldn't have left without her purse or her bible, or on foot." Jasmine was using a no-nonsense tone of voice. She could have said, *Don't test me on this one, Sonny, or you'll be sorry*, and her tone would have sounded the same.

"Call me Chris. And I'm inclined to take your word for it," he replied, surprising me.

"You are?" I asked.

He didn't take his eyes off of Jasmine when he answered me. "Yes. These women are one hundred percent sincere. And they're right; they know their friend better than anyone else. If they say she's missing, then I believe them. I just don't know if we can help find her."

Jasmine, once again, turned to her two companions, who nodded vigorously. "We have the utmost faith in you and Pamela, Chris."

"Yes, we do," May said.

"Total faith," Lila added.

"You do?" I asked.

"We do. We believe that God has given you a talent for solving things. And, I personally, believe that our Father will use this task to bring Chris into the fold."

I couldn't help myself – honestly. I rolled my eyes and began to laugh. When Lila turned to me, I laughed even harder and snorted.

"Snorting is not ladylike," Lila said, "but I understand. I've snorted a few times myself. My Edgar, bless his long-departed soul, used to tell me that it embarrassed him, along with most everything else I did."

For some reason that brought an end to my momentary lapse of sobriety. Lila's words sounded like they should have been accompanied by bitterness, but I didn't hear even a hint of that emotion in her voice. Instead, and surprisingly, I heard forgiveness.

"Okay, Bogey Man, where do we start on this one?" I asked.

Before he could answer, Lila giggled. "He really does look like Humphrey Bogart, doesn't he?"

"Well, Angel, I say we start at the scene of the crime, so to speak. After we close up tonight, let's go eyeball their friend's house. You can give us a key, right?" He glanced at Jasmine, apparently figuring that she was the ringleader. Good guess on his part.

"I have it right here," she said, digging around in her purse.

"If your friend... Addie is it? ...is really missing, then the heat's on. We can't let time slip through our fingers. And assuming Addie isn't somewhere in that house listening to the birdies sing, then we'll flap our gums at the neighbor first thing in the a.m. By the time we close tonight it'll be too late, and we can't hit the bricks right now." Chris double-checked his watch.

"If you'll cover for me, I could go talk to the neighbor now," I suggested.

"And we can accompany you," Jasmine said.

"What does *listening to the birdies sing* mean?" Lila asked.

"Unconscious." I answered her without thinking about it. I'd become pretty accustomed to Chris's forties vocabulary.

Jasmine sucked in her breath. "Could we have missed her somewhere in the house? Could she have needed us all this time and we just left her there alone?"

CHAPTER THREE

———————

"**I**'m sure you did a thorough check," I said. "I think the important thing would be to talk to the neighbor tonight. And I don't think you three should go with me. We might overwhelm her and she could forget an important detail if she thinks we're ganging up on her." It made sense to me, plus I didn't want the ladies to go with me.

"If you think so," May said.

"Are you sure?" Lila asked.

"Yes. Can you give me a ride to our house so I can pick up my car? Chris and I rode to work together."

"I have a better idea," Jasmine said. "We'll give you a ride to Addie's house and wait in the car for you." Oh, this woman was sharp. One way or the other they planned on accompanying me.

I glanced at Chris, looking for an out, and he pulled on his ear lobe before breaking out in a big grin. He thought it was funny. Since my back was now to the women, I rolled my eyes at him and mouthed the word *thanks*. He very subtly nodded his head at me.

I glanced down at my long green dress. It was satiny and floor-length with a low back and flowing sleeves, not exactly what I wanted to wear to interview someone. But it was getting late and there wasn't enough time to run home and change. I grabbed a sweater off the coat rack in my office.

"Let's get this show on the road, Ladies. Time's a wastin'."

They gathered their purses and sweaters and led the way through the restaurant. Chris and I followed.

"Be sure to ask the neighbor if she thinks there might be any way that Addie left with the goon this morning," Chris said. "Oh, and take a look inside her car. Maybe there's something in it."

"Yeah, yeah. I know all the right questions to ask. And I already planned on looking at the car. Trust me, Bogey Man."

"Oh, I do, Sugar. I really do." He gave me his best Bogey grin and gently slapped my… Well, that's between me and Chris.

"You'll take the dogs home and check on Mikey, right?" I asked.

"Constance is at our house with Mikey tonight, so we know he's okay, and I wouldn't forget the dogs, would I?"

"Of course not. Sometimes it just makes me feel better if I've said it. Besides, I know Mikey is fine when he's with Constance." Constance is my friend and babysitter. She's been a lifesaver for us because she genuinely cares about our son, and Mikey stays with her while we're at the restaurant. Sometimes he stays at her house, and sometimes she comes to our home.

I caught up to the Church Ladies who were waiting for me by the front entrance.

"I sure like the way your husband talks," Lila said.

"Me, too," May added.

Jasmine smiled in agreement.

"He's quite the character," I said. "He's a good man, and that's what really counts with me. And I have to admit that he sure does keep life interesting."

We reached Jasmine's car, a light green 1951 Chevrolet, and waited while she unlocked it.

"Chris has an older car, too, similar to this one," I said. "It's a light green forties vintage Chevy. When the Bogey Man drives down the street wearing his fedora, he draws quite a few interested stares."

"I'll bet he does," May said. "I'd bet that for just a split second people forget that the actor is gone and that Chris takes them back in time."

"I'll bet you're right," Lila said.

"Now, ladies, that's enough betting for one evening," Jasmine said.

"Oh, it's only a figure of speech. Lighten up, Jaz." May didn't seem to be intimidated by Jasmine.

I found the relationships between these women very interesting. I hoped that when I was their age I'd have a friend, or friends, that I'd feel as close to as they were to each other.

It took about half an hour in Friday night traffic to reach Addie's place. I was glad to see that the lights were still on at the houses on each side of the darkened home. I thought I might talk to the neighbor who saw Addie, and then the other neighbor, just in case they'd seen something, too.

Jasmine parked her car at the curb and switched off the ignition.

"Which house does the neighbor who witnessed the argument live in?" I asked.

Jasmine pointed at the home to the left of Addie's.

"I'll be back," I said. "Wait here for me." I glanced at each woman with what I knew was the same expression I used when I told Sherlock and Watson to *stay*.

They each nodded and I climbed out of the car, leaving my sweater behind because the weather was still warm, and carefully holding my dress up while I stepped over running water in the gutter onto the sidewalk. Patting my hair, I walked toward the front step. I usually wore my hair down, but for tonight I'd brushed it up with curls on top, similar to the famous pinup photo of Betty Grable.

Before I could ring the doorbell, the front door was opened an inch. I could see an eyeball peering out at me past a safety chain. The eye moved up and down, and back up again.

"Who are you?" a very nasal voice asked. "It's a little early for trick or treating, don't ya think?"

"I wear this dress for work," I explained, patting my hair again. "My name is Pamela Cross, and I'm here about your next door neighbor. Her friends said you saw her arguing with a man this morning, and I'd like to ask you about that."

"Ohhh," the voice said before closing the door and pulling off the safety chain. The door opened again and a very short gnome-like woman with a slightly hunched back pulled the door wide, inviting me in. She had scraggly short white hair, huge dark brown eyes, a bulbous nose that was too large for her face, and she looked around eighty. Her ears, slightly protruding, were also a bit big for her face. And she hugged a housecoat around her middle.

"Thank you for letting me in. I know it's late," I said, glancing at my vintage watch, "but Addie is still missing and we need to find her as soon as we can."

The television blared with a medical talk show in progress.

"At my age, Dearie, I don't sleep a lot." She sat down in her recliner and looked at her television. "Phooey! It's only eight o'clock. That's not late at all. Besides, they're going to talk about menopause. I'm past my prime and not interested."

I guessed that this woman could tell you what time of day it was by what show was on. At least, that's the impression she gave. She picked up her remote control and pushed the Mute button. The sudden silence was golden.

"Can you tell me what you saw today, uh, uh…"

"Elsie. My name is Elsie Montrose. And yours is Pamela Cross. Now that we have that straight, there's not a lot to tell. I heard a man yelling and peeked out the window. He was at Addie's door and they were arguing. He looked mean, if you ask me, but you didn't."

"I'd like to know what he looked like," I said.

"First, let me finish my story. Anyways, they were arguing to beat the band, although I couldn't hear everything they said. Addie pretty much told him to get lost – I did at least hear that part – which was pure bravery as far as I'm concerned. Her face looked kinda scared. He grabbed the edge of her screen door, like as to pull it open, and that's when I headed for the front door. He mighta been mean, but at least he'd have two of us to deal with, ya see. But I heard footsteps stompin' down the walkway and looked out another window. He was climbin' into a truck – one of those kind with a camper on it – and he started it up to drive away. That's all I can tell you."

"Addie's friends said you never saw her again today. Is that right?"

"Sort of."

"What do you mean? Did you see her again or not?"

"Well, when this guy was driving away, it looked like the door to the camper was being pulled shut. I coulda sworn I saw Addie's face just before it closed, but I thought it was all just my imagination. But the more I think about it…" Elsie's expression was sheepish. She'd had all day to think about what she'd seen, and now it appeared she was sorry she hadn't said anything.

"So you think Addie was in the camper when the man took off?" I asked.

"It kinda looked that way. She could have ran out of her house and climbed in there while I was running to the front door. I didn't really hurry after I heard his footsteps leaving. I wonder why she would have done that."

"Okay, tell me what he looked –"

I was interrupted by someone knocking loudly on the front door.

Elsie sighed and slowly pulled herself up off the recliner. As she trudged over to answer the door, it struck me just how slowly she'd probably gone to the front door when Addie was having problems. My best guess was arthritis in her knees. It reminded me of watching my grandmother try to walk when her knees hurt.

She opened the door a notch and peeked out. "You church nuts again?"

she said. "Why aren't you out looking for your friend?"

"That's exactly why we're here," Jasmine's voice rang out. "We want to know what you're telling Pamela."

"Well, she can tell you when we're done talking. Now go away."

"Nope. Our friend is missing and we want to know what you know."

I could see Jasmine's foot slide between the door and the door frame. It was rather interesting to watch these two women spar.

Elsie didn't say a word for a moment, and then she pulled the door open. "Okay, I guess that's fair. She is your friend, and I like Addie, even if I don't like you. I wouldn't want to see anything happen to her."

Jasmine, standing tall and straight, walked through the door with Lila and May following. "Thank you, Elsie. I know we have our differences, but Addie's life could be at stake here."

Elsie made a noise that I couldn't identify, except that it sounded like resignation or defeat. "You women may be nuts, but you're all good women. I doubt if you've ever done a bad thing in your lives. But I have, and you should know that you're not gonna convert me tonight."

"We're not here to convert you," May said.

"We'll do that after we find Addie," Lila said softly.

"I asked you to wait in the car," I said, focusing my gaze on Jasmine. "If you want Chris and me to help you, then please do as we ask in the future."

"We will," Jasmine said, very off-handedly, and keeping her eyes on Elsie instead of me.

This time I rolled my eyes and didn't care if the Church Ladies saw me or not. They didn't, but Elsie did and she chuckled.

"Got your hands full, don't ya, girlie?"

I didn't respond to that. "Okay, you were about to tell me what this guy looked like."

"He was tall, but then everybody looks tall to me. Um, I would guess he was about a foot taller than you. He had black and white hair, like this lady's." She pointed at May's salt and pepper hair. "He had a droopy mustache—you know the kind—the sides were long and hung down. He was kinda thin, but he had a belly on him, like some older men get. Maybe it was a beer belly."

"So he was an older man?" I asked.

"Not *older* older, but mebbe late fifties or early sixties. At least, that was my take on him. And he was madder than a wet hen. Whatever Addie did musta really been a doozie this time. I wondered if she tried to preach at him like she does sometimes. I just ignore her, but some people can't do that."

"You've given me a good description. You're very observant."

"Not much gets by me in this neighborhood. I keep an eye on things."

"I'll bet you do. Can you tell me what his truck looked like?"

"Well, it wasn't an old truck, but it wasn't new either. It was black, and it was one of those trucks that has two wheels on each side in the back. The camper didn't match the truck. It was white, and it looked pretty big to me. There was a ladder on the back, but half of it was gone, like it got broken off. How's that? Will that help you find Addie?"

"It couldn't hurt," Jasmine said. "Elsie, I know you don't care for us, but we really appreciate your help. We'd just die if something happened to our friend, God forbid."

Elsie reached over and patted Jasmine's hand. "I know, Dearie, I know. I wouldn't want anything to happen to her either. But let me remind you of something. If God takes you to it, He'll get you through it. So you'll find Addie."

Jasmine's eyes widened and she looked surprised. Lila giggled, and May put her hand to her mouth.

Elsie chuckled. "I have a computer and I use it. Someone sent me an email that had that saying. And you know what? I think it just might be true, and you ladies should know that better than me. Now leave this old lady to her TV show. I ain't got nothin' else I can tell you."

After a little sputtering, Jasmine and the other Church Ladies followed me outside.

"Okay," I said, "let's check out Addie's house and car."

"I can't believe that Addie might have willingly climbed into that man's camper," May said.

"Me, either," Lila said, "but since she's not here, just maybe she did."

CHAPTER FOUR

We walked over to Addie's house and Jasmine unlocked the front door. She was mumbling to herself, and I had a feeling that Elsie had gotten under her skin.

Turning to Lila and May, she said, "That little woman is right about me. Sometimes I'm too full of myself, and she didn't let me get away with it. She was preaching to the choir, and this time the choir needed it. Amen?"

"Amen," Lila and May echoed.

"Am I really that overbearing?" Jasmine asked, sounding uncertain.

"Yes, Jaz, sometimes you are," May said.

"Amen," Lila said softly. She slapped her hand over her mouth after the word popped out.

"It's okay. That stops right here and now," Jasmine said. "Better to be a good example and only speak up when it's really necessary. Preachy is out and setting an example is in."

Oh, good grief, I thought, *what are Chris and I getting into here?* I picked up my skirt and climbed up the step to Addie's house, all the while hoping that the Church Ladies weren't going to preach to me. I mentally rolled my eyes, knowing how ungracious I sounded, even to myself. After all, they meant well.

Jasmine switched on a light inside the house and I looked around. It was so neat it almost looked like a model home.

"You three know her and I don't. Would you take a look around and see if anything looks out of place?"

Without a word the women did a tour of the house and returned to my side. "Everything looks like it always does," Lila said. "Not a blessed thing out of place. I should be so neat."

I saw Addie's purse and bible sitting on the coffee table, so I knew she hadn't been back. "Okay, then let's take a look at her car."

We trooped outside to the garage and found that it was unlocked. I lifted the door and we turned on a light.

"That's odd in itself," Jasmine said. "Addie always locks the garage door. She's very careful about that. You know – thieves."

I nodded and opened the passenger side door. Her car was as neat as her house. I opened the glove compartment and found a manual describing the attributes of her 1996 Plymouth Breeze. It looked like it had never been opened.

I thought there was nothing else in the car until I noticed a piece of paper sticking out from under the passenger seat. Picking it up, I saw that it was a receipt for coffee from the place where I guessed the Church Ladies were supposed to meet for lunch. Taking a closer look, I saw that it had the current date on it.

"What made you ladies think Addie didn't show up at the coffee shop today?" I asked.

"Because when we got there she wasn't there, and she always shows up early," Jasmine said.

"Always shows up early," May said.

"Without fail," Lila added.

"Well, she was there today," I said, holding out the receipt. "She must have left before you three arrived."

"I guess we should have asked the waitress, Donna, if she'd seen her," May said.

"We didn't think," Jasmine explained.

"No, we didn't," Lila added.

"Okay, Chris and I will drive over there first thing in the morning and talk to the waitress. You said her name is Donna?" I felt like we should do something immediately, but there was nothing we could do until we knew more.

"Yes," they said, in unison.

"I'll also call the police department and talk to a friend of ours. Janet may be able to help us, although she works in the homicide division."

"Homicide?" Jasmine's face looked stricken.

"I'm not saying there's been a murder," I said quickly. "My friend, Janet Riley, just happens to work in that division. At least I have a connection."

Relief telling on her face, Jasmine sighed. "You scared me for a minute, but I'm glad to hear you have a connection."

"Sorry, I didn't mean to frighten you. It's just that Janet can look into any investigating that may have been done."

"Like I told you earlier, the police didn't do anything but look through her windows and tell us everything looked fine. I don't think they even walked over and talked to Elsie."

I glanced at my watch and saw that our restaurant would still be open. "Well, there's nothing else we can do here tonight."

I asked Jasmine to drive me to *Bogey Nights* instead of home.

"What time should we meet you at the coffee shop?" Jasmine asked, when I climbed out of the car back at the restaurant.

"What? Meet us? No, no, no. I'll contact you after we talk to Donna. In the meantime, if you hear anything from Addie, call us right away." I reached into my purse and pulled out a business card, writing our home phone number on the back.

"Okay, but what time are you going to the coffee shop?" May asked. "You know, so we know when to call to see what happened."

"We'll probably get up early and go in as soon as they open. Time is of the essence when someone has disappeared." I could have slapped myself across the face as soon as the words came out of my mouth, but I rolled my eyes instead. There was no doubt in my mind that the Church Ladies would be at the coffee shop waiting for us when it opened – probably before we got there. "Besides, I said *I'd* call *you* when we know anything."

They smiled and waved at me, looking so very innocent, while I turned to go into the restaurant. I didn't look back when I opened the door, but kept my head down and hoped Chris would understand why I couldn't stop them from showing up in the morning.

It was nine-thirty and the crowd was thinning out. Our cocktail lounge was basically just an extension of the restaurant, with music and dancing, and that crowd was winding down, too. I found Chris at the front desk, going over receipts.

He glanced up at me when I approached him. "So? What happened? Did you find out anything?"

"A little. The neighbor thinks she saw Addie in the camper when the guy she'd been arguing with pulled away. She gave me a description of both the man and his truck, which might help. And I found a receipt in her car that shows she was at the place where she was supposed to meet the ladies."

"Today?"

"Yes, today. She left before they arrived. So in the morning we're going to need to get up early and go talk to the waitress. Maybe she'll remember something. There must be a reason that Addie didn't wait for her friends."

Chris turned back to the receipts. "All in all, business was pretty good tonight. Things were busier than usual early on, and now they're slower than normal for a Friday night. We're not going to get rich, but we'll be paying the bills on time."

Knowing Chris so well, I knew that he was digesting what I'd just told him. I smiled at my husband. "Have I told you lately that I love you?"

"Thank you," he said, sounding distracted and punching numbers into a calculator. "I love you, too."

"You know I'll take care of the receipts tomorrow," I said. "You don't need to do that tonight."

"Things are quiet and I thought I could help you out."

"You really are helpful. I'm going to go out back and see the dogs. I want to make sure they have water, and they could probably use some lovin'."

I left Chris at the front desk, and after stopping to speak to a few customers, walked back to my office where I hung up my sweater and opened the door to let the dogs in. They were delighted to see me, and when two huge dogs are delighted, they can be trouble.

"Sit," I half begged and half commanded. I didn't want them jumping up on my dress and ripping it in their enthusiasm. They stopped short and sat with their tongues hanging out of the sides of their mouths, panting heavily, almost looking like they'd been practicing to do it in unison. I wondered if constant, heavy panting was a trait of the breed. My friend, Janet, has a Chocolate Lab who does the same thing.

"Now keep your distance," I said, heading for the door so I could go out and check their water. I held up my hand and gave the *stay* command. My dogs were normally well-behaved, but frequently forgot they weren't puppies anymore. And the strength of these two dogs is phenomenal, as far as I'm concerned. I recalled that even at six months old, they were stronger than any dog I'd ever been around before.

Although it wasn't empty, I refilled the dogs' water dish and set it outside. They ran out and drank like they hadn't had water in a month. Guilt. They were only dogs, but they understood what it takes to make me feel guilty. I gave them each a doggie cookie, peanut butter flavored, and felt better.

Returning to my office, I found Chris sitting behind my desk.

"It just struck me that you said the neighbor thought Addie was in the back of the camper. Did I understand correctly?"

"You did."

"Did she get a license number?" Chris asked.

"No, but the truck should be relatively easy to recognize. It's a black Dodge dually, not too old, but not new, and it has a white camper on it with a broken outside ladder."

"Yeah, Babe, easy to recognize if we ever see it amongst the million cars and trucks driving around Los Angeles."

"Good point. But if she really was in the back of that camper, then we need to move fast. The guy that was driving may have already discovered her hiding back there."

"I can't imagine why she would have hidden in the camper like that, and I wish I knew what they were arguing about. None of this makes any sense, so far. Did you ask the neighbor if she heard anything they were saying?" Chris asked.

I thumped my hand against my forehead. "I didn't ask her. I didn't think of it with the Church Ladies on my heels and Elsie needling Jasmine."

Chris looked at me, waiting for an explanation, but I didn't offer one. I honestly knew he wouldn't understand any part of it except not wanting to be preached to by the Church Ladies.

"I don't like having to wait until morning, but it sounds like that waitress might know something, and she's about the only lead we have right now. We should talk to Janet, too, but if the neighbor isn't sure about seeing Addie, I don't think the police will pay much attention to us." Chris sounded concerned.

"I feel like we've walked into a theater in the middle of a movie," I said.

"It's hard to imagine some goon putting heat on a little old lady," Chris said.

"It's even harder to imagine that same little old lady voluntarily climbing into the camper in order to follow the goon."

"*If* it was voluntary, and *if* that's what she's doing. What lame-brained idea could she have had in her noggin?"

Chris and I closed the restaurant around eleven o'clock and drove home, talking about various scenarios while the dogs slept in the back seat.

Constance, who was thankfully a night person, asked how business was and then left to drive home. I had no more than shut the door when the telephone rang. It was late, and I had that feeling you get when you know it's not going to be good news.

CHAPTER FIVE

The phone rang a second time, jarring my nerves a little.

Glancing at Chris, I said, "Maybe you'd better answer that."

He was near the kitchen and headed for the phone. Sherlock had a habit of racing Chris to the kitchen phone, and as usual, he stopped too suddenly and slid into the wall, hitting it with a loud *thunk*. Watson watched with interest from the doorway, but she never joined in the races. I couldn't understand why Sherlock didn't learn. Maybe he'd hit his head one too many times.

"It's your nickel," Chris said. "What's up?"

I watched as his face became more serious. "Okay, slow down and tell me again." He said *uh huh* a few times before responding to the caller.

"Didn't she give you a location? Some kind of clue about where she might be?"

Chris listened again as the caller replied.

"Okay, we'll let you know if we find out anything. I think you should call the police again."

He paused and listened. "I mean tonight, not after we look into it."

Realizing that he was talking to one of the Church Ladies, I guessed that they'd had a call from Addie. Unfortunately, it didn't sound like she'd given them much information.

"Who was that?" I asked.

"Jasmine. Addie called them." He didn't look happy.

"And?"

"She didn't tell them much. She said she was at the diner when she heard two thugs talking about committing a crime. She left to go home and call the coppers. It seems they realized that she was listening, and one of the two men tailed her to her house. They argued, and when he saw a neighbor eyeballing him out the window, he decided to cheese it. But he told her he'd be back and that she was in big trouble.

"Addie said she ran out at the last minute and pulled open the door to his camper, thinking if she couldn't tail him in her car, she could hitch a ride with him and see where he was going."

"What was that little old lady *thinking*?" I asked. "Does she believe this is some kind of adventure, or does she think she can save someone or something?"

"Ya got me, Toots. It seems this guy wasn't driving home. It looks like he was taking a trip somewhere. He stopped at a greasy spoon to eat and she slipped out of the camper to call her friends. Before she could tell Jasmine anything else, she saw him paying his bill and said she had to get back inside the camper. She hung up before Jasmine could ask her where she was or tell her to stay out of the camper."

I could tell by the slang that the Bogey Man was on the case, with no reservations. He didn't like what he was hearing, and he wanted to find Addie. It helped that she hadn't been discovered yet.

"Did she give any clue at all?"

"Only one. He'd stopped to chow down at a Barney's Diner, but that doesn't help because it's a chain, and who knows which one they were at?"

"Okay," I said, shifting my brain into gear, "how many Barney's Diners are there? And where are they? I know they're not just in Los Angeles County, but I don't know what kind of territory they cover."

"I know one way to find out," Chris said, heading for the spare bedroom, which we used as a home office. "I'll do an Internet search."

While Chris headed for the computer, I climbed up the stairs to take a look at my son. He just loved it when Chris and I became involved in a mystery, but I thought I might try to keep this one from him. I remembered that during the last school year, thanks to Chris and me, he got into some trouble at school for telling stories about dead bodies and talking the kids into playing a dead body/private investigator game.

Actually, he didn't come up with the game or convince anyone to play it. It was his best friend, Danny. Nobody died in their game. The kids concentrated on investigating a crime instead of dying, but the teacher still had a snit over the whole thing. It could have become ugly, but we had a friend who's a P.I. go in and talk to the class and the staff. Things eventually died down.

I watched Mikey sleeping for a moment before going back downstairs to see if Chris had turned anything up. His curly dark blond hair was sticking out in all directions, and he was smiling, maybe having a good dream. The one little dimple by the right side of his mouth brought a smile to my face. I quietly left his room.

Hopefully, if Addie had called once, she'd call again. We had to find her before the driver of the truck did. After talking to Elsie, I'd mostly convinced myself that she'd been mistaken about seeing Addie in the truck. I hadn't *wanted* her to be in the camper. Now I knew better.

When I came downstairs, Chris was just hanging up the phone. I hadn't heard it ring, so naturally I asked him who he'd been talking to.

"I called Janet. She's on duty tonight. I told her what's been going on, and she said that basically her hands are tied. We have no evidence of a pending crime, and it appears that Addie went with that guy willingly. No crimes committed."

Janet is a friend of ours who's also a homicide detective. We'd become friends when Chris and I were involved in a murder, which had consisted of a dead body being buried in the basement at *Bogey Nights*.

"I know she's right," I said, "but this is really frustrating. We know something's going on, but we don't know what and we don't know... Well, we don't really know anything except that an elderly woman overheard a conversation about a possible crime, and that she's hiding out in some stranger's camper."

"If that dizzy broad – sorry, elderly woman – is caught in the back of that camper, she could end up the victim instead of the witness. She must have bats in the belfry."

"What did you find out about Barney's Diner?" I asked, ignoring his dizzy broad comment.

"They're limited to Los Angeles and San Bernardino counties, two very large areas. That dame could be *anywhere*. The gunsel could be discovering her even as we speak. She's definitely in a jam right now."

"I sure hope he's not planning to sleep in the camper tonight." I hadn't met Addie yet, but I couldn't help comparing her to the other Church Ladies. She was, after all, one of them.

"I have to admit, Pamela, that right now I feel as helpless as any man can feel."

"I know, Bogey Man." I glanced at the clock. "It's getting late. Let's get some sleep so we'll be rested when we go see Donna."

"Who?"

"The waitress at the diner. She saw something, I'm sure."

***

Chris and I arose early the next morning. I called Constance to see if Mikey could stay with her and she said if we brought him over she'd give him breakfast and keep him for the morning. She started to laugh when she realized we were on the trail of another bad guy.

"And how are you going to keep this from your seven-year-old son? You know, the one who's every bit as curious as you are. The one who knows when you and Chris are keeping something from him. The one –"

"Okay, Constance, I get your point. I'm going to tell him that we have some restaurant business to take care of and that's why he's spending the morning at your house. So I'm counting on you to back me up on that lie. Oh, Lord, I sure do hate to lie. I need to set a good example for my son. Maybe I'll just tell him that Chris and I are going to meet someone at a diner and hope he relates that to the restaurant on his own."

"Good luck with that one," Constance said. "Your son can smell trouble even before you know it's coming. Last night he was asking me when I thought you might have another case."

I rolled my eyes and remembered my mother telling me that someday they'd get stuck that way. Lowering my eyes, I glanced at the clock. "Gotta go, Constance. We want to be at the diner as soon as it opens. I have a feeling the Church Ladies are going to be there bright and early, and I don't want them interfering with our conversation with the waitress."

"Good luck with that, too. I know those ladies and nothing can stop them." Constance laughed, but I detected just a hint of fear in her voice. She attends the same church that the Church Ladies and I go to.

We hung up and I let the dogs in. I'd already fed them and they were ready for quality time with their person, except this person didn't have time to play.

"Go get Mikey," I said to Watson. She looked up at me with her soulful eyes and left the kitchen to go wake him up. She has many tricks for making him get up, and when I heard him giggling I knew she had stuck her head under the covers and licked his toes.

"Good morning, Duchess," Chris said. "I passed Watson on the stairs. You must have sent her to wake Mikey up."

"I sure did. She does it so sweetly that he doesn't get cranky. If I'd sent Sherlock, he'd have jumped up on Mikey's bed and pushed him onto the floor."

Mikey walked in the kitchen a few minutes later, looking for his breakfast.

"You're going to eat at Constance's house this morning. Did you brush your teeth?"

"Yes, Ma'am, I did. How come I'm going to Constance's house? And how come I had to get up so early? It's Saturday, Mom." He turned to Chris, who didn't know my cover story.

"Your dad and I have to run some errands this morning so Constance said you could eat with her and spend some time together."

Mikey turned toward me, slowly, and gave me a suspicious look. "Okay, what's up, Mom? You're giving me the brush, aren't you?"

I laughed. "You've been hanging out with Chris, uh, your dad too much. You're beginning to sound like him."

Chris is actually Mikey's step-father. We'd lost my son's real father to cancer when Mikey was very young. It warmed my heart that my son had decided he wanted to call Chris dad.

"Am I getting the bum's rush or not?" Mikey asked.

"No, Son, your mother and I really do have some business to take care of this morning. We need to keep an appointment to meet with a waitress, and the place where she works opens at six o'clock. We need to talk to her before she starts working."

Why hadn't I thought of that? What could be more normal than Chris and I talking to a waitress? After all, we own a restaurant, and it was what we really were going to do. Okay, so he left out a few details, but at least it was an omission type lie instead of a flat out lie. Yeah, Chris could spin a yarn with the best of 'em.

We dropped Mikey off and drove to the diner, after checking the gates at home to make sure the dogs couldn't get out.

As we pulled up I looked around for Jasmine's car. I didn't see it, so I figured we were off to a good start.

Chris and I asked who Donna was and we asked for a table in her section, which turned out to be a window table. Donna was young, maybe in her early thirties, and she looked tired. I remembered that feeling from my own waitressing days. It wasn't an easy job, especially during the morning rush. Fortunately, it was early enough that there wasn't a huge crowd. Her dark blonde hair was cut short, probably so she didn't have to bother with it. She was a husky young woman, although not overweight, and she had a very small tattoo of a cartoon character on her left wrist.

She saw me looking at the tattoo. "It's not real. My son put it on there with one of those things you get wet and stick on your skin. It'll wash right off."

"Ah," I said. "I'm sorry if it seemed like I was staring. I really wasn't."

"Not a problem. Can I take your order?"

We ordered our breakfast and asked her if she could talk to us for a minute.

"Sure. Let me go turn in your order first though."

Returning, she asked, "Now, what do you need?"

"Yesterday a woman named Addie was here. I understand she and her friends are regulars in here. She's an older woman, and –"

"Oh, sure, Addie. I know who you mean. What about her?"

"Was she acting oddly while she was here?" Chris asked. "Did anything out of the ordinary happen? She's disappeared and her friends are worried about her."

"Do I know you?" she asked. "You look awfully familiar."

"I have one of those faces, that's all."

"Okay. Anyway, yes, something happened, but I don't know exactly what. Addie was sitting at a table, waiting for her friends, when she got a funny look on her face. I stopped and asked her if she was okay. She told me to shush, that she was trying to listen to the two men sitting behind her. She's always so polite that I was kinda surprised.

"Anyway, I left her alone. Before long the men paid their check and left. Addie threw some money on the table and walked out right behind them. She didn't even bless me when she left, which is something she always does. I've gotten used to it." She was quiet for a moment. "I sure hope nothing's happened to her. Those guys didn't look very friendly. They didn't even leave a tip."

CHAPTER SIX

"I'm sorry about the tip," I said. "Sometimes people just don't realize how important a tip can be."

"Yeah, and I waited on them really good, too. They were very demanding." She looked embarrassed, as though she hadn't meant to complain in front of us. "Say, I know why you look familiar. You own that new restaurant, *Bogey Nights*, don't you?"

"We do," I replied.

"If you don't mind me asking, what does Bogey mean?"

I laughed. She was young. "My husband looks just like a movie star named Humphrey Bogart. He used to be a really big star."

"Huh. Never heard of him. Do you have any openings for a waitress at your restaurant?"

"Not at the moment, but if you'll keep in touch with me I'll let you know when something comes up. Most of our waitresses look like famous old-time movie stars," I explained. "We had a waiter who looked like John Wayne, but he moved out of state."

"Now, I do know who John Wayne was," Donna said. "Do I look anything like an older movie actress?"

"No, but not all of our employees are look-alikes. Come by the restaurant and talk to me one day and we'll see if we can work something out."

"Can you tell us what the men looked like?" Chris asked, changing the subject and trying to move things along.

"One of them was just average. There was nothing special about him at all. Average everything from height to weight to looks – even his coloring. The other guy, well, he was kind of memorable." She went on to give the same description that Elsie had given us; over six feet tall and slender, salt and pepper hair, with a droopy mustache.

"Is there anything else you can recall?" Chris asked.

"Nooo. Hey, wait a minute. I'll be right back." Donna disappeared into the back of the diner.

"I wonder what that was about," I said, reaching across the table and patting Chris's hand.

"No telling. She looked like she remembered something important though."

Donna returned and placed a piece of paper on the table, weighting it down with a salt shaker. "The average guy dropped this on the floor when they were leaving. Well, he actually knocked it off the table. I picked it up and stuck it in my sweater pocket, figuring I'd throw it in the trash on my next trip into the kitchen. Will it help?"

Chris turned it around and looked at it, and then shoved it across the table to me. There was an address on it with the word *VIC* scrawled underneath.

"It just might," Chris said. "Thank you for your help."

Donna beamed. "My pleasure. If little Miss Addie is missing, I hope you find her." She lowered her voice. "Those four ladies are kind of pushy, but I really like them. They seem to genuinely care about people, even if no one else does. And they're always blessing me. I can use all the blessings I can get."

Donna walked over to another table and took their order. She gently slapped an older man on the shoulder, making me believe that he was a regular, too. He smiled at her back when she headed for the kitchen. Someone else waved at her. I had the feeling that she was well-liked by the customers.

She turned in the older man's order and returned with a tray bearing our breakfast. We thanked her, and she left for the door to greet some new customers.

"What do you think, Chris?"

"If the guy dropped this piece of paper, then it must have been something the two men were looking at while they sat here."

"I wonder if someone named Vic lives at this address. Addie said the two men were planning a crime. Could this Vic be involved?"

"Here's another thought," Chris said. "What if *VIC* stands for victim?"

"Ohhh, you're good. I never would have thought of that."

"I think we'd better check out this address and see who lives there." Chris dug into his hash browns. "After we eat."

I had just picked up my fork when I heard loud voices at the front door. Before I could turn around, the voices moved closer.

"There you are," Jasmine said. "Move over. We've got news, and we need to get moving."

Chris and I were sitting on opposite sides of the booth, and we each moved closer to the window. The Church Ladies slid in next to us, with Lila and May sitting to my right. Jasmine needed more room, being the larger of the three women, and she sat next to Chris.

"What's cookin'?" Chris asked, taking a bite of egg.

"We heard from Addie again!"

I thought I had a flair for the dramatic, but Jasmine's tone of voice could have earned her an award. I even thought about applauding. She'd put so much feeling into so few words.

"And what did she have to say?" Chris asked calmly. "Did she tell you where she is this time?"

"Yes," Jasmine said.

"And more," May added.

"This is big," Lila said, not wanting to be left out.

And then the women sat quietly, waiting for only heaven knew what.

Chris lost his calm. "Are you going to tell me what she said or do I have to buy you breakfast to get the skinny."

"The skinny?" Lila asked.

"The information," I interpreted.

"Breakfast would be nice," May said, "and bless your heart for offering."

"Oh, for Pete's sake," Chris said. He waved to Donna, motioning her over to the table.

Donna glanced at us and smiled when she saw the ladies. She held up her index finger indicating she'd be over in a moment.

"While we're waiting, tell me what Addie said." Chris was sounding ever so slightly frustrated.

I clamped my lips together and kept my smile to myself.

Before Jasmine could start talking, Donna arrived to take the ladies' orders. "Have you found Addie yet?" she asked.

"We know where she is, and we're going to go pick her up." May sounded quite proud of her answer.

"Well, I'm so happy to hear that. Now, what would you like to eat?"

The women knew exactly what they wanted and Donna was off to turn in their order in a moment.

"Okay, now for the last time, what did Addie say?" Chris set his fork down and turned his full attention to Jasmine.

"She's waiting for us to pick her up, but none of us can drive that far."

"Explain, please." Chris's words were coming more slowly, and he was enunciating carefully. "Tell me what she said, from the beginning."

"Well, we were going to meet you and Pamela here when the diner opened, but Addie called before we could leave my house." She glanced at Lila and May. "My friends slept at my place last night just in case Addie called again. She might have needed us, you see."

"Apparently she does, since you said you need to pick her up," I said.

No one paid the least bit of attention to me, except Lila, who took hold of my hand.

"The man in the truck stopped for gas last night, by a motel, and Addie climbed out of the truck so he wouldn't catch her. Instead of heading for the camper, he got himself a motel room. Now how much sense does that make? Why spend the money on a motel when you're carrying a bedroom on the back of your truck?"

Lila and May both shrugged their shoulders, nodded their heads and smiled.

Chris rolled his upper lip under, and this time it had a whole different meaning than it usually did. "What else did Addie say?"

"Since he wasn't going to use the camper, Addie let herself back in and slept the night there. This morning she heard him climb in the truck and she quickly let herself out. She felt she'd traveled as far as she could, and she was beginning to worry that he might catch her."

"He *might* catch her?" Chris stopped talking and I could see he was grinding his teeth. He took a deep breath and took a bite of pancake, letting himself calm down.

I was having so much fun watching the interaction between Chris and Jasmine that I'd finished my breakfast without even realizing it.

"Where is Addie?" Chris asked.

"She's in San Bernardino County, somewhere between Victorville and Barstow. She's waiting at a gas station coffee shop until we can get there to pick her up. You'll pick her up, won't you?" She gave Chris a look that said she had no doubt whatsoever that he would.

"Of course, I will. Tell me what else she said so Pamela and I can get moving."

"We'll tell you on the way," Jasmine said.

"You're not going with…" Chris closed his eyes and dropped his head. "Finish eating so we can get on the road. We'll have to take the old Chevy if we're all going to fit. Six of us won't make it in Pamela's car."

"God bless you," Jasmine said.

"Amen to that," May added.

"You're a living doll," Lila said, smiling up at Chris.

I could see a vein throbbing in Chris's neck and decided I needed to talk to the ladies while he regrouped.

"Why didn't she call you last night?" I asked.

"She didn't have any money with her. She had to borrow a cell phone from a tourist who was eating at the coffee shop. He treated her to breakfast, too. She took his address so she can pay him back."

"I'm assuming that the goon left and Addie is at the coffee shop by herself, right?" Chris asked. "Or is she hanging out with this tourist?"

"She said she barely got out of the camper before he left. The tourist left, too, so yes, she's by herself." Jasmine was beginning to watch the kitchen door with hunger in her eyes. I thought I heard her stomach rumble.

Donna brought three more orders, and the ladies dug in like loggers rather than the delicate little flowers that they were. Chris and I excused ourselves and the ladies stood up to let us out. We walked outside to talk things over.

"What did we get ourselves into?" Chris asked.

"I have no idea, but I think we're about to find out. The answer lies somewhere between Victorville and Barstow. How long will it take us to get there?"

"A few hours."

After a couple of minutes, we returned to the table and the ladies. They were just polishing off their breakfasts.

"Did Addie ever tell you what crime these men were talking about?" I asked, watching Jasmine intently.

"Oh, yes. I almost forget to tell you that part. She said that someone hired them to murder someone else."

CHAPTER SEVEN

"**M**urder?" I squeaked.

Chris dropped his head again before standing up straight and looking directly into Jasmine's eyes. "Let's go, ladies. Time's a'wastin', and we've got places to go and things to do. By the way, did she at least give you directions to the coffee shop?"

"No," Jasmine said, "but she did give me the name of it. Will that help? She wasn't really sure where she was."

If it wasn't for the fact that these were the Church Ladies, I think Chris might have said some words that they wouldn't appreciate. Instead, he turned and headed for the cashier to pay the bill. His back looked stiff and his head was hanging again.

I drive a Jeep Wrangler, which is why we couldn't all fit in it. The ladies followed us back to our house so we could pick up Chris's Chevy. While we were there, Chris looked up the coffee shop on the Internet while I called Constance to ask her if Mikey could stay until later in the day.

"Constance, I feel like I'm taking advantage of you because it seems like I'm always asking you to watch Mikey. I do apologize, but sometimes it can't be helped."

"I don't mind in the least," Constance replied. "When you and Chris are working on a case, I live vicariously through you. It makes my life a little more exciting. Maybe someday I can get involved in one of your cases." She laughed. "Besides, I can always use the extra money."

I couldn't tell if she was teasing or if she was serious.

"Well, we don't really have cases. It's just that people seem to think we can help them. We don't really *want* to get involved in these things."

"Sure you do. You're just like Nick and Nora Charles from the movies. What do you want me to tell Mikey?"

"Just say we got tied up and we'll be home as early as possible. And thank you, Constance. You're a good friend."

I hung up and turned from the phone, wondering if she was right about us. Did we really enjoy getting involved in these situations? I guess we did or we'd tell people we couldn't help them. Chris had always wished he could be like Humphrey Bogart was in his P.I. movies. Did I have a personality like Nora Charles? Before I could go any further with my thoughts, I heard Jasmine telling her friends that they'd better make a pit stop before leaving.

"The bathroom is down the hall and on the right," I said.

After another fifteen minutes, everyone was ready to leave. Chris helped the three ladies get in the car, and left me to fend for myself. I climbed in front and turned to the women. "Put on your seat belts." Like I really needed to tell them.

We were sitting at a stop light, waiting to get on the freeway, when I heard Jasmine say, "Okay, girls, time to pray."

I glanced back over the seat at them and Jasmine pointed to the freeway entrance sign.

"We always say a prayer before driving onto the freeway. Those people are nuts."

Chris and I both started to laugh, but stifled ourselves when the ladies began to pray for safety and sanity on the freeways and highways.

"Is that what you're going to be like someday?" Chris asked, keeping his voice low.

"You never know," I replied quietly, smiling at him.

We drove for a long time, passing through the San Gabriel Valley, Ontario, Rancho Cucamonga and several other cities before we finally left the 210 freeway and got onto the I-15, which would eventually lead all the way to Las Vegas, Nevada. Fortunately, we weren't going that far. We passed Wrightwood and Phelan, and Chris finally left the freeway at one of the Victorville exits.

For the most part, the Church Ladies had entertained themselves on the ride. They'd discussed Pastor Findlay's sermon from last Sunday and anticipated what he might talk about this Sunday.

Lila commented in passing that she was going to sing a solo in the morning. She'd been in the choir for a few years, but I'd never heard her sing alone.

"What are you going to sing?" I asked.

She grinned. "A standard. I'm a little nervous because I've never sung by myself in public before, but I think you'll enjoy it. Like Elsie said, God's taking me to it, and I know He'll get me through it – if I don't pass out first."

She purposely changed the subject before anyone could ask questions. "Do you think we're close yet?" she asked.

Chris pointed. "Look just up the street on the right. See that gas station? That's where we're headed."

Everyone sat back in quiet anticipation of seeing their friend. I glanced back and saw that the three women were holding hands.

Chris pulled into the parking lot, but we didn't see Addie. Of course, Chris and I had no idea what she looked like, and there was no one in the parking lot except a teenager who was busily pulling up his baggy pants. May made a clucking sound, but she didn't say anything.

"She must be waiting inside," Jasmine said. "Hopefully that man didn't come back and see her."

"I'm sure that's where she is," Chris said. "I don't see a black truck with a white camper in the parking lot so I think we can safely conclude that the guy didn't come back. Why would she wait outside in the heat anyway?"

The women were nervous and I didn't think they'd calm down until they saw their friend. We were climbing out of the car when the front door of the coffee shop opened and a very small woman walked out. She looked like she'd been through the wringer, but then I would too if I'd been hiding out in the back of someone's camper for a day and night. Her short gray hair was sticking up in all directions, her dress was quite wrinkled and she looked exhausted. She saw her friends and perked up a little, waving and slowly walking over to meet them.

"Well, it's about time," she said, obviously joking. "I was beginning to wonder if I'd ever see you three again."

"Praise the Lord," Jasmine said, pulling Addie to her bosom and giving her a bear hug. "I was beginning to wonder the same thing."

I couldn't help but wonder if the little woman could breathe. Lila and May joined in, turning it into a group hug.

Addie pushed them away. "Okay, okay, girls, give me some room. I missed you, too, but I feel so stinky after my trip. I can't wait to go home and take a shower." She waved her hand in front of herself as though her own odor offended her.

"You've never smelled sweeter," Lila said, grinning.

Addie patted her hair. "I saw myself in the mirror in the Ladies Room. Ugh. I hate to have you see me this way, but praise the Lord, here you are."

I watched Chris during this exchange and he appeared almost panicky.

I touched his arm. "It's okay, Bogey Man. They won't hurt you."

"Are you sure?" He smiled his best Bogey smile and visibly relaxed. "Let's see if we can find out what's going on."

"I have a feeling that Addie is anxious to get home. Why don't we talk in the car on the way to her place?" She'd spent enough time in the coffee shop and I knew that if it were me, I'd be ready to leave. Besides, we had a long drive back.

"Where are our manners?" May said. "Addie, come and meet our friends." She introduced Chris and me to Addie, and Addie blessed us.

Chris just shook his head. "You ladies are going to take some getting used to."

"Oh, my," Addie said. "Do you know who you look like, Chris?"

He curled his upper lip under and pulled on his earlobe. "I've been told I look like –"

"You look just like the man who runs the farmer's market out by my house. You could be brothers. Do you have a brother who runs a farmer's market?"

"Oh, Addie," Jasmine said, "he doesn't look anything like Thomas. He looks just like Humphrey Bogart."

Addie studied him. "Well, if you say so. But he looks like Thomas to me."

Chris purposely headed for the coffee shop. "Come on, ladies. Let's at least get something cold to drink before we leave. Actually, I could use some lunch right about now."

"And I could use a trip to the Ladies Room," Lila said quietly.

We turned and followed Chris into the coffee shop.

After we were seated and everyone had taken turns making themselves more comfortable, we ordered lunch and talked.

Chris looked at his club sandwich after it was delivered. He'd become more demanding about his food since we opened *Bogey Nights*, so I didn't know what was on his mind.

He took a tentative bite of his sandwich. "Delicious," he announced, digging in and taking a bigger bite.

I watched as Jasmine, May and Lila talked excitedly with their friend, drinking in the fact that she was okay and not lost to them forever.

Chris swallowed and set his sandwich down instead of taking another bite. "Ladies," he said.

No one was listening.

"Ladies," he said a bit louder.

They kept chattering.

"*Ladies!*" he said sharply.

All eyes turned to him and they stopped talking, mid-sentence.

"That's better," he said, calmly, pulling on his earlobe again. "Now, Addie, take half a shake and a deep breath and then I want you to flap those lips."

"What? Half a shake? Flap my lips?" Addie asked.

Jasmine patted Addie's hand. "Take your time, and tell him what happened, dear."

"He talks kind of funny, doesn't he?" Addie folded her napkin and set it next to her plate.

"Please," Chris said. "Just tell us what's going on."

I could hear the desperation in his voice. He was losing patience, but no one else would recognize that except me.

"Oh. Okay," Addie said. She glanced up at the ceiling, as though trying to collect her thoughts, and cleared her throat. "I was supposed to meet my friends at the diner for lunch. I was early."

"You're always early," Jasmine said.

Chris gave Jasmine a look that told her to hush. She did.

"Yes, well… Anyway, I was at my table and there were two men sitting behind me. At first I thought they were talking about a television show or a book or something. They were talking about a murder. I didn't hear the whole conversation because my ears didn't perk up until I heard one of them say something about trying to make a murder look like an accident."

She turned and looked at each of her friends in turn. "As soon as I realized that they were serious, I prayed for the intended victim."

"Can you tell me exactly what they said?" Chris asked.

"The one man – the thin one with the mustache – said he needed to make it look like an accident. The other man asked him how he was going to do that, and the thin one said not to worry, that he knew his business and no one would ever figure out it was a murder-for-hire job. That's what he said; murder-for-hire. I think I even know the person's name."

"Which person?" I asked.

"The one they're going to kill. They kept talking about Vic, so I'm guessing the man's name is Victor."

I glanced at Chris just as he turned to me. So now we knew the paper they'd dropped contained the victim's first name. Too bad it didn't list his last name.

"At least we have an address," Chris said.

"So," Addie continued, "I left the diner. I decided I'd better go home and call the police. But before I could call, the thin man came to my door. He must have followed me. He wanted to know how much I'd overheard. I tried to tell him that I didn't know what he was talking about, but he wouldn't believe me. He started yelling at me, threatening me, and then Elsie from next door yelled out her window, wanting to know if I needed help. He put his head down so Elsie couldn't see him, but before he left he told me he'd be back, and that I was in big trouble."

"Elsie didn't mention that she yelled out her window," I said.

"You talked to Elsie?" Addie asked.

"We were trying to find you," May said. "We didn't know what had happened to you."

"And your purse and bible were still inside your house," Lila said.

"We knew you'd never go anywhere without those things," Jasmine added.

"I wouldn't have if I'd had time to grab them, but the man was getting away."

"Did it ever dawn on you when you climbed into that camper that you were following a killer?" Chris asked.

Addie's eyes widened and her eyebrows shot up. "No, sir, not until just this moment. It seemed like an adventure, and it seemed like the right thing to do. Someone's life is at stake."

"And it could have been yours," Chris said. "One wrong move and we could be at the coroner's office identifying *your* remains."

"Chris!" I said sharply.

The Church Ladies sucked in their breath, collectively.

"Poor Vic, whoever he is," Addie said, placing her hands on her flushed cheeks and leaning forward.

CHAPTER EIGHT

"Excuse us, please," Jasmine said. "We need to do some heavy duty praying, and we need some privacy."

Before they could leave the table, a waitress walked over to talk to us. It wasn't the one who'd waited on us when we sat down.

"I see your friends finally showed up. Are you feeling better now?"

Addie smiled sweetly at her. "I certainly am, and bless your heart for asking."

The ladies left the table and walked outside, but the waitress lingered, watching them walk away.

"If that was my mother," she said, "I'd have the doctor check her over. She was telling us the wildest story about someone trying to kill someone else and hiding in a camper so she could follow a man. My grandmother lost her mind toward the end, and she used to make up some whoppers, too. Old people just haven't got much sense."

Our waitress had walked up and listened, nodding her head in agreement. "Not one lick of sense. Getting old is a terrible thing. Senility must be setting in."

"Sorry to burst your bubble," Chris said, "but she wasn't making up a story. In fact, she's probably saner than you two. And she isn't our mother, but if she was I'd be proud of her." I was surprised to hear him sticking up for Addie. I knew the Church Ladies were getting on every one of his nerves.

"Is that our check?" I asked, glancing at our waitress's hand. I had a feeling it might be a good time to take a hike.

"Oh, yes." She handed it to Chris.

He pulled out his wallet and counted out some money. Slapping the check and cash on the table, he walked out of the restaurant without another word. This was a side of Chris that I very seldom saw.

"Ladies," I said, working my way out of the booth, "there's a lesson to be learned here. Never talk about one customer to another customer, and never cross the Bogey Man. He may have a lot of bad habits, but loyalty is most certainly one of his best traits." I followed Chris out the door with the two women's voices buzzing behind me.

"Sometimes you surprise me, Chris. What made you stick up for Addie? I mean, you could have just let it go."

He shook his head. "Just because she's old doesn't mean she's lame-brained. Someday those women are going to be old, too. I hope someone talks nicer about them than they did about Addie."

I slipped my arm through his and we strolled toward the Chevy. The ladies were standing behind it, heads bowed, saying a prayer for Vic, whoever he was. Chris and I waited in the car.

The ride home felt shorter than the one we'd taken to go pick up Addie. There was just enough room in the old Chevy for the six of us. Addie sat in front, between Chris and me, and before too much time passed she nodded off. She'd been through quite a lot in the past twenty-four hours.

The other three ladies sat in the back and talked in hushed tones.

"Why do you think she really climbed into the back of that camper?" Chris asked.

"I think she was absolutely honest with us. I think she felt that someone needed help and it was her obligation to be the helper."

"You mean like a Good Samaritan?"

"Something like that. These women *are* pushy, and they want everyone to become a believer like they are. Their intentions are good. But whether they get on a person's nerves or not, they're always there if someone needs them. And I've never heard them complain about helping out – not even once."

Chris smiled. "You actually remind me a little of them, Cupcake."

"Yeah, like I never complain about anyone or anything."

"Not very often."

When Addie woke up, we talked to her about staying at Jasmine's house until the thin thug with a droopy mustache could be located. It took some fast talking, but we finally convinced her. We drove by her house and while she put some things together, Chris and I walked over to Elsie's to let her know we'd found Addie. We also wanted to let her know that Addie would be gone for a few days.

Chris knocked on the door and it opened an inch, just like the night before when I'd approached her, but there was something different this time. She looked Chris up and down, slammed the door and pulled off the chain, and opened it wide.

"Well! I never," she said. "Look at you. If I didn't know better I'd think Mr. Humphrey Bogart hisself was visiting me today."

She briefly glanced at me.

"Hey, Pamela. Who's this hunka man?"

I laughed. "Elsie, this is my husband, Chris Cross. I call him the Bogey Man, and obviously you can see why."

"Come on in," she said, taking Chris's arm and pulling him inside.

I could see by Chris's face that he didn't know what to make of the little gnome-like woman.

Elsie glanced over her shoulder, looking at me. "You come on in, too."

I followed Chris and Elsie inside and took a seat on the couch. Chris sat next to me and Elsie sat on his other side.

"Isn't this cozy," she said. "What can I do for you today? I saw you walking Addie to her door, so I know you found her. Where's she been?"

"In the back of that camper you told me about," I said.

"She's going to stay with Jasmine for a few days," Chris said. "If I leave you our phone number, would you call us if that stranger comes back?"

"I will, but no matter how much you look like Humphrey, you sure don't sound like him." Elsie sounded disappointed, and I knew that's all it would take for the Bogey Man to put in an appearance.

"Listen, Dollface, we gotta get the goods on this goon. It sounds like maybe he's been hired to turn some Good Joe into buzzard bait. We gotta find him first and make sure he goes to the slammer."

Elsie smiled. "Well, I'm the dame for this job. They don't call me Ol' Eagle Eye for nothin', Buster. If he shows his schnoz around here again, I'll use my wooden nickel to pick up the phone and... And... Aw, shoot! I can't think of something snazzy to say about calling you."

Chris turned to me. "Say, Angel, this cupcake is aces with me."

"Okay, you two," I said. "Elsie, if he shows his face around here you'll call us. Right? You won't try to talk to him or anything? Right?"

"Okay, if that's all you'll let me do." She didn't *really* sound disappointed about being told not to confront him.

Chris wrote down our phone number and handed it to her, and she walked us to the door.

"Now, Bogey, don't let those loony women talk you into anything crazy

– like going to church or something. They'll do their best, you know."

"Hey, wait a minute," I said. "*I* go to church. Does that mean I'm crazy, too?"

Elsie knew I was joking with her. "Not now, but wait 'til you're *their* age and then we'll take another look." She glanced at the floor before looking back at me. "No, they're not really all that bad. I just like to give them a hard time. I'm as harmless as they are, and it brightens my day to pick on them. I actually kind of like them, truth be told. Don't you dare tell them I said that though."

Chris nodded his head. "Yep, I like you, Duchess."

Jasmine was helping Addie with her suitcase when we walked back to the car. Chris took it out of Jasmine's grasp and opened the trunk of the car, gently laying it inside and closing the lid.

We drove back to our house where Jasmine picked up her car, and the Church Ladies left.

I glanced at my watch. "It's after three o'clock. We need to go pick up Mikey."

Chris nodded.

We'd called Phyllis while we were on the road, our Marilyn Monroe look-alike waitress, and asked her to open the restaurant if we weren't there in time. It meant going in a little early to set things up, but she didn't mind. It also meant overtime to her.

I hurriedly changed into my forties clothing, this time opting for a simple blue day dress with buttons down the front and puffed sleeves. With time in mind, I wore my hair down instead of taking the time to style it.

"Let's take Sherlock and Watson with us. Maybe they'll distract Mikey. If I know my son, he's going to ask questions. I don't think he quite believed the story we gave him."

Chris walked through the house and picked up the dogs' leashes while I waited in the backyard. The Labs were *very* happy to see us and it took a few minutes for them to calm down. Then I made the mistake of saying, "Let's go bye-bye," and we had to calm them down all over again. I'd found that *sit* and *down* are good commands to distract them. We were on the road within ten minutes, even with all the excitement.

When we arrived at Constance's house, Mikey needed distracting, too. He'd been waiting for us with questions. Chris took him outside with the dogs while I talked to my friend.

"As soon as you and Chris left, he started asking me what was really going on. He didn't believe your cover story for one New York minute."

"I've always wondered," I said. "What's a New York minute?"

"I think it has something to do with New York being so busy and people being impatient. Anyway, it means less than a real minute. You're stalling, aren't you? What did you find out?"

"Well, it seems that Addie overheard two men talking about bumping somebody off. One of the men realized she was listening and he followed her home and threatened her. She decided it was her Christian duty to jump in his camper and find out where he was going."

"Is that the story-in-a-nutshell version?"

"It is. We have a first name and an address for the possible victim, and we're going to check it out after I go to church tomorrow."

"What if your killer decides to do the deed tonight?" Constance asked.

"He was headed in the other direction, toward Las Vegas, so we don't think the victim is in immediate danger. I know we're taking a chance, but we don't know what else to do. The police won't listen right now because there's no real evidence of an impending crime. Right now it's all hearsay."

"Janet Riley would listen to you, and she's a homicide detective."

"I already talked to Janet. She's the one who told me there's not enough to go on. Of course, when I talked to her we didn't have an address or a name. If we can come up with something concrete, I'll call her again."

"I knew there was something going on," Mikey said from the doorway.

"Where's your father?" I asked, cringing. I didn't want Mikey to know we were working on something again.

"He's checking the plumbing," Mikey replied. "You were trying to keep me in the dark again, weren't you?"

"Oh, Mikey," Constance said, smiling. "You're way too smart for a seven-year-old. Where do you come up with this stuff? Checking the plumbing?"

"He's in the bathroom. I'm my mother's son, and she's smart, so it comes naturally. Besides, I'm seven and a half now, almost eight."

"Why, thank you, son," I said, smiling and hoping to distract him again. "You think I'm smart?"

"Yes, Mom, but not smart enough. What's this about somebody getting bumped off?"

"How much did you hear?" I asked.

"Enough to know you and dad are on another case, and that's enough for me. Who's your customer this time?"

"Our *client*, if you can call her that, is a woman named Addie. She's one of the Church Ladies."

"*The Church Ladies?* Bye, Mom. I'm going back out to see the dogs." He turned and ran out the door.

"Oh, for goodness sake! They're not *that* bad," I called after him.

Constance laughed. "Yes, they are."

Mikey accompanied us to the restaurant that night, along with the dogs. He didn't ask any more questions about our so-called case.

CHAPTER NINE

Sunday morning Mikey and I got up early to get ready for church. I was preparing a big breakfast when Chris came downstairs, wearing a nice pair of tan slacks and a blue dress shirt.

"Where are you going?" I asked.

He mumbled something that I didn't quite catch.

"What?"

"To church with you and Mikey." He sounded defiant, like he was waiting for me to say something.

Actually, I didn't know what to say. I'd always told him that if he wanted to accompany us, he was more than welcome, but he'd never taken me up on it.

"Cool," Mikey said, fingering his knife and fork.

"Why?" I asked. "I don't want to look a gift horse in the mouth, but…"

"I want to watch the Church Ladies in action, and Lila made me promise I'd come listen to her sing." Chris sat down at the table and clammed up – his jaw muscles working double-time.

Deciding not to push my luck, I went back to cooking pancakes.

"I'll be there with you, Dad," Mikey said. "You won't be alone. I'll even stay for the sermon today instead of going to Sunday School."

"Thank you, Son." Chris smiled a very tight smile at Mikey. He normally enjoyed lounging around on Sunday mornings while we were gone, watching sports and reading the newspaper – and having a little alone time. When Chris married me he got a readymade family, and I understood his need to have a little time to himself.

This Sunday morning was going to be a new experience for all of us. I was surprised to realize how much I was looking forward to him accompanying us. I glanced over my shoulder at Mikey, and he was grinning, looking very much the way I was feeling. Neither of us said another word to Chris. We wanted him to be comfortable with his decision. And, after all, it was only one Sunday among many.

When breakfast was over and the dishes were cleaned up, I picked up my purse and bible, thought of Addie, and headed for the Jeep. Chris and Mikey followed behind, taking their time and talking about an upcoming NASCAR race. I sighed and climbed into the front seat, waiting for them to catch up to me. By the time they reached the car, they'd moved on to baseball and football. At least they were going with me.

Arriving at the church I took note that the parking lot seemed fuller than normal, or maybe that was my imagination.

We trooped in and found seats next to Constance. Chris sat between Mikey and me, and I held his hand. The service began, and after opening prayers, the choir sang and we warbled with them. The pastor gave a sermon on the Good Samaritan, and I couldn't help wondering if he knew something about what had been going on. At least it was something that Chris was interested in hearing.

And then Lila's big moment came. Pastor Findlay announced that we were in for a special treat on this particular Sunday, and he introduced her. She walked up to the edge of the stage and cleared her throat. The music began to play, but Lila took a step backwards. The music stopped. She cleared her throat again and stepped forward. She looked so small and alone up on the stage.

I could see Jasmine and May sitting in the front row. Their backs were straight and they leaned forward slightly.

I glanced at Lila and saw her gaze at her friends, fear showing on her face. The music started again. Lila opened her mouth, and after a brief hesitation, the voice that came out was not that of the teeny tiny, shy woman I'd come to know. It was huge, and beautiful, and inspiring, and I saw her fear melt away. While she sang I saw the years drop away from her face, replaced by peace and soft lines. She sang *The Lord's Prayer,* as I'd never heard it before. She wasn't just singing it – she was *feeling* it.

Halfway through the song I glanced at Chris. He was smiling a Chris smile, not wearing Bogey grin.

I turned back to Lila and watched her intently. I knew there were some notes that were hard to hit because they were so high. I've heard the expression about someone having the voice of an angel so many times, but in this case it was true. As she came toward the end of the song where the words were, *For thine is the Kingdom, And the power, And the glory*, I held my breath. Her head pointed upward and her eyes were closed, and her hands were lifted up toward heaven. She hit each and every note like a pro. I knew that *Forever* was an even higher note yet. Realizing that I was squeezing Chris's hand in anticipation, I let it go, only to tent my hands and place them against my mouth. Lila sang the high note with ease and grace, said a soft *Amen*, and lowered her head.

Not a single sound came from the congregation – until Mikey started to clap. Chris glanced at him and followed suit. Pretty soon everyone was clapping, not something that happened often at our church.

Lila appeared to be embarrassed and backed away.

Pastor Findlay grabbed her arm and pulled her gently forward. "Lila," he said, "I hope you'll sing again at a future service. You've blessed us today."

Lila rejoined the choir, quietly accepting smiles and hugs, and the pastor said a last prayer before everyone stood up and began filing out the door.

Chris, Mikey and I waited outside the church to tell Lila how much we'd enjoyed her solo. Jasmine and May joined us.

"I've never heard her sing by herself before," May said.

"She's been hiding her light under a bushel," Jasmine commented.

"She's definitely got talent," Chris added.

"Even *I* liked her," Mikey said. That was quite a compliment, coming from my son. When I sing around the house, he either plugs his ears and runs outside to play or turns up the TV, and I'm not all *that* bad.

Lila joined us after a few minutes. She was smiling from ear to ear, and looking happy. The Church Ladies hugged each other while other people came up to thank Lila for her contribution. It was, well, heavenly. Lila was having *a moment*.

Pastor Findlay and his wife joined us. "You're not going to believe this," he said, "but a woman who was walking down the street heard Lila singing and came in to see what was going on. She said she was so touched that she'll be back next Sunday. She's new in town and she's been looking for a church to attend."

"Well, hallelujah," Jasmine said.

"Amen to that," May added.

"Because of my singing?" Lila asked in wonder.

"I wish we'd recorded it," Chris commented. "You really need to hear yourself."

"We did," Pastor Findlay said. "We always record the whole service. Would you like a copy?"

"You bet," Mikey said. "Now I gotta go find my friends." He left us on the run.

Chris and the pastor chatted for a moment, and Chris visibly relaxed. Our pastor was a man of God, but he was also a man who could talk about anything. He never pushed a soul to attend church, but gently prodded when the opportunity presented itself.

"Pastor Findlay, if you don't mind me asking, why did you preach about the Good Samaritan this morning? Any special reason?" I glanced at the Church Ladies who looked everywhere except at me.

"Jasmine happened to mention a friend of hers who's been trying to help someone that she doesn't even know. It inspired me because we should all do more for our fellow man."

"Did Jasmine happen to mention what her friend has been doing to help this person?" I asked.

"No, just that it was such a selfless act. Is there something I should know?"

He waited patiently for an answer, which wasn't forthcoming.

"Well, Pastor, we've got things to do. We'd better go." Jasmine grabbed Lila's hand and began pulling her away from the group. May followed.

"What did I say?" Pastor Findlay asked.

"Nothing. They'll tell you what they've been up to when they're ready, I'm sure." I didn't want to be the one to blab about Addie's great adventure. Besides, I didn't think he even knew Addie.

Chris and I excused ourselves and took out after the women. Silly of me, but I didn't trust them. I had a feeling that even though their friend was back and safe, and it was time to let go of the situation, they weren't going to stop trying to help Vic.

Jasmine looked over her shoulder and saw us following, and stopped abruptly, causing Lila to trip.

"So what's today's plan?" Jasmine asked. "Are you going to follow up on finding Victor?"

"What would you suggest we do?" Chris asked.

"Why, look for him. He needs to be warned," May said.

"He's in danger," Lila added.

"And didn't you say you have an address for him?" Jasmine asked.

"We have what *could* be his address," I said.

"So you're going to drive over there and talk to him. Right?" Jasmine was pushing.

I had a feeling that I knew what was coming next.

"And you're going to take us with you, right?"

Did I know my Church Ladies or what?

"No!" Chris said. "We're going alone."

I almost laughed because I could tell by the look of chagrin on his face that he hadn't meant to confirm our agenda for the day.

"Well, no you're not," Jasmine said. "We're going with you. We started this whole thing, and we want to be in on it when it's finished. I guess Addie actually started it, but she's exhausted. She won't be going with us, but I know she'll want *us* to go."

"What about Mikey? We can't take him with us. Who knows what we'll be walking into? We simply can't go today." I figured that would put things into perspective. We actually couldn't go until Monday when Mikey would be in school. Problem solved.

All heads turned to me. Chris appeared to be relieved. The ladies had other ideas, and turned their backs on us while they whispered amongst themselves.

Turning back, May said, "Addie can keep Mikey while we're gone."

"I thought you said Addie was exhausted," I reminded them.

"She's never too tired for children. She has ten grandchildren and she says they're what keeps her young at heart." Jasmine appeared to think that would settle the matter.

"We have to go home and take care of the dogs, too," I said.

"You can do that while we go home and change clothes," Jasmine said.

"And then we'll all meet at Jasmine's house," May added.

"After lunch would be best," Lila suggested.

Chris tucked his upper lip under and pulled on his earlobe before placing his hands on his hips. "You dames ain't goin' with us on this caper. Not today and not tomorrow. See? I know you think I'm being a heel, but that's the way it is. You're makin' me goosy, and I ain't at the top of my game when I'm feelin' goosy. If I was in a jam, and we could end up in a jam here, I don't want you church ladies for back-up. See? End of story."

***

You know what they say about the best laid plans…

After we dropped Mikey off with Addie, I pulled the address out of my purse and gave Chris directions while the Church Ladies sat in the backseat of the Chevy and buzzed like little elderly bees.

"I was a mailman, Pamela. I know this area like the back of my hand." Chris was not in a good mood, and I decided not to push.

He found the street we wanted after taking a shortcut that took us out of our way, and turned right. Things were quiet in the backseat while the ladies took in our surroundings. I watched the street numbers, but I soon realized there was something wrong.

"Is this what they mean when they talk about the *other side of the tracks*?" Lila was staring at a prostitute standing on a street corner. The hooker stared back and Lila looked away first. The woman on the corner laughed as we passed by, knowing she'd won the war of the wills. "Right about now those big dogs of yours are sounding pretty good. Maybe we should have brought them along."

We were definitely in a seedier part of town.

"This can't be right," Chris said, pulling into a parking lot. "The address on that piece of paper is a sleazy motel, not a house. I thought we were looking for a house."

CHAPTER TEN

"**W**ell, maybe we'd better go in and see if there's a Victor staying at that sleazy motel. This is the address those two men at the diner were interested in. There has to be a reason they were discussing it," I said.

After some lengthy discussions, we finally talked the ladies into staying in the car while we walked to the office to ask about Victor.

The office was empty, but there was a bell on the desk. Chris rang it, but no one appeared from the back room. He rang it again. Nothing. He rang it twice in rapid succession.

"Hold your horses," yelled a gruff and gravelly female voice from the other room. "I'll be there in a second."

We waited patiently and finally a scrawny woman of indeterminate age poked her head around the door frame. Her greasy blonde hair had turned to yellow, and she was as thin as a rail.

"We ain't got any rooms right now," she said, turning to go back to whatever she'd been doing.

"We're not looking for a room," Chris said. "We're looking for a person."

She popped her head around the door frame again, got a better look at Chris, and ambled over to the counter. "Well, look what the cat dragged in. Ain't you the one? Anybody ever tell you that you look like –"

"Yeah, yeah. I've heard it before, Cupcake."

I could tell by his tone of voice that Chris was in Bogey mode. He was going to play it up with this woman for all it was worth – and she'd eat it up. There was no doubt in my mind, because I'd seen him use this act before, and it always seemed to get results.

"What can I do for ya, Sweetcakes?" She moved forward and leaned on the counter, smiling. She was missing a few very prominent teeth, and those she had left were spotted with dark red lipstick. Her face was drawn and it looked like she was at the tail end of recovering from a black eye.

I got a very strong whiff of cigarette smoke and backed up a step. I don't generally have a problem with people who smoke, but this woman reeked. I noticed that her fingers were stained a nicotine yellow, much like the part of her teeth that showed through the lipstick.

Chris rolled his upper lip under and pulled on his earlobe. "We're lookin' for a Joe. You got a sap named Vic stayin' in this flophouse?" He rolled back on his heels and stuck his hands in his pockets.

"Whaddaya want him for?" Ms. Nicotine asked, suddenly sounding suspicious.

"Nothin' you'd care about. We got some personal business to take up with him. You got anyone by that name or not?"

"Nah. I gotta a Dick, and I had a Nick, but no Vic. Say, why don'tcha lose Red and come on in back with me?" She was pointing at me when she suggested he lose Red, but she never actually looked at me.

Chris made a clicking sound out of the side of his mouth. "No can do. This here is my Gal Friday. She goes where I go."

The woman thought about it for a moment. "Nah, I ain't into three-somes. I like a one-woman man."

"That's exactly what I am," Chris said, taking my arm and leading me out of the office.

We walked toward the car and never looked back, although I was sorely tempted.

"I feel like I need a shower," I said. "Did you notice how dirty that place was? I'll bet they haven't vacuumed or dusted in years."

Chris started to laugh, but stopped abruptly. "Hey, who's that standing by the car? Is that the hooker we saw standing on the corner?"

I took a closer look and began walking faster. "It sure is. And those screwball Church Ladies are out of the car and talking to her. I know we told them to stay in the car, no matter what."

I noticed Chris's step picking up, too.

We reached the car and Chris stopped next to Jasmine in a protective stance. "What's going on here?"

The tall blonde hooker wore an extremely short skirt with a skin tight blouse. She had on enough make-up to choke a horse, but when I looked closer I could see that she was very young. I wondered if she might be one of the runaway teens you hear about from time to time. She hadn't had time to develop a legitimate hard look yet, although the make-up helped.

"Oh, lighten up," she said. "These ladies remind me of my grandma. We were just having a little chat."

Lila smiled angelically. "We were just telling her about Jesus and how much He loves her."

"And how she needs to get herself out of this environment," May said.

"I think she was listening until you came back," Jasmine said, her words almost sounding like an accusation.

"Well, it's time for us to leave," Chris said, trying to herd the women back into the car.

Jasmine pulled away from him and handed the girl a piece of paper. "Here, young lady. This is my home phone number. If you want to talk more, you can call me any time. If I'm not home, leave me a message and I'll call you back. I wrote the number of the church on there, too. And you know your grandma would probably agree with us."

"I'm sure she would." Before I could grab the paper, the hooker stuck it in her bra. "You ladies take care," she said, walking away. "I enjoyed talking to you."

Lila was beaming. Jasmine and May were looking pretty happy, too.

"Such a nice young woman," Jasmine said.

"Do you understand what she does for a living?" Chris asked.

"Love the sinner, hate the sin," May said. "Yes, we know. And she's still one of God's children. She's just lost her way for now."

He sighed, helping May into the car.

"Let's get out of here," I said. I'd noticed what looked like a young gangbanger watching our vintage Chevy with longing in his eyes. *Not today, kid*, I thought.

Chris stopped the car at the parking lot exit and waited to turn left, out into traffic.

I had a sudden epiphany. "Hey! What if Vic is at this same address, only at the west end of the street instead of the east end? This is a major boulevard, so I'll bet the numbers repeat to the west."

I didn't think Chris had heard me until he turned right and headed west. I sat back and relaxed as the scenery began to perk up, which included more houses and better businesses. We found the right address, and it was a nice, older home, white with green trim. Chris pulled up to the curb.

He turned and pinned the three women in the backseat with a no-nonsense look. "Ladies, do not speak to women of the night, bums or anyone who looks like a gang member. Do not try to convert anyone while we're here. In general, do not speak to strangers. And above all, do *not* get out of this car!"

"Yes, sir," Jasmine said, looking at Chris with big, innocent eyes.

"Okay," May responded.

"Not on your life," Lila added.

Chris and I left the car, and I glanced at the house across the street where I saw a sweet little old lady in her front yard watering her flowers. She waved at me before wiping the sweat from her forehead with the back of her gloved hand.

"You probably should have given the Church Ladies that speech at our *last* stop," I said.

I smiled and waved back at the woman.

I saw Chris's eye twitch and his jaw clench, and decided to let it go.

We climbed the front steps and Chris pushed the button for the doorbell. We waited, but no one responded. He pushed it again. Still nothing. There was a window by the front door. Chris leaned over and tried to see inside.

"The curtains are too heavy to see anything."

"I have an idea. Wait here for a minute," I said. I walked over to see the woman who was watering her plants.

"Good afternoon," she said, looking at me. "Can I help you?" She fanned herself with her hand. It was warm out.

"Yes, ma'am. I wondered if you can tell me if a man named Victor lives in that house." I pointed at the white house where Chris waited for me.

"Oh, yes. That's Victor's house alright. Are you looking for him? Because if you are, he left about an hour ago. He's retired, you know, so he comes and goes when he wants to. He got to retire young, at fifty-five. He's been a nice neighbor and he's always helping me out with little things. Why, he fixed my faucet for me just this morning. Nice man, nice man. I don't have any family, at least that I care to talk about, so I guess I'm pretty lucky to have him for a neighbor."

I held out my hand. "I'm Pamela Cross. That's my husband, Chris, waiting for me over on Victor's porch."

The woman set down her watering can. "I'm Florence Nash. It's a pleasure to meet you. I can tell Victor that you were here," she offered.

"Oh, that's okay. Do you have any idea when he might be home?"

"In the evening. He's always home in the evening. He doesn't like to go out after dark, from what he tells me. He always chats with me while he fixes things around here. You know, these old houses always have something going wrong with them. Yes, he really is a good neighbor. I always offer to pay him for his help, but he won't take my money." She wiped her brow again.

"Well, thank you for your help, Florence. I don't think we can come back tonight, but maybe we'll stop by tomorrow."

"Oh, I'll look forward to seeing you," she said. "I so seldom have company. I'll make some cookies for you, and tea. You will come back to see me, won't you?"

"I'll make a point of coming to see you tomorrow." I glanced at her face and noticed that her cheeks were turning pink. "It's awfully warm out here. Maybe it's time to go inside?"

"I think you're right. I should have started watering earlier. It does seem warmer than it should be for this time of year." Florence picked up her watering can and headed for the front door of her house.

I walked back to the car and motioned for Chris to meet me. Looking in the back window of the car, I could see three faces watching me expectantly. I didn't have much news for them, except that we'd found Victor's house, and I knew that would be a disappointment since he wasn't home.

Chris and I stood by the car and talked for a moment. "Florence, Victor's neighbor, said he won't be back until this evening. From the way she described him, he sounds like a genuinely nice guy. I can't imagine why someone would want to bump him off. Anyway, I can't keep leaving Mikey with friends. Do you think Victor will be safe until tomorrow?"

Chris looked at me like I was out of my mind. "How would *I* know that?"

"Well, I guess you wouldn't." I grinned at Chris. "I'll ask the ladies to pray for his safety tonight."

Chris made a noise that sounded similar to a growl. I chose to ignore it and climbed into the car.

"Chris and I will have to come back tomorrow," I explained, "so please say a prayer for Victor's safety tonight. You ladies, I'm sure, have other things to do tomorrow. And we can handle this by ourselves."

"We have nothing to do tomorrow," Jasmine said. "What time do you want us to be at your house?"

The noise that Chris made this time sounded a lot more than just similar to a growl. I hadn't rolled my eyes in a long time, so I decided now was as good a time as any. I threw in a sigh, too, for good measure.

"I think we can handle things by ourselves tomorrow," Chris said. "You ladies sleep in and enjoy your day."

I hoped the ladies would pay attention to Chris and take his advice.

And I hoped we'd be in time to save Victor.

CHAPTER ELEVEN

"**M**aybe we should have left a note on Victor's door asking him to call us right away," I said over dinner.

"Who's Victor?" Mikey asked.

"Just a guy," Chris replied.

"What if that hit man comes after him tonight?" I asked.

"Hit man?" Mikey said. "A real hit man? Like in the movies?"

"No, Son, your mother's just joking."

I looked from Chris to Mikey and back again. What was I thinking, talking in front of Mikey? I'd become too blasé about *everything*. "Yeah, I really am joking, Mikey."

"Uh huh." My son is so smart, and he didn't believe me for a minute.

We finished eating and I began cleaning up the dishes. "Mikey, don't you have homework for tomorrow?"

"I did it on Friday."

"Well, then, you'd better go straighten up your room and take your shower."

"I can tell when I'm getting the bum's rush," he replied. "I'll be in my room if you want me." He really did listen to Chris's slang too much, and I noticed that he was using the terms more often.

"Oh, Mikey. I didn't mean to make you feel that way. Come back and we'll have some dessert. I have some leftover peach/apricot cobbler in the refrigerator. But then you really do have to go take your shower."

Over dessert we talked about how things were going at school, leaving Victor and the hit man behind. Mikey had a new teacher this year, and he really liked her. "Miss All makes learning kind of fun," Mikey said. "She tells stories to go along with what she's teaching us."

"I had a teacher like that once," I said. "I loved his class."

Chris smiled. "Seventh grade. Art class. My best teacher was a knockout – a real dish. Every boy in school wanted to take her class. And we actually learned from her, too."

I just looked at him.

"Well, we did," he said, sounding defensive. "She was talented and shared her knowledge with us."

We finished dessert and I carried the dishes to the sink. Chris was watching me, and Mikey was petting Sherlock and Watson. I glanced toward the doorway and back at Chris. He looked confused and shrugged his shoulders at me. I looked at the doorway again, then at Mikey, and finally inclined my head toward the door a couple of times.

The light dawned in Chris's eyes. "Mikey," he said, "your mother was right. It's time to get ready for bed now. Go take your shower."

"But, Dad, it's still early." I knew whining when I heard it, and Mikey was whining.

"Tell you what, Ace, you go take your shower and I'll play checkers with you before it's lights out. Okay?"

Mikey sighed. "Okay. But can I play with the dogs for a few minutes first?"

"If you take them outside," I replied. "Fifteen minutes, and then you take your shower."

Without another word, Mikey whistled to the dogs and they joyfully followed him outside, tails wagging in every direction.

"I wasn't thinking," I said, turning to Chris. "I shouldn't talk about what we're doing in front of him."

"I know. It's easy to slip."

"He takes it all so calmly that I forget he's just a child. Sometimes he's too grown up for his age."

"That he is." Chris smiled at me. "You're a good mother, Pamela, and it's not going to hurt him if he hears some of what we're doing, but I don't think talking about a hit man in front of him is the right thing to do."

"No, it's not. He already sees enough of that type of thing on television. When I was his age I wouldn't have known what a hit man was."

"We need to regulate what he watches. I'm glad he's not one of those kids who's glued to the TV though."

"Okay, Chris, back to my original question. Shouldn't we have left a note for Victor? It seems like we should have done something."

"I know it sounds farfetched," Chris replied, "but what if this is the wrong Victor? I'm sure it's not, but we don't want to scare him if he's not the man we're looking for."

"But we have that address…"

"I know. I'm sure it's the right man, but we need to talk to him in person. We'll drive back over there after we drop Mikey off at school tomorrow morning."

***

The next morning arrived and things went smoothly for a change. Mikey and Chris got up on time and the dogs were little angels – not that they're ever any trouble. I had to laugh to myself. Sherlock, at one hundred two pounds, and Watson, at eighty-six pounds, are not little and they're frequently trouble.

We ate breakfast, Mikey found his backpack, and we were out of the house about ten minutes earlier than usual. Since our restaurant is closed on Sundays and Mondays, we knew we'd have all day to take care of business.

We were headed for the Jeep when I heard something. I stopped dead in my tracks and hoped I was wrong.

"Yoo hoo," a familiar voice called. "We're here, and it looks like we're not a minute too early."

I turned around and saw Jasmine walking up the driveway, followed closely by May and Lila. They were all wearing expectant happy faces, which made it more difficult to feel annoyed.

I turned to Chris. He sighed loudly and said something I couldn't hear, closed to door to the Jeep and headed for the Chevy. I guess he knew when he was licked. Mikey followed him with his head down, and I was pretty sure he was trying not to laugh at whatever Chris had said.

"What did your dad say?" I asked quietly.

"I couldn't hear all of it, but it was something about his nightmare coming true."

I started to laugh, unable to stop myself. "The Church Ladies are the Bogey Man's nightmare?"

Mikey stopped and turned to the ladies. "Good morning. How are you today?"

"Well, bless your heart, young man, we're all fine as a fiddle. Or is that fit as a fiddle? No matter, we're all ready and raring to go."

Chris opened the back door of the Chevy and helped Jasmine in. Mikey, on the other side of the car, helped Lila and May in, and gently closed the door.

Mikey climbed into the front seat and I slid in next to him. He quickly glanced at me, then Chris and the ladies, before dropping his head to stare at his lap. Smart kid. He knew it wouldn't go over well if he started laughing. Chris was aggravated enough already.

Chris cleared his throat. "I didn't know you ladies would be here this morning."

"Why, I thought it was expected," Jasmine said.

"Me, too," May said.

"I wasn't sure," Lila added.

"Well, you're here now." Chris sounded resigned. "We'll take Mikey to school and after that we'll head for Victor's house."

"Sounds like a plan to me," I said.

"Is that where the hit man lives?" Mikey asked.

Reaching over, I put my hand on his mouth and said, "*Shhhh!*"

"Oh, your son knows what's going on?" Lila asked.

"*No!*" Chris and I said in unison.

Chris turned around and glanced over the car seat, giving the Church Ladies a warning glance.

Jasmine clamped her lips together and May closed her mouth and folded her arms across her chest.

"Tic-a-lok," Lila said, using her fingers to make the sign of closing a zipper across her mouth.

"Mikey," I said, "why don't you tell the ladies about what a cool teacher you have this year. I'm sure they'd like to hear about Miss All."

Mikey twisted around as best he could, which wasn't that easy with his seatbelt on, and spent the whole ride telling them some of the stories Miss All had told to illustrate some of their lessons. The women were wonderful and responded positively in all the right places. They added a few short stories of their own about what school was like when they were young.

We arrived at the school and I climbed out so Mikey could exit the car.

"Those ladies aren't so bad, Mom. I *like* talking to them. And I'm going to tell Danny about sock hops. He'll never believe me. I might tell Miss All, too."

"I'm glad to hear that you like the ladies, Mikey. Now you have a good day at school, and we'll be back to pick you up later."

Some friends ran out to meet him as we watched him walk up to the school. Chris pulled out of the parking lot and headed for Victor's place.

The Church Ladies chatted all the way, and once again prayed before we got on the freeway. Chris said he knew a shortcut now that he'd figured out the way to our destination.

Forty-five minutes later we pulled up in front of Victor's house. Being the loving wife that I am, I didn't mention that it should have only taken us half an hour.

"Okay," Chris said, turning around in his seat, "I want you ladies to wait here. Do I need to remind you not to talk to strangers?"

"No," Jasmine said. "We remember the pep talk you gave us yesterday." She sounded a little annoyed.

"Just so we understand each other." Chris sounded a tad annoyed, too.

"We do," May said, "but we'd like to know when you're going to let us get out of the car and join in. After all, we're the ones who got you involved in this in the first place. And we know we can help."

"We're going to go talk to a man who might be the intended victim of a major crime," Chris said, through very tight lips. "I don't think that's the time for a whole passel of us to show up at his door."

I could tell that the ladies weren't happy, but he'd made his point. They sat quietly while Chris and I headed for the house.

"There's a car in the driveway," I said. "It looks like he's home this time."

"Looks like it," Chris said.

"How are we going to approach him?" I asked. "We can't just walk up to the door and say, 'Hey, pal, we think someone's gonna try to kill you.'"

"We should have discussed this before driving over here. Okay, let's just play it by ear."

Chris knocked on the door and it opened almost immediately. Victor must have been watching out his window. "Can I help you?"

"Are you Victor?" Chris asked.

"I am. What can I do for you?" He stood in the doorway, and if looks mean a thing, then I couldn't see anyone wanting to get rid of him. At about five feet and eight inches tall, he had thinning, light brown hair and brown eyes. He had a medium build, with just a little paunch around the middle. And he had one of the most pleasant faces I've ever seen. He simply looked friendly. I took an immediate liking to him.

"We think someone's gonna try to kill you," Chris said.

My mouth dropped open and I gave Chris a look that said, *Have you lost your mind?*

Victor's eyes widened and his eyebrows nearly shot off the top of his head. He took a step backward.

"Excuse me?" he said, sounding shocked. "Who are you and why would you say something like that to me. Explain yourself."

All of a sudden he didn't look so friendly.

"I'm sorry my husband was so abrupt," I said, trying to smooth things over, "but there is an indication that someone may want to harm you. May we come in and talk to you?"

Victor hesitated for a moment, and I figured he was probably wondering if we were the ones who wanted to hurt him. He finally stepped back and motioned us to come inside.

I glanced back at the car before entering the house and saw that the women had rolled the window down to watch us. Three elderly faces peered at us from the rear of a light green vintage Chevy. I saw May stick her thumbs up in the air.

CHAPTER TWELVE

W e followed Victor inside the house, where he sat down in an old dark brown recliner. Chris and I planted ourselves on the even older brown and tan couch. I glanced around the room and saw that although it was clean, Victor's furniture appeared to be old and a little dingy. He didn't appear to be a man of means, so I crossed money off my mental list of possibilities of why someone would want to kill him.

"Now, what's this all about?" Victor asked. He appeared to be very uncomfortable, which didn't surprise me.

Chris leaned forward, looking into Victor's eyes. "Some friends of ours, actually one lady, overheard two men talking about killing someone and making it look like an accident. When they were leaving the diner, one of the men dropped a piece of paper. It had your name and address on it. Of course, we could be wrong, but that leads us to believe that you may be the intended victim."

Victor sat quietly for a minute, obviously trying to digest what Chris had just told him. "Who is this friend?" he asked. "Is it someone who knows me?"

"Oh, no," I said. "She's an elderly woman who was at the wrong place at the wrong time, or at the right place at the right time, depending on your point of view. And one of the two men realized that she overheard them and followed her home. From what she tells us, he threatened her. Fortunately for her, a neighbor was watching. I have a feeling that he was going to come after her again, but we've hidden her away for now."

Victor reached for the telephone that was on an end table by his chair. "I'm going to call the police."

Chris and I waited while Victor's hand lingered on the receiver. He moved his hand away from the phone and placed it in his lap, fingering the fabric of his slacks.

"Before I call, tell me what these men looked like. Maybe I can figure out who they are. I'd like to be able to tell the police as much as I can."

Chris leaned back. It appeared that Victor was taking us seriously. "The waitress we talked to said one was over six feet tall and slender, with salt and pepper hair and a long mustache. She said it drooped. We got the feeling that he was probably middle-aged. She couldn't tell us much about the other one. She said that everything about him was average; coloring, build, size. I'm sorry we can't give you more than that."

Victor appeared thoughtful again.

"Does either of those descriptions sound familiar to you?" I asked.

"Well, the description of the all-over-average man doesn't give me much to work with; however, the other man could be..." He stopped talking, shaking his head. "No, it doesn't make sense. There's a guy who frequents the same bar I do, but I don't even know him. He certainly couldn't have anything against me."

"What bar is that?" Chris asked.

"Del's, over on Pico," Victor said. "Nah, it couldn't be him. I've only seen him around there a few times. And like I said, I don't know him."

Victor reached for the phone again. He tapped the receiver with his fingertips before pulling his hand away. "No, I'm not going to involve the police. I think there really must be some kind of mistake. I haven't done anything to piss anyone off lately. This just doesn't make sense. But thanks for the warning. I'll keep my eyes open and be careful – just in case."

"But that note had your address on it," I reiterated.

"You know, this same address would exist at the other end of the street," Victor said, sounding hopeful.

"We've already been there," Chris said. "It's a sleazy motel, and there's no one named Victor registered there. I think you might be in trouble, Pal."

Victor turned to Chris with a solemn look on his face, and blinked. He didn't say anything, but blinked again. Call me silly, but I was pretty sure he was blinking back a tear or two. His eyes appeared watery. Maybe he really did know who might be after him and he didn't want to share the information with us – or with the police.

Before I could go any further with that thought, there was a loud knock on the front door. Victor shook his head and excused himself.

"Yes?" he said.

"You must be Victor. Nice to finally meet you in person. I'd like to see the Bogey Man, please. It's urgent." Jasmine's unmistakable voice rattled me, and she sounded breathless. What now?

"I'm sorry, but you want to see who?" Victor sounded confused, and I couldn't blame him. He looked like he was ready to close the door on Jasmine.

To his credit, Chris didn't groan or growl, or say anything at all. He simply stood up and headed toward the front door.

"That would be me, Victor. Some people say I bear a resemblance to Humphrey Bogart."

Victor opened the door wider and studied Chris as he took a step back.

"What is it, Jasmine? I thought you were going to wait in the car?"

"It's important. Can you come outside for a minute?"

Chris stepped outside, pulling the door shut behind him, and Victor returned to his recliner.

"Is that the woman who saw the two men?" he asked. "Maybe I should invite her in and ask a few questions."

"No, she didn't see a thing. It was a friend of hers who heard the two men talking. Jasmine never saw them."

Victor looked disappointed, but he didn't say anything. He watched the door, waiting for Chris to return. So did I. Victor began picking at the fabric of his slacks again. He was agitated and I couldn't blame him. We'd handed him a bowl of sour grapes, and he wasn't up for it.

I turned around and watched Chris out the front window. He followed Jasmine to the curb where he stopped and looked in the direction that Jasmine was pointing. Her mouth was going a mile a minute, but I never saw Chris open his. He nodded his head and returned to the house after helping Jasmine climb back into the car. Knocking on the front door, he entered the house without waiting for anyone to open it.

"What was that about?" I asked.

He turned to Victor instead of answering me directly. "Do you know anyone who drives a black Dodge dually with a white camper on it?"

Once again, Victor appeared to be confused. "No, should I?"

"I don't know, but that's the truck that Jasmine's friend described as being the one the guy with the droopy mustache was driving. And Jasmine and the other ladies just saw it drive by. By the time I got out there, it was gone. She said the driver fit the description and that he was eyeballing your house when he drove by."

"What other ladies?" Victor was beginning to sound frantic. "How many people are involved in this?"

"Let me explain," I said. "There's this group of four Church Ladies who meet for lunch every once in awhile. It was one of those ladies who overheard the conversation between the two men we're worried about. The ladies came to us for help, because initially they were worried about their friend when they couldn't find her. That's a longer story, and I won't go into it right now. But this whole thing leads up to someone being after you. It seems that your life really is in danger."

Victor turned to Chris, and Chris nodded his head. "I know it sounds kind of loopy, but that's the story in a nutshell."

Victor stood up and paced across the room and back again. He sat down on his recliner. "Okay, here's what I think. I think it's all a big mistake. My name is Victor Rogers. Are you sure you've got the right Victor?"

Chris shrugged, not having an answer for that question. "All we have is a piece of paper with your name and address on it."

"On the off chance that it's not a mistake, I'm going to drive up to Del's and ask the bartender if he knows anything about the guy with the mustache. If I think there's really anything to this, then I'll talk to a friend of mine who's a retired police officer."

"We have a friend who works in the Homicide Division at –"

"No," Victor interrupted, "I'll talk to my friend. He'll know what to do. I appreciate your warning, but I don't think there's anything else you can help me with at this point." He stood up, obviously ending our encounter. It was time for us to leave.

"I hope you'll take this seriously. Let us know if we can help in any way." Chris handed Victor one of our business cards after writing our home telephone number on the back. "Call us anytime."

"Thank you," Victor said, sounding stiff and formal while he walked us to the front door. "I really think you've scared me enough for one day."

We didn't know how to reply to that, so we left, remaining on the front porch while we talked.

"He sure did an abrupt turnaround," I said. "One minute he was concerned, and the next it felt like we'd stepped on his toes."

"He's scared," Chris said. "He started out having a nice day, and then we showed up on his doorstep with bad news. How would you expect him to act?"

"All I can say is that if it were me –"

"But it isn't," Chris pointed out.

"– I'd be on the phone to the coppers right now. I wouldn't waste my time driving over to a local bar."

Chris glanced toward the car and groaned. "What are they up to now?"

I followed his gaze and saw Florence, Victor's neighbor, standing on the sidewalk talking to the Church Ladies. She was smiling, so I assumed the ladies hadn't done anything wrong.

"They're just talking," I said. "That's Victor's neighbor, Florence. She invited me for tea and cookies today, and I'd forgotten about it in all the flurry of the morning's events."

"Tea and cookies? I don't have to go, do I?"

"I'm not even sure I'm still invited since there are four of us now. Let me go see what's going on."

Chris hung back a little while I forged ahead and joined the ladies.

"Florence, I'm so sorry. I forgot we'd have the ladies with us when I accepted your invitation," I said.

"Oh, there's plenty for everyone," she said brightly. "The more, the merrier, as they say. Would your husband like to come, too?"

The Church Ladies had quieted down and were watching me expectantly.

"What do you ladies think? Are you in the mood for tea and cookies?" I asked. Silly me.

"Oh, we'd love to have tea with Florence," Jasmine said.

"What a treat," May added.

"And we do enjoy cookies," Lila finished.

"Let me talk to Chris and I'll be right back." I could see by his face that he'd been listening.

"How long do you think this will take?" he asked, before I could open my mouth.

"Maybe an hour. Would you mind?"

"I'll make you a deal. You go have tea and crumpets with the ladies, and I'll go visit Del's and see if I can find anything out. I'll be back in an hour."

"Cookies," I corrected him.

"Whatever."

I couldn't blame him. In fact, I'd have liked to go to Del's with him. But maybe the bartender would be more willing to talk to Chris without me interfering. And the ladies seemed so happy about our little tea party. I gave Chris a quick kiss and my blessings, figuratively, and headed back to the women.

I glanced back at Victor's house while I walked to Florence's home, and the curtain fell into place. Victor had been watching us. I believed that Chris and I had shaken him up more than we'd intended. Of course, with what we'd told him, I couldn't expect any other reaction.

Sometimes Chris can be too blunt. But, then, how do you gently tell a man that someone wants to kill him?

CHAPTER THIRTEEN

I sat in the dining room while the Church Ladies helped Florence get out extra cups and saucers. Two sets, along with a sugar bowl and creamer, were already sitting on the dining table which was covered with a white lace tablecloth. I could see that Florence had been looking forward to my visit. The women bustled and chatted and enjoyed themselves, making the most of this unexpected social occasion.

As I listened I heard Florence tell the ladies that she used to go to church, but it had become too difficult to attend because she didn't drive anymore. Jasmine asked about her age, and Florence said, with pride, that she'd be eighty-eight on her next birthday.

"So if you don't drive, what do you do about groceries and doctors' appointments and things like that?" Lila asked.

"Victor takes me," Florence replied. "He's been so good to me since he moved into that house. If he doesn't see me out in the yard, he checks to make sure I'm okay. He's just like the son I never had."

"Don't you have any family to help you out?" May asked.

"Not really. Well, I do have some nieces and nephews, but they don't come around. They call once in a while, but we're not very close. They have busy lives." The look on her face suggested that she wasn't happy with her family. I wouldn't be either if they never came to visit me.

The ladies brought two teapots, the extra cups and saucers, dessert plates, and a platter covered with cookies to the table. We indulged ourselves with homemade oatmeal and chocolate chip cookies.

"These are delicious," Jasmine said. "Did you make them yourself?"

"Yes. Believe it or not, I still enjoy baking. It's one of the little ways that I can pay Victor for his kindness. He does love my pastries."

"Does Victor ever have company?" I asked. Maybe I should have worked into that question more slowly.

"He has a couple of gentlemen friends who stop by from time to time," Florence replied.

"Have you ever seen him argue with anyone?"

Florence looked surprised. "Why, no. What's this all about?"

"Oh, nothing much. We'd just heard that someone was angry with him, and after talking to him it's hard to imagine anyone taking issue with him."

Jasmine kicked me under the table and I couldn't tell if she'd been crossing her legs or if she was trying to get my attention. I turned to her, but she was watching Florence.

"So what do you do for entertainment?" May asked, changing the subject.

"I have my soaps, and I enjoy the game shows, too. And on Monday nights I have a mystery show I watch. It's about a gentleman who writes mysteries and becomes involved –"

The doorbell interrupted her description of Monday night television.

Florence excused herself and left to answer the door.

"Jasmine, why'd you kick me?" I asked.

"Even *I* know you should have been a little more discreet with your questions, bless your heart. I know you meant well, but do you really think we should drag Florence into this?"

"Who's in a better spot to see who comes and goes?" I asked. "Victor doesn't seem to be taking this seriously enough, so I thought I'd see if Florence knew anything. Jasmine, that man's life is at stake here. Questions have to be asked."

"She's right, Jaz." May was sticking up for me and I was surprised. "You and I both know that little old ladies keep an eye on the neighborhood. We're good at that. Florence could have seen all kinds of things going on around here."

"May's right," Lila said. She seemed to withdraw into herself after her comment, as though she wasn't sure if she should have spoken up or not.

"Well, what's done is done. I guess I'm the only one who disagrees with your method, dear." Jasmine patted my hand. "You ask whatever you need to."

Florence returned with Victor in tow, and he didn't look too comfortable when he saw us.

"I didn't mean to interrupt your tea party," he said apologetically. "I just wanted to check on Flo. I hadn't seen her out in the yard this morning."

"Oh, she's fine," I said. "I met her yesterday when we drove over here and she invited me back for tea and cookies. Or tea and crumpets, as Chris likes to say."

Victor looked around the room, taking in each of the ladies' faces. "Oh. Where is your husband?"

I evaded the question. Victor might feel that Chris was sticking his nose in where it didn't belong. "He ran an errand while we ladies enjoy ourselves."

"Ah. Well, I'd best be going then. I'll check in with you later, Flo."

"I'll see you this afternoon." Florence waved at him as he let himself out.

"What a nice man," Jasmine said. "It's wonderful that he takes the time to watch out for you."

"He really is like a son," Florence replied.

"How long has he lived by you?" I asked.

Florence picked up her cup and took a sip. "Oh, I'd say he's lived here for about two years now. He came over one day and offered to mow my lawn for me, and we've been good friends ever since."

"Well, I'm really happy to hear how good he's been to you. We should all have someone who cares so much about us." I picked up my cup and realized that I'd already finished my tea, so I reached for the platter to take another cookie. It was bare. Pulling my hand back, I picked up my napkin, folded it and placed it on the small dessert plate that Florence had placed in front of me.

The doorbell rang again. "I'll get that for you," I said. "Sit and relax for a few more minutes."

I could hear the ladies chattering like parakeets while I walked through the house to the front door. I opened it and found Chris standing there.

"Has it been an hour already?" I was surprised.

"Yeah. How time flies when you're having fun, huh? Are you about ready to go? We've got to pick Mikey up at school before long."

"Give me a couple of minutes to help Florence clear off the table and we'll be ready. Do you want to come in?"

Chris looked like he was in *fright*-or-flight mode when his eyebrows shot up and his lips tightened. "No, I think I'll wait in the car." It was definitely the fright mode.

Walking back to the dining room, I couldn't help but chuckle. My big bad Bogey Man was afraid of a group of little old ladies.

"Well, Florence, let me help you clear off the table. My husband is back and waiting for us. We've got to pick our son up at school." I glanced at my watch and saw that it was later than I'd realized.

"Oh, please don't bother," Florence said. "I can do this myself. It'll keep me busy."

"Are you sure?" Jasmine asked. "I don't want to walk out on you with all these dishes on the table."

"I'm sure. I'm so happy that you all came to visit me today. I hope you'll come back again. And, Pamela, feel free to bring your son along. I do love children."

I could see by her expression that she really meant it.

"If we take surface streets instead of that silly freeway, we could come again," May said. "We just can't drive on those freeways anymore."

"We'll be here whenever you want us," Lila said.

"Let me give you my phone number," Jasmine added, pulling a piece of paper out of her purse.

"And I'll give you mine," Florence said.

With phone numbers exchanged, several Bless Yous said, and purses over their shoulders, the ladies followed me out of the house.

"What a lovely lady," Jasmine said.

"Such a sweetheart." May smiled at Chris as he handed her into the backseat of the car.

"A joy to be around," Lila said, taking Chris's arm.

"You will have to come see her again," I said.

"And you'll have to come with us." Jasmine pulled her skirt out of the way of the door before Chris closed it.

"Actually, that's not a bad idea. You could help keep an eye on Victor." Chris had walked around to the front passenger side of the car and stood next to it talking to me.

"Why would I want to keep an eye on Victor? If something happened, there's nothing I could do."

"You could call the coppers. I don't think Victor really wants to believe there's a problem here. Besides, you're always calm in an emergency. You'd know what to do."

"Okay, Bogey Man, you've made your point. I can watch him from Florence's house. And just where would you be?"

"Probably parked down the street. If I drove your Jeep, he wouldn't recognize the car. And this way we could keep an eye out for the black truck. Thanks to Jasmine we know that at the very least it's been cruising his house."

"Yes," came a voice from the backseat. "Thanks to me."

I hadn't realized that the women had opened the window and were listening to us. "We'll come with you to see Florence, and we can keep her busy while you watch Victor."

"I don't think so," I said. "I'm not even sure this is really a good plan."

"Sure it is," Chris said.

"What about the restaurant? We can't sit here all day and work the restaurant at night, too. We'd be exhausted. And what about Mikey? I can't keep leaving him with Constance. She already takes care of him in the evening."

"We'll work it out," Chris said.

"Sure we will," May said.

"Where there's a will, there's a way," Lila added.

"We can do this," Jasmine said, with finality. "And, don't forget, Florence invited your son to come visit, too."

Since I was standing outside of the car, I turned my head away from prying eyes and rolled my peepers.

Chris chuckled. "You're rolling your eyes, aren't you?"

I repeated my annoying habit and rolled them again, refusing to answer him.

We headed for Mikey's school and the ladies spoke to each other about Victor and black trucks with white campers. They weren't listening to Chris and me, so we were able to talk about the morning.

"What did you think of Victor?" I asked.

"I think he's got his noggin buried in the sand. I guess that's a common enough reaction – denial. He doesn't want to admit that someone might be trying to drop the final curtain on him."

"My take exactly," I said. "Did you find out anything at Del's?"

"The bartender knows who Victor is, but he said the night bartender would know more. He suggested I come back in the evening and talk to the other guy."

"Are we going to a bar?" Lila asked. I had no idea that she'd been listening.

"*No!*" Chris said adamantly.

Lila turned back to her friends while we stopped for a red light.

"Next time you say your prayers, pray for patience for me," Chris said, quietly.

Surprised, I turned to stare at him. He was looking in the rearview mirror at the Church Ladies.

Someone yelled and I turned to find a teenager in the car next to us signaling for me to lower my window. I rolled it down.

"Nice ride," he said. "Wanna sell it?"

"Nice ride?" Lila asked.

"It means he likes the car," I explained.

"Thanks, but it's not for sale," Chris called back to the young man.

"Too bad."

Smiling at the kid, I rolled up the window.

We turned left and the teenager pulled into our lane and did the same. A right turn came up and Teen Boy stayed with us. We pulled into Mikey's school. I was watching the kid and he pulled up to the curb.

"Chris, I think that boy is tailing us. Maybe he's going to follow us home and try to steal the car."

A young girl came out of the school and walked up to the teenager's car, opened the door and climbed in. Coincidence. He'd been picking up his little sister. Apparently, he wasn't a thief. I was becoming too suspicious for my own good.

CHAPTER FOURTEEN

Monday night Jasmine called us at home because Addie had remembered something. Jasmine put Addie on the phone.

"When I was hiding in the camper, I didn't have anything to do, and I found some mail lying in the sink. So I sorted through it. I remembered that the man with the mustache is named John. At least that was the name on the mail. I can't recall his last name, but it was something like Jenkins or Jacobs, or maybe Jackson. All I can remember is that it began with a *J*. I hope this helps."

"It might. Let me have you talk to Chris."

I handed the phone to Chris, figuring he might have a few questions, and while he talked to Addie I let the dogs in the back door. They were scratching to come in and it was becoming annoying.

"Did you happen to notice his address when you looked at all of those bills?" Chris was asking when I returned to the kitchen.

I saw his face darken and took that as a *No*.

"Uh huh," he said. "Did you notice anything else?"

He was quiet while he listened to the answer. Sherlock sat at his feet and watched him intently. Chris rolled his upper lip under in Bogey fashion, but I had a feeling it might be more in frustration than him moving into Bogey mode.

"Well, Addie, I'm glad you called us, but the fact that he's a 'mess pot' isn't going to help us much. Being messy isn't a crime. If you think of anything else, let us know." He handed the phone back to me.

"Thank you, Addie," I said. "We'll get this figured out. Are you feeling better yet?"

"No," she replied. "When I realized what a foolish thing I'd done, it just sapped me of all my strength. I can't believe what a dumb thing I did. I guess it was the heat of the moment. It's going to take some time before I start feeling like my old self again. And I'm a little afraid to go out right now, just in case that man is out there. I wouldn't want him to see me. But thank you for asking."

"We'll do everything we can to get this guy off the street. You just take care of yourself and don't worry too much. He doesn't know where you're staying," I said.

Watson licked my ankle and I pushed her away with my foot. She seemed to like the taste of the body lotion I used. After a second cursory lick and another shove from me, she ambled away and sat down by Sherlock.

"I called Elsie to see if he'd been around, but she didn't know. She's glued to that television most of the time." Addie sounded frustrated with Elsie's TV viewing habits.

"Okay, we'll be in touch with you, and if you think of anything else, call us." I hung up and turned to Chris.

"How's she feeling?" Chris asked.

"It finally dawned on her that she'd done something very stupid, and very dangerous. She's tired and she's frightened, as she should be. Other than that, I think she's okay."

"We should check back with that neighbor and find out if she's seen that truck hanging around Addie's house."

"She said she already talked to Elsie, and she hasn't seen anything."

"Then it's back to Florence's house for a stakeout."

"Chris," I said, "we've got too much to do at the restaurant right now. I don't see how we can fit all of this in."

"Is there anything I can do to help?" Mikey's hopeful voice came from the top of the stairs.

"You're supposed to be in bed, Ace." Chris had given Mikey the nickname of Ace because, well, Mikey liked it. It was part of the forties jargon that Chris used so often.

"I was," he called down the stairs. "I heard the phone ring and couldn't get to sleep."

"So you eavesdropped?" I asked.

"No. Well, yeah. I like to know what's going on around here."

"Back to bed, Squirt," I said. "And it's rude to listen in on other people's conversations. Don't do it again."

"Yes, Ma'am."

I could hear my son's footsteps pounding across the floor upstairs. That was his way of letting us know that he didn't like being left out.

I looked at Chris and he shrugged. "Kids!"

***

Chris left to take Mikey to school and I was cleaning up the breakfast dishes when the phone rang. Sherlock raced for the phone and slid into the wall, as usual. Would he ever learn? Watson sat back and watched his antics, licking her paw. I had a feeling that if I could read her mind, she'd be saying, *What a doofus*. I agreed with her.

"Hello," I said, answering the phone.

"Is this Mrs. Cross?" The voice sounded familiar.

"Yes, this is Pamela," I replied.

"Uh, this is Victor. Victor Rogers. Remember me?"

"Honestly, Victor, I won't forget you anytime soon," I replied. "What can I do for you?"

"I've been doing a lot of thinking, and if there's any possibility that you and your husband are right about someone being after me, then I'd better take steps. I'm calling my retired police friend this morning. He'll know what to do."

"I think that's an excellent idea. You really would be better off in the hands of someone who knows what they're doing."

"I also wondered if I could ask a favor," Victor said.

"What would that be?" I couldn't imagine what he could want from virtual strangers if he had a friend who could help him.

"I know that my friend won't be able to watch over me twenty-four hours a day, and I wondered if I could call on you and your husband to help out."

I didn't know what to say. "Victor, let me have your phone number. I'll talk to Chris and call you back. He's out of the house right now."

Sherlock apparently decided it was time to play. He leaped onto my foot like it was a stuffed toy. "Stop that," I ordered, trying to push all hundred and two pounds of him away.

"Excuse me?" Victor said.

"Sorry. I have a very playful dog underfoot right now."

"Oh. I'll bet you have one of those ankle-biters, don't you?"

"Not exactly," I said, trying to push a very determined Sherlock away from my foot again.

Victor gave me his phone number and I wrote it on a chalk board by the phone. "Please don't wait too long. Now that I think I might be in danger, I want to take action right away."

"I'll call you back within the hour," I said.

We hung up and I grabbed Sherlock's collar. "What's the matter with you, Pal? You pick the darnedest times to want to play."

He lunged for my foot again, and Watson came over to see if she could play, too.

"Outside! Both of you." I herded them to the back door and let them out. Then it struck me. I hadn't fed them yet. No wonder they wanted my attention. I prepared their dishes and set them outside the back door and refilled their water dish. Labrador retrievers are known for their even tempers. The dogs ate with relish, tails wagging, without giving me a look of scorn. I chuckled to myself, wondering if I'd even recognize a dog's dirty look.

Sitting down on the back porch while the dogs ate, I waited for Chris to come home. I finally heard him pull into the driveway and walked through the house and to the front door to meet him.

"Everything okay with Mikey?" I asked.

"Sure. Why?"

"He seemed kind of quiet at breakfast. I wondered if he was upset about last night."

"Ace wants to be a part of things. He can't, and that frustrates him. I gave him a couple of tidbits that he can share with Danny today. Those kids love a good mystery."

I nodded. "That they do. Victor called while you were gone."

"What did he want? To tell us to get a life and leave him alone?"

"Not quite. He's thought things over, and he's asked for our help. He's going to call his copper friend, and he wants us to help out. What do you think?"

"I think we'll help out in any way we can."

"I thought you'd say that. He gave me his number and I told him I'd call him back."

I called Victor and explained that while we would help, we were only available in the morning because we had a business to run. Chris motioned for me to tell Victor to hold the line for a minute.

"Victor, hold on for a sec. Chris wants to tell me something."

"We should have discussed this," Chris said. "I can go over in the evening if you can cover the restaurant. Maybe not every night, but at least part of the time."

I turned back to the phone after pushing the speaker button. "Chris says he can help out in the evening, too. Exactly what do you want us to do? By the way, you're on speaker phone now, so we can both hear you."

"It may sound silly, but mostly just keep me company. I don't want to be alone right now."

"Don't you think it might be wiser if you called the police?" I asked.

"I called my friend after I spoke to you and he's on his way over. He said I shouldn't worry too much; that this whole thing is probably a mistake. But after thinking everything over, I'm inclined to believe you and your husband. I don't believe in coincidences, so I'm sure that address you and your husband found is mine. I still can't think of anyone who might come after me though."

"We'll do everything we can to help," Chris said. "Will you call us back after you talk to your friend?"

"I will. I see him pulling up to the curb right now, so I'll get back to you later on."

We hung up the phone and sat and looked at each other.

Chris spoke first, after checking his watch. "It's only nine o'clock. We've got some free time this morning. Why don't we drive over toward Victor's part of town and keep an eye out for that black truck. If that goon is hanging around anywhere near Victor's house, maybe we can spot him and follow him."

"That's not a bad idea. Besides, if we see the truck, then we'll know what this John person is up to, which means Victor will be safe."

We took my Jeep because it was better suited to surveillance – not so recognizable – and drove to the general vicinity of Victor's place.

While driving past a large department store parking lot, I spotted the black Dodge dually with a white camper attached to it. "Chris! There it is."

Chris pulled into the lot, leaving plenty of distance between the truck and us, and parked. We'd wait John out and follow him. He could lead us to some interesting places, or he could lead us on a wild goose chase.

Only time would tell.

CHAPTER FIFTEEN

We waited. And we waited. After over an hour, I walked into the mall and looked around for someone fitting John's description. Chris sat in the Jeep and watched in case I missed him. Fortunately for me, it wasn't a big mall. I walked in and out of every store, but no one fit John's description. I returned to the car.

"Any action out here?" I asked.

"Not a thing, other than a mall cop who wanted to know why I was sitting here. I told him I was waiting for my wife, which is the truth. We chatted. He kept glancing over at the truck, so I finally asked him if there was something wrong. He said that he was keeping an eye on the truck because it had been parked there since yesterday."

"Really! I wonder if John met someone here and left in the other vehicle. I'd think he'd be coming back soon, if that's the case."

Chris shrugged.

I tend to roll my eyes, and Chris shrugs. We all have our little habits.

"I don't know, but if he's not back soon, we're going to have to give it up for today. I have business to take care of at the restaurant."

"I've got a few things to finish, too, like paying bills," I said. Glancing at the truck I took note that Addie had been right about the ladder. I kind of hoped this guy was on it when it broke.

We waited for another half hour and left, driving by Victor's house before heading for the restaurant. We didn't see anything suspicious.

Arriving at *Bogey Nights*, we let ourselves in and began the process of making sure everything was in order. Our chef, Luis, was already in the kitchen setting ingredients out, ready to prepare a repast for the evening crowd. His sous chef would be in later. Our restaurant was actually rather exclusive, only opening for dinner, and of course, we had the cocktail lounge. Our prices were high, but people didn't seem to mind paying for gourmet food and atmosphere, which included being around Chris and me.

Our amateur detective status had helped the business.

"Chris, I've been thinking. Maybe we should start opening for lunch, too."

"I've had the same thing on my mind, Babe. We'd have to hire more help and give more hours to our staff, but I think we can do it. Luis and I were talking about it the other day. He can't be here for both lunch and dinner, but he knows someone who would probably be willing to take on the lunch crowd. I'll talk to him about it."

"And I'll speak to Phyllis and Gloria to see if they want more hours. I'm pretty sure they'd be up for it. Gloria has been talking about taking on a second job."

Chris walked back to the kitchen with me. He stopped to talk to Luis, and I kept walking. My office is located behind the kitchen.

I sat down at my desk, pulled the business checkbook out of a drawer, and began paying bills. I knew I should start doing this online, on the computer, but I was stubborn. I figured it was just a matter of time before someone figured out how to hack into everyone's account. My suspicious mind was always working double time.

After finishing my paperwork, I leaned back and thought about Victor. At first he hadn't seemed to believe us about someone being after him. Fortunately, he'd had second thoughts about it and he seemed to feel it would be best to be more alert and careful. I wondered why the killer hadn't come after him yet. The only explanation I could think of was that since Addie had overheard him, he was taking his time and being more careful. He didn't want to take unnecessary chances. I figured that he'd let things die down and then give it his best shot – unless we could find him first.

Chris walked into the office. "I've been thinking about Victor."

"Me, too."

"I'm sorry we couldn't wait for the goon to make an appearance. It bothers me that we know where his truck is, but we had to leave."

"Chris, why don't you drive back over there? I can cover things here. I feel like we're being way too blasé about this. Not only is Victor in danger, but Addie's in danger, too, and she probably feels like a prisoner in Jasmine's house since she's not comfortable going out in public."

"Good idea," he said. "If the truck is still there, I'll wait. If it's gone, I'll head home and change into my work clothes and come back here."

I chuckled. Chris's work clothes consist of a forties-style suit with a vest, and sometimes a fedora. "Okay. If you don't come back I'll ask Phyllis to cover so I can go home and change."

Chris glanced down at the floor and then back at me. "I think I'll bring the dogs back with me. We've been hanging around Victor's place a lot. This guy may have seen us, and he could come after you, as well as Victor and Addie."

"I think that's a stretch, but you never know. Mikey will be at Constance's house, so we don't have to worry about him. I think we've got it all covered."

"I'll stop by Victor's and see what his friend said, too." Chris leaned across the desk and gave me a kiss before leaving.

"Oh, what did Luis say?"

"He'll call his friend, Nathaniel, this afternoon. He says Nate is a retired chef who's bored and wants to go back to work."

"Cool," I said. "I had another thought, too. I think I'll call Donna, the waitress at that coffee shop, and see if she might be available."

"Good idea."

Chris took off and I called Phyllis and Gloria at home. They both said they'd be happy to take on extra hours.

Next I called Donna.

"Oh, Mrs. Cross. I was just about to call you. The guy with the droopy mustache was in late yesterday afternoon. He was asking a lot of questions about Addie."

I was surprised, and yet I wasn't. He had to be worried about what Addie might know. "What did you tell him?"

"I told him I didn't know who he was talking about. He pushed me about it, but I stuck to my story. I didn't let him know that she comes in here a lot. The other ladies were in for lunch yesterday, but Addie wasn't with them. They bought some food to take home for her. They told me she's afraid to go anywhere because of that schmuck, and that really makes me mad. Did I do the right thing?"

"You did. I wish you'd have called us sooner, but no harm done."

"I would have called but some things came up and… Well, I hate to say it, but I forgot in all the confusion." Her next words sounded like she was close to tears. "The owners of this coffee shop are retiring and they've sold the place. It's not going to be a coffee shop anymore and I'm out of a job in two weeks."

"Great timing," I said.

"*What?*"

"I'm calling to offer you a job. How about it? Would you come work for us at *Bogey Nights*? Of course, you'll have to wear a period costume for the job. All of our waitresses dress like they did in the forties."

"Oh, Mrs. Cross, you're a lifesaver! I can't thank you enough. I'm a single parent and I was really worried about what my son and I would do. My husband left right after my son was born. And I sew, so I can make some costumes for the job. This is going to be fun."

"Please, call me Pamela. And *you'll* be a lifesaver for us. We're going to start opening for lunch soon."

I told Donna that two weeks was perfect and she could move right from her old job to the new one. On a whim, I decided to have her work the dinner shift. Tips would be better, and I could relate to her as a single parent. I'd been there.

Most of our staff resembled past actors and actresses. Phyllis and Gloria resembled Marilyn Monroe and Myrna Loy. George Chandler looked very much like George Raft, and the female patrons loved him. Susan French didn't resemble anyone in particular, but she looked great in her forties costumes, and she'd been wishing she could work an earlier shift. Donna would take over her spot and I'd move Susan to lunchtime. I'd still need to find at least one more for the noontime shift, but that shouldn't be a problem.

Phyllis came in early so I could head home and change clothes, and Gloria came with her. Unfortunately, I'd forgotten that Chris took the car. Gloria graciously offered to give me a ride home, and I took her up on it.

We pulled up to the curb and I saw that Chris was home, so Gloria headed back to the restaurant.

"Chris," I called out, entering the house. "Where are you?"

"Upstairs, changing clothes."

Climbing up the stairs, I met him at the top. "I didn't expect you to be home so early. Was the truck gone?"

"No, it was still there. The mall copper recognized me and came over to flap his gums. He said he didn't like the truck sitting there for so long, so he put a warning on the windshield. It told the owner to move it or it would be towed away."

"I wonder what's going on. Maybe John decided the truck was too visible and found something else to drive."

Chris shrugged. "I told the mall copper that you weren't really shopping, and that we were watching the truck because it could be involved in a crime. He just assumed I was a copper. I gave him my cell phone number and he said he'd call me if there was any action with the truck."

"I talked to Donna and offered her a job. It turns out she's losing the job she has anyway, and she was thrilled."

Chris looked at me. "Why is she losing her job? Something wrong there?"

I pulled a dress out of the closet and began changing. Chris whistled at me, and I grinned. "No. They're closing down the coffee shop. Anyway, she said John was there yesterday asking a lot of questions about Addie."

Chris looked worried. "What did she tell him?"

"Absolutely nothing. She acted like she didn't know who Addie was."

Chris smiled and the worry lines disappeared. "Let's give her a raise."

"I think it's a good thing we had Addie stay with Jasmine. She'll be safe there. I still think the police should be brought in on this though."

"So do I, but we can't force anyone to call them, and the only information you and I have is hearsay."

We finished changing clothes, and I swept my hair up into a forties style. We took separate cars back to the restaurant, with the dogs riding in the Jeep with me, just in case something came up and one of us had to leave. I put them in their fenced area behind my office with their dinner and some water. Before they ate they ran around the perimeter to make sure no one had invaded their space. Satisfied, they ate their dog food while I went to work.

Phyllis met me at the front desk. "A lady called to make a reservation for a party of four. I told her we were booked tonight and she said she was a very close personal friend of yours." She picked up the reservation book. "We've got a party of twelve coming in for a birthday party, and another party of six coming in for a pre-wedding dinner. The rest of the tables are full, too. It's going to be a busy night. Anyway, I did some finagling and managed to fit them in."

"Thank you, Phyllis. Good job. What was the lady's name?" I had a feeling I probably knew who it was.

"Jasmine Thorpe. Was that okay?"

I sighed. "You did the right thing." Was I ready for the Church Ladies tonight? I wasn't sure. And if it was a party of four, then Addie was probably coming along. I was sure she needed a night out and a break from her confinement at Jasmine's house. Everything would be okay.

I actually believed that until Chris and I were talking later and his cell phone rang.

"Yeah," he said, answering it. He listened and I saw his face harden.

"Have you called the police?" he asked.

Again, he listened.

"I'm on my way."

CHAPTER SIXTEEN

"**W**hat is it?" I asked.

"That was the mall cop. He said he was checking out the camper again and there's a very nasty odor coming from inside."

"What would that mean?"

"It could mean nothing, or it could mean somebody's goin' home feet first tonight."

"Why would you think someone's dead?"

"He described the odor. I smelled something like that when I was a mailman. An elderly man's mailbox was filling up, so I stopped to do a check on him. He'd been dead for a few days, and it was summertime. I'll never forget the stench as long as I live."

"Oh, Chris, what's going on?"

"I don't know, but I'm bound to find out."

"Call me as soon as you know anything," I said.

Chris left and Phyllis and I opened the restaurant. I checked the reservation book to see who was coming in. Looking up, I saw two faces that I recognized.

"Mr. and Mrs. Longworth," I said. "It's so good to see you. It's been a while."

Mrs. Longworth smiled. "We've been on vacation in the Mediterranean. What a wonderful trip."

She filled me in as I showed them to their table. Mrs. Longworth was involved in several charities and worked hard for her community. She deserved a trip and time to enjoy herself. I told her as much. Mr. Longworth was a well-known criminal defense attorney. If I were to do something illegal, I'd definitely want him in my corner.

"We've been so fortunate. This city has been good to us, and I like giving something back." Mrs. Longworth sat down on the chair I'd pulled out for her.

Mr. Longworth gave his wife a smile of approval. "I have to admit that we didn't find another restaurant to rival this one while we were gone."

"Well, bless your heart," I said. "Thank you."

I returned to the front desk after talking for a moment longer, and they were settled in with menus. I placed their drink orders and glanced at my watch. I hoped it didn't take too long for Chris to call me. Patience isn't my long suit.

The door opened and the party of twelve walked in. They were happy and chattering and ready for a celebration.

"And which one of you is having a birthday?" I asked.

A gentleman stepped forward, slowly, and declared he was the culprit. "I'm ninety-six today," he said.

"Well, you don't look a day over eighty-six," I said.

They all laughed and Gloria showed them to their table.

The party of six came in and were seated by Phyllis.

And the party of four was right behind them. "Pamela, Dear, God bless you and what's your special tonight?" Jasmine looked different. It took me a moment to figure out what had changed.

"Why, you're the only thing special in this place. You look wonderful in your forties dress. All of you do," I said, taking in each of their outfits, all from the same era. Jasmine was wearing a light blue shirtmaker dress with small red bows throughout the fabric. She had her hands tucked into the front pockets and smiled at me.

"Oh, you," Lila said, patting the skirt of her grey day dress, the kind that homemakers wore while they cooked and cleaned. At least it fell in soft folds. Her tennis shoes definitely looked out of place.

May grinned and pushed Addie front and center. They each wore soft cotton dresses. May's was black with soft pink roses throughout the fabric. Addie's was off-white with a flower I couldn't identify decorating the fabric. Both dresses had shoulder pads and caplike sleeves, and a V neckline with a winged collar. It almost seemed like they'd hit a two-for-the-price-of-one sale, but they looked adorable.

And all four women wore hats. Lila's was big and floppy, and the rest were smaller and just covered the top of their hair.

"We'd like a fancy dinner tonight," Addie said.

"Is it a special occasion?" I asked.

"Yes. I'm out of the house and I don't believe that John person will see me here. I can't help wondering what went wrong in his life to turn him into a killer though."

Hopefully he'll run his car off a cliff and never see you again, I thought. I glanced at the Church Ladies and chastised myself for having an unchristian thought. They were getting to me. Addie was beginning to think of him in terms of being a person with circumstances that had turned him into a potential murderer. But we all have circumstances. That doesn't mean we plan to kill someone. Victor might agree with me on that one.

Phyllis arrived and showed the ladies to their table. I continued greeting people at the door, and a few made their way into the lounge. The Sugar Daddies would start their music soon.

I carried my cell phone with me, waiting for Chris to call. My patience was beginning to wear thin. What had he found?

I was debating with myself about calling Chris, when he walked through the door.

"Chris, I didn't expect you back this soon. What happened? What was in the back of the camper?"

"No dead bodies. Let me check with Luis and make sure things are running smoothly in the kitchen and then I'll tell you what happened."

At least there were no dead bodies. I could wait for the explanation for a few more minutes.

I made the rounds and checked on the customers to be sure they didn't feel neglected. The birthday group had ordered a cake ahead of time and all of our employees gathered and sang the birthday song to our honored guest. He was absolutely glowing – until he grabbed his chest and fell off his chair taking silverware and several dishes with him.

Bending over and leaning close, I briefly studied his face. The initial glow had turned into a pallor. I dropped down and felt for a pulse. Nothing. I was preparing for CPR when his daughter put her hand on my shoulder.

"He left a Living Will. He didn't want to be resuscitated. He knew he had a heart condition. At his age, well, he said he'd just as soon go and be with my mother. We lost her twenty years ago." Tears streamed down her face. "He was a good man, but he was tired."

So our birthday boy expired – right there. In *Bogey Nights*. I was just about ready to start clutching at my own chest.

Chris ran out from the kitchen, Phyllis ran to call the paramedics, and when I looked up I saw the Church Ladies approaching. My heart dropped to my feet when I considered what they might do or say. Would they preach at the family? Drop on their knees and pray at the top of their lungs for the elderly man's salvation?

Oh, ye of little faith.

The ladies comforted the family with loving words and kind gestures. They were wonderful.

And people being people, the rest of the diners just kept eating while throwing several curious glances over their shoulders at the unfolding drama. After all, there was no blood and no screaming, so how bad could it be? Mr. and Mrs. Longworth were the exceptions and came to ask if they could help. I thanked them and shook my head, indicating it was too late.

The paramedics arrived quickly, and the family left heartbroken, but comforted by four wonderful little old ladies who understood their grief.

"Well," May said. "That man's daughter told me he was celebrating his ninety-sixth birthday. At least he went out with a bang."

"May!" Jasmine exclaimed.

"Well, she's right," Lila said. "He was having fun with his family, and there was a lot of commotion when all the dishes broke."

I turned my head away and rolled my eyes. What next?

"Pamela," Chris said, "I'm going back to the office to fill out some paperwork about this incident."

"I'm right behind you," I said. "Phyllis can take care of things while you tell me what happened with the truck."

"Truck? Not *the* truck." Addie looked into Chris's eyes and nodded her head. "Yes, indeed, he's talking about the black truck. I can see it in his eyes."

Three other heads turned to Chris and all bore questioning expressions.

"You might as well all come back to Pamela's office. That way I'll only have to tell the story once."

We followed him through the kitchen and back to the office.

"Are the dogs here tonight?" Lila asked.

"Yes, but I'll leave them outside," I said.

"No, it's okay. You can bring them in. I need to lose my fear of dogs, and I've been praying about it. Your pets can be my test case. They're so darned big – if I can get along with them, then I can get along with other dogs."

"You have dogs?" Addie asked.

I nodded. "Two Labrador retrievers."

"Oh, my favorite breed. I've had dogs over the years, and I had a Lab some years ago. She was the best dog I ever owned. If I wasn't so old, I'd buy me a couple." She glanced at me suspiciously, maybe having second thoughts. "How old are your dogs?"

"About a year and a half," I replied. "Why?"

"I just wanted to make sure they're past that puppy stage. My Lab was hell on wheels as a puppy, but when she grew up? She was the best companion a woman could ask for."

Lila cringed when Addie said *hell on wheels*.

Jasmine reached over and patted her hand. "It's okay, Lila. She didn't mean to say that."

"Yes, I did," Addie said. "That dog was an absolute terror until she grew out of the puppy stage."

"Addie's the wild one in our little group," May explained.

"Do you ladies want to hear what happened or not?" Chris asked. "I can wait if you want to talk about puppies some more." His frustration was showing again. First he went looking for a dead body, and then he returned and found an unexpected body and a gaggle of Church Ladies. He was probably wound pretty tight.

"Go ahead, Bogey Man. Tell us what happened."

While he spoke I let the dogs in and told them to sit. They looked at the ladies and sat, but their behinds barely touched the floor. I figured they knew if they played their cards right they'd be in for some attention.

Chris cleared his throat after rolling his upper lip under and pulling on his ear lobe, a sure sign that the Bogey persona was about to put in an appearance.

"Okay," he said. "I had this pegged as a crime scene, with someone down for the count. So I hightailed it over to the mall —"

"What mall?" May asked. "And what crime scene?"

"We found that black truck that Addie told us about sitting in a mall near Victor's house. It appears to have possibly been abandoned. The mall copper called Chris and told him about a nasty odor coming from the camper on the back of the truck."

I glanced at Chris. He was rolling his lip under again and rocking back and forth from heel to toe.

"So Chris drove over to see what was going on. Chris?" I pointed at him, indicating he could pick up the story.

He quit rocking. "Thanks, Cookie. Okay, so the mall copper meets me by the camper. We walk around the truck and I take a sniff after eyeballing the whole thing. The smell ain't good, but I don't picture a heavy inside and bleeding. See?"

"Heavy?" Addie asked.

"A bad guy," I interpreted.

"Oh."

Chris pursed his lips before going on. "Yeah, a bad guy. The smell is putrid, but something ain't right. I remember that Addie climbed right into the camper, so maybe it could be unlocked. See? So the mall copper and me, we try the back door of the camper. It opens like a charm. He's thinkin' he better go call the Paddy Wagon. I tell him, 'Hold the phone, I don't see no dead body in here.' So he settles down and hands me his flashlight."

Chris stopped and shook his head.

"I don't know where that bozo went after you got out in Victorville, but somewhere along the way a raccoon climbed into the camper. And it died."

"A raccoon?" Jasmine asked.

"Dead as a doornail." Chris rolled his hand into a fist and pointed downward with his thumb.

"So that means the bad guy is still out there," May said.

"It sure does," Addie said, sadly.

"Uh oh," Lila said.

Jasmine opened her mouth but I cut her off. It seemed like these women *all* had to make a comment every time something happened.

"Okay, so Addie, you're going to have to continue to lie low for a while." I watched her for a reaction.

"You're right," she said, suddenly standing up straighter. "I need to stay where he can't find me. But I'm not afraid. You need to understand that."

"A little fear can be healthy sometimes," Lila said, sounding very wise.

CHAPTER SEVENTEEN

Apparently Watson recognized that the ladies were charged with emotion. She walked over to Addie and held out her paw. Not to be outdone, Sherlock padded over to Lila and turned his back to her to give her something to scratch.

Lila watched the dog for a moment before setting a tentative hand on his back. He wiggled a little and she got the hint and gently stroked him. He wiggled a bit more before dropping and rolling onto his back. Lila relaxed and grinned, and gave him some well-deserved scratching.

I handed each of the women a doggie cookie to give to the dogs. Addie held hers out for Watson, and Lila held it much more tentatively. Sherlock didn't disappoint me. He took it from her hand very gently.

"That's *it*," Addie said, shaking Watson's other paw. "As soon as I can go home, I'm going to look for an older Lab who needs a home. I'll go to one of those rescue places you hear about. We'll finish growing old together. I'd feel so much safer."

"Safer?" Chris asked. "The most a Lab would do is lick the bad guy to death."

"Chris, why don't you take the ladies to the lounge while I put the dogs back outside? Lila can have a glass of wine – it has such a calming effect – and the other ladies can have whatever they want. On the house. That'll be our way of thanking them for their help with the birthday tragedy."

"Oh, it was our pleasure," May said. "We've all lived long enough to have lost loved ones. We knew how those poor people were feeling. I just hope, and pray, that they understand their loved one is in a better place now. I know how that sounds to some people, but it's true. It's not a cliché."

"No, it's not," Jasmine said.

"He's happier now," Lila commented.

"And he got to celebrate his birthday before he left us," Addie said, smiling. "How wonderful is that?"

Chris almost looked panicky when he turned to me. "*You* take the ladies to the lounge, and *I'll* put the dogs out."

"Oh, brother," I mumbled, leading the ladies out of the office.

Daniel, the bartender, took the ladies' orders while I got them settled at a nice table in the corner, not too close to the band. They loved to chat and the band made that difficult.

I sat down, planning to visit with them for just a few minutes before I had to get back to work. We talked about the upcoming church social and Jasmine said the ladies had been put in charge of the homemade ice cream. Strawberry was her specialty, and May said she'd take care of the chocolate while Lila made the vanilla.

"I'm going to be attending," Addie said. "Our church doesn't do anything like that and I think they should. But, then, we don't have as many children who attend our services. Your church has plenty of children, and I like that."

Addie stopped talking and her face began to turn reddish. Her jaws were clenched and I could see the muscles working. She appeared to have quit breathing. The other three ladies were still talking and hadn't noticed that anything was wrong. I hoped we weren't losing another patron. One in a night was enough.

"Addie? Are you okay?" I asked. "What's wrong?"

She turned and looked at me, her eyes wide. Pointing toward the doorway to the lounge, she moved her mouth, but no words came out.

"Addie?" My heart beat harder than normal. "What is it?"

"It's *him*," she said softly.

By this time the other ladies had figured out that something was wrong and they were paying attention.

"Who?" Jasmine asked.

"*Him!*" Addie said adamantly, shaking her finger in the general direction of her gaze. She grabbed Lila's wine glass and took a big swallow. "Go get the dogs!"

There was no doubt in my mind about whom she was referring to as I turned to face the doorway.

But there was no one there.

"Was it the goon?" I asked.

"Oh, yes. It was the goon okay. He was standing right there, looking straight into my eyes." Her hands were shaking. "Are you going to go get those dogs or what?"

I jumped out of my chair and ran to the door, looking in every direction as I passed through it. I couldn't see anyone who resembled John… John… Whatever his name was. I ran outside, and Chris saw me and followed behind.

"What's going on, Babe?" he asked.

"That John guy was here. Addie saw him." My head flew from side to side, looking for the man or the truck and camper.

"There!" I yelled, watching his truck pull out from the side of the restaurant and onto the street.

He didn't seem to be in any big hurry.

"Chris, go after him," I said. "Don't just stand there."

"Pamela, by the time I get to the car he'll be gone. But at least we know he's picked up his truck, not that it makes any difference."

I looked into Chris's eyes. I knew he was right. "Addie is really scared. I think one of us had better follow them home tonight and make sure *he* doesn't follow them."

"I'll do that," Chris said. "And I'll go inside with them to look through the house. I wouldn't want to see anything happen to any of those women."

They were growing on him. They frightened him in an odd way, but he liked them.

"I'd better let the ladies know he's gone," I said. "And I'll let them know that you're going to follow them later. Phyllis probably thinks we've deserted her, so why don't you go back to work until the ladies leave?"

"How did he know she'd be here?" Chris asked, walking from the street toward the restaurant. "Was it a coincidence or did he see her somewhere and follow her?"

"I can't see any way that he could know she was staying with Jasmine," I replied.

"Unless…," Chris said thoughtfully.

"Unless what?"

"Maybe he saw the mall copper and me reconnoitering his truck. Maybe he followed me home and then here. This is *not* a good thing, Pamela. If that's the case, then he knows where we live, where we work, and that Addie is a friend of ours. No, this is not a good thing. Now Victor's predicament has reached out and moved too close to home."

"Mikey," I said. "We can't let this man come near Mikey. I hope you're wrong about him following you. I'm going to call Constance right now and ask if Mikey can stay with her for a few days."

"Good idea," Chris said. "You can take some fresh clothes over to him in the morning. Just make sure you're not being followed. In fact, maybe *I'll* take them over to him."

Although it wasn't cold outside, I still felt a shiver run through me. I didn't like where this whole situation was heading. Now we had more than Addie and Victor to worry about. I didn't like it at all.

We walked inside and although it took a moment to sink in, I heard someone singing with the band. Occasionally the wife of one of the band members came in and sang, but it wasn't her voice. Although it sounded different than it had in church, I knew it was Lila.

Lila was singing *Symphony*, one of my favorite songs, although not from the forties. She couldn't have known how that song turned my heart inside out. I sat down and listened, calming as she sang each note to perfection. The love song made me think of Chris.

It was so odd to watch her in her plain forties housedress with her limp gray hair, singing like a canary. The woman's appearance and her voice didn't seem to go together.

When she finished, she turned to the band and spoke quietly. They nodded and set their instruments down, moving in around her, and they harmonized with *Coming in on a Wing and a Prayer* – a song from World War II about waiting for word from a missing plane. All of a sudden a voice comes on the radio and says the plane is coming in on a wing and a prayer. I could almost see the anxious faces waiting around a radio and it gave me an unexpected chill.

They sang a capella, with no instruments. Only voices. It brought a tear to my eye. Glancing at the other ladies, I saw that it touched them, too.

As I listened I wondered if I'd been born in the wrong era. Chris and I cared so much about all things related to the forties. It seemed that people had a more common goal and that they pulled together instead of fighting each other. There was innocence and romance linked to that era in my mind. If I'd actually grown up in the World War II years I might feel differently, but reading books, watching vintage movies and listening to the music, it seemed like a time I would have enjoyed.

I looked up and saw that diners had left their tables to stand at the door and listen to Lila.

She didn't see them. She looked over their heads and sang her little heart out.

Jasmine nudged me. "Lila thought the music might take Addie's mind off the goon, as Chris likes to call him."

"Good idea," I said. "I know it sure took *my* mind off of things. By the way, Chris is going to follow you home tonight and check your house before he leaves."

I could see the relief on her face. She nodded assent.

We turned back to Lila and listened to the rest of the song. When she finished singing, everyone applauded – loudly. Lila turned to the band and thanked them, and when she left the stage I could see that she was blushing. I could hear the buzz of conversation as people returned to their tables. I found it interesting that they tried to ignore a man who had dropped dead right in front of them, and yet they left their tables to hear Lila sing. Maybe Lila's singing was Beauty and death was the Beast? I wasn't sure.

Addie jumped up and met Lila halfway across the dance floor. "That was outstanding, Lila! I had no idea you could sing like that. You've been hiding your light, my friend."

"The Lord gave me a gift, my voice, and I thought maybe this was one of the times I should be faithful and use that gift." Lila could be so humble sometimes – most of the time, actually.

"You were aces," I said, "and you can sing here anytime you want to."

"Aces," Lila said. "I like that. I'm aces." She grinned before she buried her face in her hands, embarrassed.

Leaving the ladies to their own devices, I returned to the dining room to look for Chris. The Longworths were leaving and he was at the front door shaking hands with Mr. Longworth.

Hurrying over, I just missed them as they opened the front door and left. I caught the door before it closed and leaned out to wave good-bye, but pulled my hand back when I caught sight of a black truck with a white camper driving by.

"Chris!" I called. "That bum is still hanging around."

"I'll take care of this," he said, picking up the telephone receiver.

I listened while he called the police department and told them that there was a strange man lurking around outside the restaurant. I knew the department was short-handed, and I didn't know if they'd be able to get here before we closed. I was sure they had other, more important calls to take care of all over town. Glancing at my watch I saw that we had about half an hour to go before we could start locking up.

Chris hung up.

"What did they say?" I asked.

"The coppers will be here as soon as they can. We'll probably be closed by then." He curled his upper lip under and appeared thoughtful.

"What?" I asked.

"I think we need to outsmart this sap."

"And how are we going to do that, Bogey Man?"

"Watch and learn, Dollface." He looked very smug. I couldn't imagine what he might be up to.

CHAPTER EIGHTEEN

While the customers began leaving in small groups, Chris kept his eye on the street outside. The truck had passed *Bogey Nights* twice and then seemed to disappear. Chris didn't trust that he was really gone. He left by the rear door of the restaurant, after turning off the back lights, and hot-footed it to the front to check out the street. I watched out the window with some amusement – Chris was doing a male version of tiptoeing.

He returned through the rear as I was locking the front door.

"Did you see him?" I asked, meeting him in the dining room area.

"I did some fancy footwork and saw him parked down the street."

Hiding a smile, I said, "Yeah, I saw some of that fancy footwork."

"He's going to have to cool his heels for a while. We're not leavin' this juke joint until I have a few things put in place."

I almost rolled my eyes, but caught myself in time. "We're not a cheap bar so don't call Bogey Nights a juke joint. We're a supper club with a cocktail lounge."

"I know, I know. But juke joint sounds more forties."

That stopped me cold. Chris never actually talked about trying to *sound* forties. He just did it.

"Okay. So what's the plan?" I asked, recovering.

Chris pulled on his ear lobe and grinned his best Bogey grin at me. "I want you to take Lila and May for a ride. The big lug is going to follow Jasmine's car when she leaves, thinking Addie's in it."

"But if he followed *us* here, which is what we think, then he's not going to know what her car looks like."

"I've got that covered. I'm going to pull Jasmine's car up out front and the women will all climb in, with Addie making a big show of it. Then I'm going to have Jasmine get back out and look through her purse, like she forgot something. She'll pull into the driveway and she and Addie will switch places with you and the dogs."

"The dogs?" Now I was really confused.

"I want Jasmine's car to look full. I don't want the palooka to realize we've pulled a switch. When you leave, turn left out of the driveway. That way you won't be driving past him and he won't see that two of the passengers are dogs."

"Gotcha." I was beginning to catch on.

"While you and the ladies are taking him on a wild goose chase, I'll take Jasmine and Addie home. After you've driven around, in the opposite direction from Jasmine's house, you can take Lila and May home. We can leave your Jeep here for the night, and then switch cars tomorrow."

"I don't suppose you have a simpler plan," I said hopefully.

"Take it or leave it, that's the plan."

"Okay. You know, our employees must think we're nuts. There's always something going on."

"If they don't think we're goofy now, they soon will."

I found the Church Ladies in the lounge, standing up and ready to leave. I explained the plan to them. You'd have thought I'd given them chocolate truffles wrapped in hundred dollar bills.

"Finally," May said. "We're going to be part of a plan."

"Well, praise the Lord," Lila said.

"Amen to that," Jasmine said, grinning. "It's about time you let us be involved."

Addie looked more than pleased – she looked relieved.

"Ladies," Jasmine said, "let's hold hands and pray for everyone's safety." They grabbed my hands in the process, and we all prayed. Actually, I felt a bit better after the last Amen. Jasmine took off her glasses and placed them in the pocket of her dress.

I checked in with Luis, in the kitchen, and he was ready to leave. Phyllis and Gloria were already halfway out the door when I called good-night to them. The three of them walked out to the parking lot together. Our other employees had already left for the night.

Chris pulled Jasmine's car around to the front of *Bogey Nights*, directly under the street light, and left the motor running. I unlocked the front door and the ladies waved good-night to me. I was hoping they wouldn't overact.

I ran to my office and grabbed the dog leashes before calling them inside. Clicking the leashes into place, we scrambled out the door and down the driveway so I could see what was going on.

"Thanks for a wonderful evening." Addie yelled and waved in the general direction of the restaurant, certainly gaining the goon's attention. She was the last one to enter the car.

Jasmine climbed out of the car and set her purse on the hood, searching through it. She leaned toward the car window and pointed at her eyes and then at the restaurant, indicating she'd lost her glasses. She climbed back into the car and pulled into the driveway. All in all, it was quite a performance. The best part was that the women were convincing.

As soon as they couldn't be seen from the street, Jasmine and Addie climbed out and Chris led them back to his classic green Chevy. I loaded the dogs into the rear seat with May, and Lila sat in front with me.

"Are we having fun yet, girls?" I asked.

Lila tittered.

"You can count on it," May said.

Glancing up, I saw the three employees standing in the parking lot watching, and shaking their heads. I waved before turning around and driving toward the street. At the end of the driveway, I looked both ways before pulling out and turning left. I saw the truck's lights flick on before the thug pulled away from the curb and hung a U-turn.

"He fell for it," I said. "He's going to tail us no matter how long it takes."

Checking my rearview mirror, I saw the nose of Chris's car pull up to the edge of the parking lot. He held back until we were well down the street before he turned right and headed for Jasmine's house. So far his plan was working.

I had no idea where I was going to go. I just drove. The only thing that mattered was that I stay in familiar territory so I always had a way out if the goon caught up to us and tried to cause trouble.

Everything was going so well – until the black truck pulled up next to us at a red light. He did a double-take when he saw the dogs in the car. I could almost see him mentally counting people in the car and looking at profiles. His face turned dark with anger. I did a quick inventory to make sure everyone had on their seatbelts. Unfortunately, there was nothing I could do to protect the dogs.

Watson must have picked up on my sudden fear. She whined and pawed the back of my seat.

"It's okay, girl. Lie down." I spoke over my shoulder. "Sherlock, you lie down, too."

Sherlock followed my gaze when I turned my head to look at the bad guy. He let out a huge, deep, protective growl before he obeyed. I glanced in the rearview mirror. May was crushed between the two big galoots. If anything went wrong, at least they gave her some padding.

Looking up, I saw the light change to green.

"Hold on, everyone," I said between clenched teeth. "We're about to go for a joy ride, only I don't think it'll be all that joyful."

Lila grabbed the sides of her seat. May gripped the back of my seat. The dogs, well, the dogs didn't do anything but lie there.

I checked out the traffic. Only one car was headed toward us, and it was moving slowly.

Laying rubber, I pulled away from the signal and made a hard left turn, even though I wasn't in the left turn lane. It took the goober longer to turn because of the oncoming car, but he managed to pull up behind us. He got right on my tail and shined his bright lights on the car. It was blinding in the rearview mirror. I stepped on the gas and headed for the freeway. I knew that my Jeep could outrun his dually truck any day of the week, but I wasn't sure about Jasmine's car. I needed to fly, and the freeway wasn't all that far away.

"Lila," I said. "Pull my cell phone out of my purse and call Chris."

Looking at me with wide-eyed innocence – and fear – she finally pried one of her hands off the edge of her seat. She leaned over and took a look at my speedometer.

I grinned at her.

She opened my purse and fumbled around, finally pulling out the phone. "What number do I use to call Chris?"

I told her how to use my speed dial, and she gave it a shot. "It's going to his answering machine."

I'd have rolled my eyes, but I was picking up speed and I didn't want the ol' peepers sticking that way now. Why on earth had my mother ever told me that story about sticking eyeballs?

"Okay, leave a message on his voice mail and tell him to call us right back. Tell him it's urgent."

Voice mail started and I heard Lila say, *"Chris! Come rescue us! That bad man is chasing us all over town. Pamela is going to take us on the crazy freeway again. Call me back fast."* Then she remembered, and added, more calmly, "Oh, by the way, this is Lila. I'm using Pamela's cell phone."

I hung a sharp right at the next street and began to pull away from the truck and camper. He must have had some kind of engine in that truck, because within a block he began to creep up on me again.

"Freeway ahead," I yelled, seeing the sign I'd been looking for. "We're home free now, ladies."

And then a copper pulled in behind me with his lights flashing.

And the cell phone rang.

CHAPTER NINETEEN

lancing in the rearview mirror, I saw the truck duck down a side street. Could I convince the copper that we'd been in danger? I didn't really care. At least he'd gotten rid of the goon for us.

Pulling over, I asked Lila to answer the cell phone. "It's Chris," she said.

"Would you tell him I'll call him back in a few minutes?"

"Pamela says she'll call you back after the police officer lets us go," Lila said, turning back to the cell phone. She moved the phone away from her ear and I had the distinct feeling that Chris might be yelling.

I reached out and she handed me the cell phone. "I'll call you back." I closed the phone and hung up on my husband, probably not the best way I could have handled things.

By this time the copper was tapping on my window. Two yellow Labs were grinning and panting, watching my every move. They'd both plopped their heads on the back of the two front seats. They'd never met a stranger, so to speak, and moved their gaze from me to the police officer. They appeared to be very excited.

"Officer," I said, rolling the window halfway down, "would you mind if I get out of the car? One of the dogs is beginning to drool on me."

The copper looked inside the car and saw two elderly women in vintage clothing and two very happy dogs. I glanced back and saw that May's hat was now lopsided, almost falling off her head.

"Have you ladies been drinking?" he asked.

"No, sir. Well, one of the ladies had a glass of wine, but that was about an hour ago."

He motioned me to climb out of the car.

"You were driving awfully fast. Why was that?"

"Well, Officer, you see, it's like this. There was this man following us, and we thought if we could —"

"What man?" he interrupted, glancing around.

"He turned the corner when you pulled up behind us. I swear that there really was a man. We were frightened."

"Why was he following you?" the officer asked.

"I have no idea," I lied, "but he didn't look very friendly."

"What are you ladies doing out at this time of night?"

I glanced at my watch; it was almost eleven-thirty. "My husband and I own a restaurant in town and I was giving my friends a ride home."

"What restaurant?" This copper sure could ask a lot of questions, but then that's his job.

"*Bogey Nights.*"

"I know that place. My wife has been bugging me to bring her in sometime. How's your food?"

"Excellent, and the ambiance is great, too. We have music and a dance floor." Never pass up an opportunity to advertise. I'd have offered him a free meal, but he might have misconstrued that as a bribe.

I hadn't rolled the window back up and by this time Sherlock had climbed into my seat and had his head hanging out the window. Drool was dripping down the lower half of the window. I'd have to pay for a carwash for Jasmine.

The copper didn't miss the action; he was grinning. "Okay, I'm going to let you go this time with a warning. Take the ladies home and get those dogs out of your car before they ruin it." He shook his head. "I have Labs, too. I know firsthand what they can do."

My first reaction was relief. My second was fear. "Is there any chance you might be willing to follow us as far as the freeway? It's only two blocks away."

"So you were really being followed?"

"Yes, sir. The man was in a black truck, a dually, with a white camper attached. If you should happen to see him, could you stop him to stall him until we can put some distance between us and him?" I did my best to appear helpless and bewildered. It seemed to be working. "You can't miss the black and white combination."

"You don't want much, do you?" He shook his head. "Get in your car and I'll follow you until I know you're safely on the freeway."

Before opening my door for me, he glanced inside one more time. May had coaxed Sherlock back to the rear of the car. The two dogs' long thick tails were wagging wildly, and the two ladies had their heads bowed with their hands clasped together. Watson's tail kept hitting May's hair, causing the hat to slip even farther.

"Is there something wrong with them?" the copper asked.

"No, they're praying for our safety since we'll be driving on the freeway." *I* recognized a freeway prayer when I saw one. Besides, Lila kept glancing up at the freeway sign.

"Maybe I should start doing that," he replied, smiling politely before he turned and headed back toward his cruiser.

Climbing into the car, I turned to the ladies. "Okay, he's going to follow us for a few minutes. We won't have any more problems tonight."

I pulled away from the curb and watched in my rearview mirror as the copper pulled in behind me. Relief was right up there with my feeling of let's-get-this-over-with-I-want-to-go-home.

May gave me directions to her house and I dropped her off after checking and double checking to make sure we hadn't somehow caught the goon's eye again. There had been no sign of him.

"God bless you," she yelled from her front porch.

Lila turned in her seat to look at me while we drove to her house, a few blocks away. "You know, Pamela, I have to admit that I did feel a trifle bit safer with the dogs in the car. Why, if that nasty man had made us pull over, I think the dogs would have protected us."

I laughed. "Sherlock and Watson? They probably would have licked him and then held up their paws to shake hands."

"Really?"

"No, I'm joking. They surely would have watched out for us."

"Well, no matter. I know the good Lord was watching over us. And I want to thank you, Pamela, for putting up with us silly old Church Ladies, as everyone likes to call us. I know we can be annoying, but we mean well. We just want the best for everyone."

"I know that, Lila, and you're certainly not annoying me."

"I'm not sure about your husband though," she said quietly.

"Oh, I can guarantee that he likes you ladies. He's just not used to people who bless him and pray about everything."

"But you pray, don't you?" Lila asked.

"I do, but I generally don't pray in a group. I'm kind of private about it."

"Oh, you should open up a little. We may be old, and we may be the Church Ladies, but we do have a lot of fun. The Lord blessed us with our friendships with each other." Lila was grinning, a beautiful sight if I'd ever seen one. Her eyes were bright and she appeared totally at peace with life and herself. Her timidity had melted away for the moment. "Who knows? One of these days someone may be referring to *you* as a Church Lady."

"You never know," I replied, pulling up in her driveway.

She blessed me and climbed out of the car before our conversation went any further. I had to admit that I was sorry to see her leave – in a way.

"Church Lady," I said to Watson, who'd climbed into the front seat. "Can you imagine anyone calling me a Church Lady?"

She tipped her head, trying to figure out what this human was saying to her. "*Woof,*" she replied.

Pulling back onto the freeway, I kept my eyes open for the black truck. Surprisingly, I didn't see any black trucks at all. I took the off ramp that would help me find my way home, glad I was moving closer to familiar surroundings.

My cell phone rang and it suddenly struck me that I'd never called Chris back. "Uh oh. I'm in for it now." I pulled to the side of the road.

"Hi, Sweetie," I said, as cheerfully as possible.

"Where have you been?" he demanded.

"Uh, I was taking the ladies home."

"First I get a frantic call from Lila, and then she tells me the police have stopped you, and you tell me you'll call me back – which you didn't do, by the way. What the hell is going on? Where are you?"

"I'm only about five minutes away," I said. "I'll explain everything when I come home."

"Why did the police pull you over? Lila said the police would have to let you go. What's going on?"

"Trust me, Bogey Man. Everything is fine. I'll be there in a few minutes, but for now I'm pulled over talking to you. I'd like to hang up and drive home. The dogs are tired of riding in the car, too."

"Oh. The dogs. Yeah, hang up and hotfoot it home. Wait. Really, why did a copper pull you over?"

"Because that John guy was chasing us and I was speeding."

"What…?"

I hung up and pulled back onto the street.

A black truck pulled in behind me.

CHAPTER TWENTY

Fortunately there wasn't a white camper on the back of the black truck, but for just a moment my heart wasn't sure it could take all the excitement. I patted my chest, willing it to slow down. The truck turned right after one block and my breathing returned to normal, along with my heart rate.

Pulling into the driveway, I glanced up and saw Chris standing on the front porch waiting for me. I walked around to the passenger side of the car and let the dogs out. I knew they'd distract Chris at least long enough for me to pull myself together. Running over and jumping up on Chris, they almost knocked him over. Fortunately, he'd braced himself against the side of the house. After all, they are a combined weight of around one hundred eighty-five pounds.

Chris figured out my ploy though. He opened the front door and shooed the dogs inside. Walking across the lawn, he met me halfway. "I want to know what happened tonight, and I want to know right now. Pamela, I honestly thought something had happened to you."

"It almost did." I told him about the goon and how he'd pulled up next to us at a red light, and how the chase was on when the light changed.

Chris walked inside with me while I told the story, after checking up and down our street for the truck in question.

I kept talking while I let the dogs outside. "So, at least he wasn't killing Victor or chasing Addie tonight. Well, I guess at first he thought he was chasing Addie. "

"Not funny, Pamela." He'd said my given name too many times during the course of the evening. He usually called me Cookie, or Angel, or some other nickname. It made me nervous because it told me how upset he was. "Why didn't you check in with me at some point?"

"I was a little busy. Besides, what could you have done?" I said, beginning to fume. I could take care of myself – but did I want to?

Chris sat down at the kitchen table, looking defeated. "I guess I couldn't have done anything. It would have all been over by the time I got there."

"Yeah. Well…"

"But understand. You're lucky that copper pulled you over or there's no telling *what* might have happened."

I smiled. "I had two of the Church Ladies with me. There wasn't any luck involved. You know how they pray about everything. Why, I'll bet they were praying the whole time that guy was chasing us. And don't forget Sherlock and Watson. You know they'd stick up for me; protect me."

"Uh huh." Chris had crossed his arms across his chest and leaned back in his chair. He wasn't going to budge an inch.

"Let's go to bed," I suggested, suddenly feeling overwhelmingly tired.

"You go on up and I'll be there soon. I want to check the dogs' water and think for a few minutes."

I didn't argue with my husband, but climbed the stairs, ready for some sleep. It was a long time coming, as was Chris.

***

As much as I would have liked to sleep in, I didn't. Chris and I were both up early, ready for whatever came our way.

We fed the dogs outside and then let them back into the house. It was a warm day and I figured they could hang out in the house with us for a while.

I called Constance's house and spoke to Mikey. "How'd you sleep last night?"

"Fine. When can I come home?"

"Soon, Sweetie, very soon."

"You and dad are on another case, aren't you? You don't need to answer me. I figured that one out. It has to do with a hit man, doesn't it, Mom?"

"You're one smart cookie, Mikey. I'm just not sure it's safe here right now. You can stay with –"

"If it's not safe for me, then it's not safe for you and dad either," Mikey interrupted. Intelligent kid.

"We'll get it all figured out. I don't want you gone any longer than you have to be," I said. "Just give us a couple of days. I'll call you and come by Constance's house this afternoon on my way to work."

Chris tapped me on the shoulder. "Tell Ace I said to trust us. I'll go see him, too."

I repeated Chris's comments to our son.

Mikey had to get ready for school, so we didn't talk much longer. I could hear the worry in his voice and that concerned me. We shouldn't be in this position, but it was our own fault for becoming involved. I voiced my thoughts to Chris.

"Pamela, you were trying to help your friends. When we first got involved, we had no idea that Addie had overheard a gun-for-hire talking about a job. We can't walk away now and leave those ladies unprotected."

"You're right, although I'm thinking more and more that we should call the police in on this." It certainly couldn't hurt to talk to Janet Riley. After all, she is a friend and she works in the Homicide Division.

"Call Janet. Tell her what we know and ask if there's anything she can do." Chris had read my mind again. Actually, he knew me so well that he could follow my thought processes without much effort.

"I'll call her today."

We decided on cold cereal for breakfast, which was out of the ordinary for us. I usually prepare a healthy meal before we begin the day.

The phone rang and Chris stood up. Sherlock sat up, alert and ready to race Chris to the wall phone. He never tried to beat me to the phone, just Chris. I wondered briefly what that crazy dog might have on his mind. You'd think he'd learn that every time he ran in the kitchen he slid into the wall. Maybe he'd knocked himself silly once too often.

"Sit down," I said. "I'll get it. I don't know how many times Sherlock can race you for the phone before he knocks a hole in the wall."

Chris sat down and continued eating.

"Hello?" I said, picking up the receiver.

"Mrs. Cross? This is Victor. I wanted to let you and your husband know that things were quiet here last night."

"I'm not surprised," I replied. "Your attacker was busy following me and my friends."

"Oh, no! Are you okay?"

"We're fine. One of L.A.'s finest stopped me for driving too fast and scared him away."

"That's a relief. Will you be coming by to see me anytime soon?"

"Yes, and I'd like to stop to see Florence, too. She's such a sweetheart."

"That she is," Victor said. "She tires easily though. You might want to keep that in mind."

"I will. Victor, have you seen anything of the truck we described to you?

It was parked at a mall not too far from your house for a couple of days. And what about your retired cop friend? Is he spending time with you?"

"No, I haven't seen the truck, but I haven't been watching that closely. My friend was here yesterday and he stayed until late last night. I feel pretty safe. Since I haven't seen the truck, I'm beginning to wonder if this is all just a big mistake."

"I don't think so," I said. "This guy has been trying to get to the lady who overheard him talking, and he chased us last night, thinking that she was in the car with us. I think he wants to deal with us before he comes after you. If anything happened to you, we'd be here to point the finger at him."

"Good point," Victor said.

"We'll be over to see you in a while. But, Victor, keep your eyes open for that truck. It's more important than you seem to realize."

"I will."

We hung up and I repeated what Victor had said to Chris.

"I could guess what he was saying by hearing your end of the conversation," he said. "For some reason this guy doesn't seem to be taking things seriously enough. Doesn't he get that his life is in danger?" Chris seemed frustrated, as he'd frequently sounded throughout this situation.

"Here's the thing," I explained. "He can't understand why anyone would want to kill him. Therefore, it doesn't seem real to him. I don't think he'll take it seriously unless something actually happens. Even seeing that truck might wake him up. He's heard about it, but he hasn't seen this guy cruising by his house. He needs something concrete before he'll wake up and watch out for himself."

"You're pretty smart, Cookie. I wish I understood people as well as you do."

"It's a gift," I said, smiling. "Now let's get moving."

We picked up the Jeep at the restaurant and I returned Jasmine's car. I didn't want to disturb the ladies, knowing they'd had a busy night, so I left the car key in the mailbox without knocking. I'd call her later and tell her where I'd left it. Within an hour Chris and I were on our way to Victor's house. He took the route that I suggested instead of his shortcut and we cut fifteen minutes off our trip.

At my request, Chris stopped at the mall so I could pick up some mascara. I was running low. There was a sale going on and we took a little longer than we'd meant to.

Arriving at Victor's, we could see him peeping out of the curtains, apparently watching for us. He opened the door before we could knock.

"Come in. Quickly! That man just drove by my house about five minutes ago. You were right." He sounded surprised, and frightened. "I was out in the yard and as he drove by he aimed his hand and finger at me and acted like he was firing a gun. I don't understand. I've never seen this man before."

"So it wasn't the man you thought it might be? From the bar?"

"I don't think so. I guess I actually couldn't see him that well. I was too busy watching the finger he was aiming at me."

Chris walked over to the window and pulled the heavy curtains apart, looking out. "I'll be back," he said. "He's driving by again."

He ran out the door, slamming it behind him. Victor and I watched out the window while he ran to the Jeep and jumped in. He pulled away from the curb and raced off in pursuit of the black truck with the white camper.

"I wonder why that guy has a white camper instead of a black one to match his truck," I said, still watching out the window.

"He got a deal on the camper," Victor said. "At least, that would be my guess."

"Good guess. You're probably right."

We continued to watch, and we waited for Chris to return.

My cell phone rang and I walked over to the couch to answer it.

"Pamela, is that you over at Victor's house?" Jasmine asked.

"Jasmine? Where are you?"

"The girls and I are visiting Florence."

I hadn't noticed Jasmine's car when we pulled up.

"Is Addie with you?"

"No, she's hiding out again, bless her heart."

"I didn't see your car," I said.

"We're using May's vehicle now because that man has seen mine."

"Ah. Well, I'll be over as soon as Chris gets back."

"Where did he go in such a hurry?" Jasmine asked.

"Didn't you see the black truck drive by?"

"No! We just saw Chris run out and leave in a hurry. If we'd seen the black truck go by we would have given chase ourselves."

"*No, no, no!*" I said adamantly. "No following, no chasing, no getting into trouble. We've got enough of that already."

"You can say that again," Victor called from the window. "Here he comes again, but I don't see your husband."

CHAPTER TWENTY-ONE

Chris wasn't behind the truck? "Gotta go," I said, hanging up on Jasmine. She could wait.

"No Chris? Are you sure, Victor?"

I couldn't understand why my husband wouldn't be right behind the guy. I ran to the window and snatched the curtain out of Victor's hand, pulling it back and letting the sun in. I could see the tail end of the truck turning right at the corner, just as Chris drove in from the other direction. Running outside, I pointed to the corner so Chris would follow the goon.

"Go get him," I yelled through the window.

Instead, Chris pulled up to the curb and turned off the engine. Well, *that* was anticlimactic.

I ran to the curb and yanked the Jeep's door open. "Chris, he's getting away. Again. Aren't you going after him?" I climbed into the car while I spoke, ready to give chase.

"No."

"No?"

"We've been so busy that we forgot something," he said.

This time I was the one who was frustrated. "And what would that be? Chris, he's getting away. What could we have forgotten that would stop us now that we're so close to him?"

"We forgot to keep an eye on the gas gauge. If we're lucky, there's enough to get to a gas station. In fact, I think I'll ask Victor to follow us in case we run out of gas before we find a station. Maybe he's got a gas can I can borrow."

I put my head back and rolled my eyes. No stopping me this time. "I can't believe we'd be that careless."

Chris turned his head and looked out the window and groaned.

"Okay, I didn't say we're stupid, just careless. You don't have to turn away from me."

"That's not what I'm groaning about." He pointed out the car window.

"Oh. Yeah. I forgot to mention that the Church Ladies are here." Jasmine, May and Lila were hurriedly walking across the street with Florence in tow.

"Is something wrong with the car? Why didn't you follow that man?" Jasmine sounded out of breath.

"Not enough gas," Chris said.

"You can borrow my car," May offered.

"It's too late," Chris replied. "That sap is long gone by now, but thank you for the offer. You're a peach, May."

By that time Victor had joined us. "You're out of gas?"

"Almost," Chris replied. "Would you mind following me to the nearest gas station? Just in case I don't have enough to make it. And do you happen to have a gas can that I can borrow?"

"Certainly. I told Flo I'd run an errand for her, so I have to go out anyway. Besides, if I'm not home, maybe that guy will quit driving by. He's beginning to get on my nerves."

Beginning to get on his nerves? I kept my mouth shut.

Florence had walked around the car and stood next to Victor. "You're such a good man, always ready to run errands for me." She patted his back and smiled up at him. "By the way, what man is everyone talking about?"

"Oh," Victor said, "just a guy driving an unusual truck we've seen in the neighborhood lately. Nothing to worry about." He *was* a good man. He didn't want Florence to worry needlessly. We could worry enough for her.

"Chris," I said, "why don't you go fill up the gas tank and then come back for me? I'd like to stay and visit with the ladies for awhile."

He turned to me and nodded. I gave him a kiss and climbed out.

Victor pulled his car out of his garage after telling Chris where the nearest gas station was, waved a gas can out the window, and Chris took off with Victor following him.

I walked back across the street to Florence's house with the ladies chattering in my ear. They wanted details.

"There are no details," I said, glancing meaningfully at Florence. "There's been a black truck with a white camper driving around the neighborhood lately, and it's just odd looking. Nothing to worry about; it's just a truck. The guys were curious about it, that's all."

The ladies understood my look and knew that mum's the word. I knew they'd save their questions for later.

We visited with Florence for about half an hour. She talked about what a nice neighborhood this was and what a low crime rate it had. She said she'd heard that other parts of Los Angeles were scary – her word, not mine.

"A friend of mine who moved away called and said that she hears guns going off during the night. Can you imagine that? I wouldn't even know what a gunshot sounded like. I have a feeling that they sound different in person than they do on television."

Chris finally came back and parked in front, honking the horn. I didn't see Victor, so I figured he was running his errands. I ignored Chris. It wouldn't be the end of the world if he had to come in and talk to the ladies. He finally gave up and knocked on the door.

"Are you ready to go?" he asked, when I answered his knock.

"No. Come say hello to everyone," I suggested.

He rolled his upper lip under and walked through the doorway, mumbling. He seemed to be doing that a lot lately.

"Hello, ladies," he said, putting on his best Bogey smile. He glanced around the table at the tea cups and cookies. "Looks like you're cooking with gas today. You've got all kinds of goodies sitting here."

"Oh, no," Florence said. "I have an electric range. In fact, my house is all electric."

"Florence, in this case *cooking with gas* means we're having a good time and you've done just the right thing in serving the cookies with the tea," Jasmine explained.

"I see." But she didn't. Her expression was one of confusion.

Chris tried again. "Well, everything looks ginger-peachy to me. Mind if I help myself to a cookie?"

"Please do," Florence said, picking up the plate and holding it out to Chris.

He took a bite of a cookie and, liking it, reached out for another. Turning to the Church Ladies, he said, "You gals were sure gussied up last night. If I were single…"

"Oh, you," Jasmine said, smiling. "We wanted to fit in and we'd noticed on our last visit that some of the customers dressed up like they did in the 1940's. Did we really look okay?"

"You betcha, Shweetheart. Those glad rags turned you ladies into real glamour girls."

Shweetheart was one of Chris's favorite Bogey words, and he always said it with a crooked smile on his face.

He turned to Lila and surprised me. There was a look of affection on his face. "And you, Doll, you set the place on fire with your songbird act. You can warble at our place anytime you want to. Your singing was aces."

Lila beamed and actually looked Chris right in the eyes. "I do enjoy knocking one out every once in a while."

I chuckled. Lila had surprised me, too. Was she coming out of her shell?

"Knocking one out?" We'd lost Florence. She had no idea what we were talking about.

"Lila sang at our restaurant last night," I explained. "She's got a voice and range that are unbelievable. I heard someone say that she hides her light under a bush. But she sure didn't last night."

"Well, Doll," Chris said, turning toward the door, "we'd better get moving. I'd like to stop to see Mikey on our way home. He should be out of school soon."

That got my attention. "I'm seconds behind you." I set my plate and teacup in the kitchen, picked up my purse, told the ladies to have a nice day, and followed my husband out the door.

"You know, Bogey Man, you made Lila's day with your comments about her singing. You're a good man, too, just like Victor." I took hold of his hand. "Even your comments about the way they were dressed were awesome. I know she wore that plain housedress, but maybe next time she'll try something a little classier."

He smiled down at me. "Thank you, Sweet Cheeks. I have to admit that I like those ladies, even if they do make me nervous. I think I like Lila the best though. She's kind of unassuming and sweet."

"I gather from things I've heard that her husband didn't treat her very well. I think he used to say things to her that made her feel awful about herself. Again, from what I've heard, and to put it in your terms, I think he might have been a lowdown heel who did a hatchet job on Lila every chance he got."

"A hatchet job? What do you mean? Did he ridicule her or what?"

"He made her feel like she wasn't worth much. From what I've heard, and this is gossip, he'd tell her she was plain and ugly and stupid, and not worth the spit in his mouth."

"Whoa, that's cold. That kind of treatment shouldn't happen to a dog, much less Lila."

"She took her lumps from that weasel, but you made her feel good today, Bogey Man. And I'm proud of you."

Chris's chest puffed up a little as we climbed into the car. "Yeah, well her husband sounds like a royal pain in the posterior."

"You're so polite sometimes," I said, smiling. "I would have said something a lot worse than that."

"Let's take a pass by that mall on our way to see Mikey," Chris said, changing the subject. "I have kind of a hunch about that place. Like maybe it's meeting place for the goon and his partner."

"Could be," I said. "It's close to Victor's house. Maybe that's why they chose that location. I wish we knew something about the second guy. We have absolutely nothing to go on except for this goon with the droopy mustache."

As we pulled into the parking lot at the mall, we saw a black truck with a white camper – and several police cars. And the mall cop, who looked up and saw us and waved frantically at Chris.

"Uh oh." Chris slowed to a crawl.

CHAPTER TWENTY-TWO

The police wouldn't let us drive up to the scene, so we found a parking space and the mall cop ran to meet us. Chris and I left the Jeep and walked over to him.

"What's going on?" Chris asked.

"Don't you know? Isn't that why you're here?" he replied. "I mean, aren't you a police detective or something?"

The light dawned on me slowly. The mall cop had thought Chris was a copper, and Chris had never corrected him. I wondered how my husband would get out of this one.

"Wait a minute," Chris said. "I never said I was a *city* copper. I'm a *private* Dick. I was watching this guy for someone."

"You're getting yourself in deeper and deeper," I whispered into Chris's ear. Chris isn't a detective of *any* type, private or government.

But the mall copper didn't look at all disappointed. In fact, he was watching Chris with a renewed respect. "I always wanted to be a Private Eye," he said longingly.

"Yeah. So what's the skinny here? Did the goon finally get himself in trouble?" Chris was rocking back on his heels and acting tough, with his thumbs hooked through his belt loops.

"You could say that," the mall copper replied. "He's dead."

"*Dead?*" I repeated. "As in bit the dust?"

"You got it, Ma'am. Someone shot him, and it was at close range, too." The mall copper – I really should ask him his name – seemed quite proud that he knew something about the crime.

"Excuse me," I said, "but what's your name. I can't keep thinking of you as The Mall Copper."

"It's Wade," he replied. "Wade Smiley."

"Well, Wade, are you sure he's really dead?" I asked.

Almost on command, an ambulance drove away and a coroner's van followed it out of the parking lot.

"That answer your question?" He watched the two vehicles drive away.

"Hey! Smiley. We need you over here." A copper was motioning him over. "And tell those lookers to move back."

"Oh, they're not –"

"Let it go," Chris said quietly, reaching out and shaking Wade's hand. "We have to get moving anyway. I'll call you in a while and you can give me the lowdown on all of this." He gestured toward the crime scene. "The coppers and I, well, we go way back. I don't want to get in their way."

Wade nodded and moved off toward the truck and camper.

"You and the coppers go way back?" I asked. "Since when?" I was proud of myself. I hadn't rolled my eyes this time. I'd looked at Chris and crossed my eyes.

"I just wanted him to trust me. As much as I've jawed with him, I think that might do it. He feels like the coppers look down their noses at him because he's a mall copper."

"There's nothing wrong with being a mall copper," I said. "It's honest work and they make me feel safer when I'm shopping. I know they're really security guards, not coppers, and they don't carry a gun, but..."

"Uh huh. Anyway, I want this guy on our side so he'll spill his guts when I call him later."

We were pulling out of the parking lot when I could have sworn I heard someone yell my name. I knew it had to be my imagination, so I didn't ask Chris to stop.

We drove over to Constance's house, but she and Mikey weren't there. Glancing at my watch, I saw that we were too early. My son wouldn't be out of school for another half hour. I was disappointed, but came up with a plan so I could spend some time with him. I'd call Constance and work something out with her. She was such a good friend to us, and she'd known Mikey and me for a long time because we used to live next door to her. She and Chris had become good friends, too. Maybe we could bring Mikey home now that the bad guy was dead.

The drive home was a quiet one. I knew Chris was thinking things over, and so was I.

"I sure wish we knew who the goon's partner is. This is going to make things a lot more difficult," I said. "We don't know anything about the other guy, including what he looks like. All we've been told is that he's totally average, in every respect."

"I was just thinking the same thing, Doll. Before we leave for the restaurant I'll call Victor and let him know what's happened. I need to warn him not to let his guard down. If the partner killed John, then I think things just got worse. We know it's not a game or a misunderstanding on Addie's part. John was harassing Victor by driving by and aiming his trigger finger at him. He was dragging it out for some reason – trying to scare him before he bumped him off. Maybe he wanted to see Victor squirm. I don't know."

"And now things are different," I said. "I have a feeling that the partner isn't going to play the same game. He'll go after Victor and get the job done."

"Right – I think. It boils down to the fact that we just don't have enough information to go on. You didn't call Janet, did you? Do you know if she's working today?"

"No. I haven't had time to call her, and I'm not even sure she's on duty." I glanced at my watch again. "In fact, I guess I'll have to call her from work. We've got to change clothes and get to the restaurant. I'll need time to tell her everything. It's not a conversation we can have in two minutes."

I never thought I'd end up with a friend who was a homicide detective, but we had worked with Janet on another case and we'd become quite good friends in the process. We even trained her dog, a chocolate Labrador retriever named Friday, to behave once in a while. Friday is a female with a very stubborn streak, and once in a while was the best we could do. She likes things her way, even though she's a dog.

I changed into a pair of forties-style slacks and a blouse. The brown slacks had a slightly higher waist than normal and were full-legged which was popular in the 1940's. The eggshell-colored blouse had a somewhat large collar with pointed ends, and it sported the shoulder pads that were part of the dress of that era. I felt like a football player, but Chris assured me that I didn't resemble a jock in any way.

Turning my attention to my hair, I wore it in a long pageboy, although I pulled one side back and brushed the bangs to the side. I have some curl in my long, auburn hair, which added body to the style.

On the weekends we dressed to the nines, but this was Wednesday, a day for me to be more comfortable. Chris always wore a forties-style suit, no matter what day of the week it was. His only concession was that during the week he took his jacket off and let his vest or suspenders speak of the forties. He usually had a fedora nearby, but he only wore it outside or in the cocktail lounge.

We put the dogs in the car so they could stay in the rear yard at the restaurant. With everything that had happened, I thought it would be a good idea to have our backs covered. The dogs would take care of that for us.

Arriving at the restaurant, I put the dogs in the fenced yard and made my way to the office to call Constance to ask if she and Mikey would like to join Chris and me at the restaurant for dinner. She was delighted and said they'd be there with bells on.

Before I could contact Janet, Chris walked into the office to call Wade. We wanted details, and the most important one was whether or not the coppers had any suspects or if they'd caught the killer.

While he was on the phone, I made my way through the restaurant, checking napkins, silverware and table settings to make sure everything was in order for the dinner crowd. Back in the kitchen, I found Chef Luis watching over the shoulder of a man I'd never seen before.

"Luis? Who's your friend?"

"Oh, Pamela. Come meet Nathaniel. He's preparing a luncheon fit for a king for you and Chris. Chris said he wanted to sample his cooking before you hire him."

"The timing couldn't be better. We haven't had time to eat anything yet."

I shook Nathaniel's hand and received a firm handshake in return. Our new luncheon chef appeared to be in his late seventies, but age didn't matter if he could do the job. Even at his age, he still had light brown hair, which surprised me, although it was thinning. He wasn't too much taller than me. There was something appealing about him; he had a friendly smile.

Luis had mentioned that Nate was retired but bored. The new chef wasn't very tall, and yet his self-confident demeanor gave one the feeling of being around a larger-than-life man. I took an instant liking to him.

Wandering back out to the dining area of the restaurant, I stood behind the reservation desk, thinking. The whole situation didn't make sense to me. With everything that had happened, I would think that Victor *must* have some idea of who might be after him. But thinking back to our conversations, I believed him. He may have stepped on the wrong toe and never realized it. Or, on the other hand, maybe he was a terrific actor. Maybe he really knew who was after him and why.

Someone knocked on the front door of the restaurant, interrupting my thoughts. I'd have to explain that we're only open in the evening for the time being. I knew it wouldn't be a delivery, because they always come to the back door.

"I'm sorry," I began, opening the door, "but…" I stopped talking when I realized it was Janet Murphy. She didn't look happy, and I had a feeling this wasn't a social call.

"Come on in," I said. "It's good to see you. Actually, I'd planned on calling you this afternoon."

"And what were you going to call me about? John Jackson maybe?"

"John Jackson?" Could the goon's surname be Jackson?

"Yeah. The dead guy at the mall. I understand you and Chris were quite interested in him."

Now I knew why Janet didn't look happy. She probably thought we'd been keeping things from her. We were, but not on purpose. There hadn't been anything that we could tell her before.

"Come on in and sit down," I said, indicating one of the dining tables. "I'll go find Chris. I really was going to call you this afternoon."

"Uh huh."

As I passed through the kitchen to find Chris, Luis stopped me. "Are you ready for a feast?" he asked.

"Not now, Luis. Give us a few minutes." I stopped, rethinking things. "On second thought, there's a woman sitting at one of the tables in the restaurant. She'll be joining us. You and Nate can begin serving right now." Maybe I could soften Janet up with a tasty gourmet lunch.

"Chris," I said, walking into the office, "Janet is here."

He held his hand up, motioning for me to wait.

"Okay, Wade, thanks. You've really been a big help." He hung up.

"Janet's here, and she's not a happy camper. Somehow she's found out about us watching the dead guy. By the way, his name is John Jackson. Anyway, I've got her seated at one of the tables. Luis and Nate, the new lunch chef, are going to start serving samples of Nat's dishes. I thought maybe it would soften her up if we talk over a tasty meal."

"Good idea. She knows about us because she saw us leaving the scene, and she asked Wade what we were doing there. He was afraid to lie to her, and I told him he did fine."

"Did he tell you anything about what happened?"

"Let's talk to Janet first, and then I'll tell you what he said."

Walking back to the dining room, we found Janet standing next to the table, tapping her foot. Nate was placing a platter bearing appetizers on the table.

"Thank you, Nate," I said. "You can bring everything else out in a few minutes."

"Please," Nate said rather haughtily, "when I'm in the restaurant I'm Nathaniel."

Chris and I both turned a wary eye on the potential new chef. Did we want someone with an attitude working at *Bogey Nights*? I saw that Janet was regarding him with a hesitant look, too. I was surprised because when I'd met him in the kitchen, he seemed so easygoing.

Nate laughed. "However, when it's social, I'm just plain Nate. I was just teasing you."

"Well, Nate," Chris said, "let's keep our conversations on a social level. When we speak to the patrons, we'll refer to you as Nathaniel. Deal?"

"But, of course," Nate said. Smiling at Chris, he turned and headed back toward the kitchen. I had a feeling that Nate might be somewhat of a character.

Chris pulled a chair out for Janet. "Actually," he said, "Nathaniel does sound more professional than Nate."

"If you think food is going to get you off the hook, you're dead wrong. And speaking of dead…" She sat down, and taking a good long look at the platter, she began to fill her plate.

Food is always a good ice breaker.

CHAPTER TWENTY-THREE

The three of us were quiet while we served ourselves portions of the appetizers. Nate had placed a sample of each item on the plate instead of the amount that would normally be served. I started with roasted eggplant served with roasted garlic dip, and quickly added some stuffed mushrooms. Before I could reach for the fried calamari rings, Janet and Chris dove into them.

Nate had added shrimp cakes, and chicken and duck pâté served with onion chutney and Greek-style Petrou olives. Lastly, there was stuffed antipasto bread, and stuffed grape leaves. Who needed a main dish?

Janet took a bite of a shrimp cake and groaned. "Oh, this is sooo good! But it's not going to get you off the hook."

"Maybe this won't, but wait until he serves the entrée." I hoped it was something wonderful – food to soothe the angry beast, or copper as the case may be.

"So tell me what you know about John Jackson, and don't leave anything out." Janet took a bite of the stuffed antipasto bread and closed her eyes while tilting her head back in appreciation.

While we ate Chris and I told her about the Church Ladies, what Addie had overheard, and what we'd done so far. We told her about Victor, the intended victim,, and that he didn't seem to know why anyone would want to bump him off.

She lifted her right eyebrow every so often while we talked.

"So why didn't you call me right away?" she asked.

"Because we didn't have anything concrete," Chris replied. "What was I going to do? Call you and say, 'Hey, we know some Church Ladies who have a friend who *might* have overheard a murder-for-hire conversation. Yeah, she hid out in the back of a camper that was being driven by a possible killer. And, by the way, the intended victim hasn't got a clue about who might want him dead.'"

"You really don't have any more information than that?" Janet asked.

"We've met with Victor, and he has some retired cop friend who's watching out for him," I said. "He asked us to do what we could, when we can. Have we told you anything that would have made you become involved in this case before now?"

"Not really," she replied, sounding reluctant to admit she wouldn't have listened to us. "But now that Jackson is dead, I've got to look at all sides of this thing. Are you sure these Church Ladies, as you call them, are a reliable source of information?"

"Who knows?" Chris replied. "They're a bunch of little old ladies who pray at the drop of a hat. But so far they've been mostly reliable, even if they are a nightmare to me."

"I knew it!" I said. "I knew you felt that way. Why, these are some of the nicest ladies I've ever known, Christopher Cross!"

"Don't get mad at me, Babe. You know they've been under our feet through this whole thing. I like them, too. But you have to admit, they can be as cockamamie as anyone we've ever met. And they can be downright intimidating sometimes."

Before anyone could say anything else, Nate arrived with a cart and more food.

"Saved by the chef," Chris mumbled.

Nate cleared off the appetizer platters and began placing serving plates and bowls on the table. "Here we have our salads," he said, setting the scene. "We have Grilled Chicken Summer Salad, the standard Caesar Salad, and a fresh fruit plate. Of course, I will be providing other salads, too. And your soups. For today you have your choice of Vichyssoise, Lobster Bisque, Creamy Sauerkraut or Tomato Florentine. *Bon appétit!*" He left to return to the kitchen to work on his presentation of the entrees.

"You'd better snatch this guy up in a hurry," Janet said. "If you have Chef Nathaniel preparing lunches, and Chef Luis here in the evening, you're going to have to beat off the crowd with sticks. Hey, wait a minute. You're not open for lunch."

"We will be starting soon," I said. "Nate is a retired chef who's bored and said he'd take the lunch crowd for us."

"Okay," Janet said, "back to our situation. I can't do anything about Victor because I don't have anything to tie him and the murder together. Nothing solid, that is. I want —"

"Can't you have someone watch him?" I asked, interrupting.

"Not enough manpower right now."

Chris smiled. "So we're still in the game then."

"It's not a game, and yes you are," Janet said, grudgingly. "I want you to share anything and everything you find out with me. Understood? And you're not to take unnecessary chances of any kind."

She turned to me. I knew that technically Janet could tell us to back off, but she knew we wouldn't. A warning was the best she could do at the moment.

"You do recall almost being murdered some months back, right?" Janet was playing dirty by reminding me.

"Yes. How could I forget? We're not taking any dangerous chances. John Jackson had apparently found out about our business. We think he followed us. On the off chance that he'd figured out where we lived, we sent Mikey to stay with Constance for a few days, but I think he can come home now. We don't know anything about the partner, and he's probably figured that out since we haven't been watching him.

"The only one who's seen him is Addie, and she's in hiding. He'll never find her at Jasmine's house." I was proud of the way we'd taken care of things.

Janet's expression was skeptical, at best, but she refrained from saying anything.

Nate returned with his cart and the entrees.

"You're hired," Chris said, patting his stomach.

"But you haven't tried the –"

"We will, but the fact remains that you're going to be a blessing for *Bogey Nights*."

Janet and I turned to each other.

"Did he just say *blessing*?" Janet asked.

"I believe he did," I replied, "which tells me there's hope for him yet."

"It was a slip of the tongue," Chris said. "I've spent way too much time around those Church Ladies."

Nate returned to the kitchen, smiling and whistling, and we gawked at the dishes he'd brought to us. Grilled Eggplant Parmigiana, bacon-wrapped Cornish hens with a raspberry balsamic glaze, grilled salmon, and ratatouille, accompanied by carrots with shallots, sage, and thyme and green beans with a sweet onion vinaigrette. Just to make sure we couldn't walk away from the table, he'd also left a Shoofly Pie.

"No dinner for me tonight," Janet said.

"Me, either," Chris added.

"I may not eat for a week," I commented.

"I'd like to meet these lady friends of yours," Janet said. "Maybe I can glean something from talking to them that you missed."

"Can you come back here tonight?" I asked.

"If I have to, but I'm so full that the sight of more food is going to be a problem."

"We'll seat you in the lounge with the women," Chris suggested. "You might have to smell food, but you won't have to look at it." He was grinning. He knew from Janet's reactions that hiring Nate had been a smart move.

Janet left after finishing her food, shaking her head in disgust because she'd eaten so much, and I called Jasmine. "Can you and the other ladies come to the restaurant tonight?" I asked.

"Any special reason?"

"I have a friend who's a homicide detective, and she'd like to talk to you."

"*Homicide detective?* Did those men finally catch up to Victor? Oh, my goodness, Florence will be heartbroken. She just thinks that man walks on water, although you and I know of only One who can do that." She chuckled.

"Before you start praying for Victor's soul, he's okay." Oops. I didn't mean to hurt her feelings, and that sounded kind of snide. "I'm sorry, Jasmine. That came out wrong."

"Don't worry about it," she said, kindly. "But what's going on? What does your homicide detective want with us?"

"The goon that drove the black truck, John, has been murdered. She's looking into his death, and obviously we think it had something to do with the whole Victor thing."

"*No,*" she said, sounding surprised. "Someone killed the bad guy? I'll get the girls together. His is one soul that does need prayer." She tsked-tsked, and I rolled my eyes, glad we were on the phone instead of face to face. "I'll also make sure everyone can be at the restaurant tonight. What time do you want us there?"

We talked for a moment longer and I said that dinner would be on us; to bring their appetites along. Jasmine blessed me and said goodbye, already talking to Addie as she hung up the phone.

She called me back about ten minutes later. "We'll all be there except for Addie. This whole thing has really taken it out of her. She even made an appointment to see her doctor. Poor thing; she took on a lot more than she bargained for when she climbed into that camper. But as scared as she was of that bad man, she's still going to pray for him with us. Of course, I wouldn't have expected less from her."

"No, I guess you wouldn't. Maybe Janet can visit Addie at your house. She's the one she really needs to talk to since she overheard the two men."

George Chandler, our waiter and George Raft look-alike, arrived shortly after I returned to the dining room. Phyllis and Gloria had Wednesdays and Thursdays off. George was joined about five minutes later by Susan French. Susan doesn't resemble anyone but herself, although she does dress the part, and she's rather exotic looking. I watched the two working together, and it briefly crossed my mind that they'd become somewhat of an item since they'd come to work for us.

Ah, the world of restaurants. It seemed like there was always something going on.

The phone rang and Susan tore herself away from George long enough to answer it. "Pamela, it's for you. He says it's personal. Someone named Victor?"

She handed me the receiver. "Victor? What's up?"

"Plenty," he replied. "The police were just here to see me."

Oh, crap! Chris and I had forgotten to call the intended victim. Some private eyes *we* were.

"They told me that someone named John Jackson was murdered and they wanted to know if I knew him. Who's John Jackson?" He sounded beyond irritated. "They didn't tell me anything and they wouldn't answer my questions. They just wanted to know if I knew John Jackson."

"He's the man who drove the black truck with the white camper. He's the man we suspect of being hired to murder you."

"Oh? So he's dead? Then I guess things are all over and my life can go back to normal." His tone of voice had definitely changed from aggravated to friendly.

"Victor, don't get too excited. You're forgetting that Jackson had a partner. You're not out of the woods yet, I'm sorry to say."

CHAPTER TWENTY-FOUR

Victor sighed, loudly and dramatically. I figured that was for my benefit. "What now?" he asked.

"The ladies are coming to the restaurant tonight to talk to a homicide detective. She's going to be working on this, too, although she'll be coming from the direction of the murder investigation. We don't honestly know that Jackson's death had to do with the threat against you."

"Well, make room for me, too. What time is everyone meeting? I want to be in on this. After all, we're talking about my life here."

"Good idea," I replied. "Can your retired cop friend come, too?"

"Unfortunately, no. He had a family emergency to attend to. But at least I'll be safe if I'm with all of you at the restaurant."

After telling him what time the ladies would arrive, we hung up. I told him that dinner was on the house. We were going to be offering a lot of free dinners, but what the heck. Maybe we'd finally accomplish something. I also suggested that he park in back and come in through the office door so he wouldn't be seen, just in case Jackson's partner was nearby. I explained about the dogs and told him they were friendly, but I'd wait for him outside so they couldn't jump all over him.

Hanging up the receiver, I turned to find Chris standing behind me.

"We forgot to call Victor," I said. "I can't believe we *both* forgot him. He's what this whole thing is about."

Chris looked sheepish. "We dropped the ball, but it won't happen again. I won't let it."

"This had been an extremely busy day." I sat down on a chair in the waiting area. "I can't wait to finish things up and go home to our nice, warm bed."

Chris grinned at me. "Come here, Doll." He pulled me up and held me close. "Maybe we can find some new ways to keep that bed warm tonight."

"Don't you ever get tired?" I asked.

"Nah. All this drama keeps my blood flowing and my brain on the alert."

"You big lummox. Doesn't anything ever get you down?"

"Nope. Why don't you go have a glass of wine to calm you down while I open the restaurant? Just this once."

"No, I'm tired enough already. A cup of coffee would make more sense."

"Then take a cup of coffee with you back to the office and relax. I'll take care of things for awhile." Chris unlocked the front door.

"You're sure you don't mind?" I asked.

"It'll be slow for now. You go unwind."

What a guy. He really cared about me.

Luis had coffee ready for the customers and he poured me a cup to take back to the office. "You look tired, Pamela. No offense," he added quickly. "You're always a vision, but you do appear tired tonight."

"It's been a busy day," I replied, "and it's not over yet." Glancing around, I noticed that our sous chef, Phillip, was already hard at work. I carried my mug and headed toward the office for a few minutes of peace and quiet.

After closing the door between the kitchen and the office, I opened the back door to let the dogs in. I always hesitated to do this because I knew if the Health Department found out I'd probably be sorry. Sherlock and Watson shed constantly. I kept a small vacuum in the corner and frequently cleaned up the office. The last thing we needed was for someone to find a dog hair in their food.

These were my thoughts when I opened the back door. The dogs were just finishing the food that Chris had put out for them and they ignored me until the last bite was gone. After that, it was every man, woman and child for themselves. They came racing in to wallow in the attention they knew I'd give them. Throwing herself on the floor, Watson rolled onto her back and waited for some scratching. Not to be outdone, Sherlock offered me his paw for a shake.

"My babies," I said lovingly to each of them. "You're good dogs. Yes, you are. Mikey will be here soon." Watson scrambled up and sat watching me.

They recognized the name and gave me a look, trying to figure out what

I was saying about the boy they considered one of their playmates. Sherlock dropped his paw and turned toward the doorway. Watson jumped up and ran outside. Someone was coming. Sherlock let out a sound of recognition and followed her.

I heard childish giggling and knew that my son and Constance had arrived. So much for quiet time, but that didn't matter as long as my son was with me. I followed the dogs outside where I found them smothering Mikey with doggie kisses.

"*Mom!*" Mikey yelled, pushing the dogs down and running forward. He threw his arms around me. "I've missed you and dad."

"We've missed you, too." I hugged him back. "And you can come home now."

"I can?" He sounded excited. "No more danger?"

"Yes, Pamela, what about the danger?" Constance asked.

We walked into the office and I closed the door so Sherlock and Watson would have to stay outside. I heard one of them scratch at the door in an attempt to get me to open it.

"It's, uh, been eliminated. No more safety problems." I patted Mikey on the back while giving Constance a pointed look. Would she get my meaning?

"Oh," she said. "Do you mean what I think you mean?"

"Probably. We'll talk while Mikey…" My voice trailed off, not wanting my son to think I was hiding something from him – which I was.

"While I what?" he asked.

"Why don't you go help your dad greet the customers?" I knew he wouldn't be able to resist that, and interestingly Constance had told Mikey to dress up for the evening. Well, he never did show up at *Bogey Nights* in jeans, a t-shirt and flip flops. After all, that wouldn't fit in with our motif. Besides, Mikey liked dressing the part. He was wearing slacks with cuffs and loose legs, topped off by suspenders over his pin-striped shirt. I smiled. He looked like a mini-Bogey Man.

Constance, who felt completely at home in the restaurant, walked into the kitchen and poured herself a cup of coffee. Returning, she sat down on the small sofa we'd put in the office.

"So what happened?" she asked. "When you say your trouble was eliminated, do you mean that he was really eliminated or has he been arrested?"

"He's dead. Somebody bumped him off."

"Pulled the curtain on his last act?" Constance was smiling.

"Is there something funny about it?" I asked.

"No, it's just the way you talk sometimes. It cracks me up. You and Chris are perfect for each other. And you never used to use forties slang until you met him. I like it."

"Yeah, well…"

"So the guy is buzzard bait."

"See? You talk like we do."

"So does Mikey. And, by the way, he's started rolling his eyes a lot. Sound familiar? You might want to break him of that habit."

"Well," I said, "there are worse habits he could pick up from me. And don't try to tell me his eyes will get stuck that way."

"Okay, enough about Mikey. So what happens now? Does this guy's death mean that your client is safe?"

"Not really. The dead guy had a partner. I'm guessing that the two men had some kind of falling out, and now the partner will go after Victor. He and the Church Ladies are coming in tonight to meet with Janet. She has a lot of questions."

"The Church Ladies? When are they going to be here?" Constance sounded almost too calm as she slid forward on the sofa.

"Are you thinking that you and Mikey will eat and run? You know these women are harmless. We all attend the same church, and you've known them even longer than I have."

"Exactly. I've known them for a long time. I love them to pieces, but I don't wear blinders. I know how pushy they can be when they want something."

"Then you're safe. They don't want a thing from you. They're totally focused on me and Chris right now."

Constance walked over to my desk and patted my back. "Poor baby. They've brainwashed you."

For the first time since Constance and I had become friends, I was annoyed with her – and I looked up and rolled my eyes.

She backed away. "Okay, Pamela, I know I'm not being very nice. But they've suckered me into more than one job at church events that I didn't want to become involved in. I try to steer clear of them as often as possible."

"They mean well," I said for the umpteenth time. It seemed like that had become my job – to tell everyone that the ladies didn't do things out of malice, but out of love for people.

"You're right. If they're coming early enough, Mikey and I will stay and make nice with them. Lila and May are okay. It's that Jasmine. She's so demanding." She paused with a faraway look in her eyes, possibly remembering moments of irritation involving Jasmine.

She blinked her eyes and turned her focus back to me. "And you're going to pick Mikey up tonight, is that right?"

"Yes. I can't wait to have him home, sleeping in his own bed. The dogs have missed him, too."

Mikey stuck his head around the doorframe. "Dad says you need to come out now because the Church Ladies are here. He needs your help."

Constance laughed and followed me through the kitchen and out to the reception area where we found Chris surrounded by three very talkative ladies. I noticed that this time they hadn't worn vintage clothing, but had decided to wear slacks instead. Except for Lila, who never wore anything but a dress or skirt and blouse.

"One at a time," Chris was saying. He saw me and looked relieved.

"Is he really dead?" Jasmine asked.

Chris turned to me. "Pamela, would you please seat the ladies while I take care of the other patrons?"

"Follow me, ladies," I said. "And Mikey, you come along, too."

He looked disappointed, but he and Constance followed me to a table near the lounge. Knowing Mikey, he really wasn't looking forward to spending the evening at a table packed with elderly ladies.

"I'm going to seat you all here because Janet will be meeting with you in the lounge when she arrives. You've got about an hour to eat before she'll be here." I pulled up a sixth chair and placed it at the end of the table, and set a menu in front of each woman. I knew what Mikey would want, but I set one in front of him, too.

"Are we expecting someone else?" Jasmine asked.

"Victor is going to join you for dinner. He wants to know what's going on, too. Is that a problem?"

"Certainly not," Jasmine replied. "If I were him, I'd want the inside dope, too."

"Yes, the inside dope," May echoed.

"After all, it is his life that's in jeopardy," Lila added.

Constance put her hand to her head as though she had a headache.

Susan approached the table just long enough to take drink orders. I noticed that Lila was having wine again, while everyone else ordered iced tea.

"Victor should be here any minute. I told him to come in by the back door, so I'd better go watch for him. I don't want the dogs to knock him down."

"Would they do that?" Lila asked.

"Not purposely, but they do get excited when a new *friend* comes to visit. Especially if I'm not there to keep them calm."

"Can I come with you, Mom?" Mikey asked. "I'm good at keeping the dogs under control."

"Sure."

We walked back to my office and the first thing I heard was a man yelling for help.

"Uh oh," I said.

Mikey opened the door and ran outside.

I followed him and found Victor pushed up against the fence with the dogs up on their hind legs, licking anything they could reach for all they were worth. One of the Lab traits is that they use their tongue and mouth as often as possible. Things can get messy when a happy Lab is on the scene.

Victor looked about as stressed as I'd seen him, which was saying a lot since someone wanted to kill him.

CHAPTER TWENTY-FIVE

I grabbed a couple of doggie treats off my desk on my way out of the door and handed them to Mikey. My dogs were suckers for a good doggie cookie.

"Sherlock! Watson!" Mikey called. "Come get a *cookie*."

Their ears perked up and two heads swung toward my son.

"Come on, you big galoots. Come get your cookies." Mikey has such a way with words.

We calmed the dogs down and apologized to Victor, who graciously said everything was okay. I doubted that, but decided to take his word for it. I scolded the dogs and I could see that their feelings were hurt. After all, they didn't think they'd done anything wrong. They were just being friendly, and we'd rewarded them with cookies. I could almost read their minds.

Mikey showed Victor to the Men's Room so he could wash up, and told me that he'd escort our guest to the table when he was done. Sometimes my son seemed so grown up for a child.

I was standing by the table chatting with the ladies when the boy and man arrived, and I had to admit that Victor looked a lot happier than he had ten minutes earlier.

"Well, if it isn't God's Safety Squad," Victor said, looking from face to face. "Flo told me you're all churchgoers, and I know you're all trying to keep me alive. But where's the other lady? I understood there were four of you watching out for me."

"She's not feeling well," Jasmine replied. "She's staying at my house until this is all cleared up. Gosh, you should have brought Florence with you tonight."

"Florence doesn't like to go out after dark. Besides, since she doesn't know about my problems, I'd like to keep it that way. I know your friend saw Jackson, but if she's still at your house, does that mean she saw his partner, too?"

"Yes, indeedy," May said. "She'll be able to help the police with her description of the man. I'm sure the detective will talk to her soon. We're all getting older, and we all have problems, but the good Lord blessed Addie with amazing vision." May put on reading glasses and began to peruse the menu. Apparently she hadn't received the same blessing.

"Well, thank heaven for *that*!" Victor said. "It's about time someone came along who can get me out of this mess."

Leaving the table, I walked back to the Reservation Desk to see Chris. The restaurant was beginning to fill up and I felt guilty about not helping. I saw Susan approach the table where our friends were sitting and she dropped off the drinks, and I also saw the ladies examining Susan's forties outfit. If body language meant anything, the ladies were asking her where she got her blouse and slacks. I chuckled to myself. Susan made all of her own clothing.

After dinner had been served and everyone was through eating, I moved the ladies and Victor to a table in the lounge, seating them as far away from the band as I could so they could hear each other.

Mikey approached the Reservation Desk. "Mom, can I go home soon?"

"Is something wrong?" I asked. He usually enjoyed hanging out at *Bogey Nights*.

"No. Well, yes. For starters, I can't go in the lounge because I'm not old enough. And those women keep asking me about school and do I have a girlfriend, and stuff like that. It's embarrassing, Mom. I'm ready to leave."

"I see. Well, let me talk to Constance. By the way, Janet will be here in a few minutes. Wouldn't you like to wait and see her before you leave?"

Mikey's face brightened up considerably. "Janet's going to be here? Yeah, I'll wait a few more minutes."

My son not only liked Janet, but he liked to brag at school that he had a friend who was a real live homicide detective. During the previous school year he'd had a teacher who made his life miserable because he talked about a murder that Chris and I were involved in, among other things. This year he had a teacher who got a kick out of Mikey's forties slang and the fact that he was so open about everything.

The front door opened and Janet walked in. Mikey ran over to greet her, and he took her hand to lead her back to the lounge. I heard him say, "I can't take you in there, but I can point out where they're sitting."

Janet glanced over her shoulder at me and winked. "Thank you, Mikey. You're a very good host."

He turned his head to look at her and I could see him smiling.

"Chris," I said, "why don't we ask George to cover the front desk for a few minutes and go listen in? I'd like to hear what Janet and the ladies have to say."

"It's too busy right now. Why don't you go listen in and you can fill me in later."

"I feel guilty, Chris. It seems like you're doing all the work tonight."

"That's okay. I'd rather be up here than with your Church Lady friends anyway." He quickly turned and studied the reservation list, knowing he'd said too much.

"They pray for us all the time, Bogey Man."

"That's nice."

I sighed before turning and walking toward the lounge. Constance and Mikey were headed in my direction and Constance had her purse slung over her shoulder. I returned to the Reservation Desk with them. "Pamela, we're going home now. Thank you so much for the dinner. You can leave Mikey with me another night if you'd like to. I've kind of gotten used to having him around."

"Thanks, Constance, but I'm ready to have him come home. We'll pick him up when we're done here. Do I need to repeat how much I appreciate your help?"

"No, I know you do." She grinned, and she and Mikey left.

I looked up into my husband's face. "You know, Chris, I'll stay here with you. I've already heard everything the ladies have to say, so it would be silly to sit in on the meeting."

Chris smiled, pleased with my decision. "You're a heck of a dame, you know that?"

"I try."

Chris and I welcomed guests, seated people, and chatted with customers. I kept an eye turned toward the lounge, wondering what was being said. I couldn't help myself.

Nate made an appearance, saying he wanted to see how we ran things from a customer's point of view. I was pleased that he cared enough about the restaurant to take an interest. He hadn't made a reservation, but I found a nice table for him.

About forty-five minutes later I heard Lila's sweet voice emanating from the lounge. She was singing again. Was this going to become a habit? Maybe I needed to offer her a wage. This time she was singing *Rockin' Chair* which had originally been sung by jazz singer Mildred Bailey in the 1930s. It was the song of an old woman sitting in a rocking chair singing her blues. Lila had a very different voice from Bailey's, but she did the song justice. I was amazed that The Sugar Daddies, our band, knew this song. I walked over to the doorway and saw that this time Lila had brought music with her. She apparently liked singing in the lounge.

As before, I saw customers walk to the doorway of the lounge to listen. I grinned when I saw Nate standing at the door smiling, enjoying the music.

I made a mental note to talk to Chris about removing the wall between the lounge and the restaurant, like I'd seen in forties movies. I liked the idea of the openness between the band and the diners. That would enlarge the dance floor, too.

Lila finished her song and the applause was awesome to hear. She was quite a hit, and I saw that this time she didn't look quite as embarrassed. Our little Lila was coming out of her shell – in our restaurant. I was pleased, not that my opinion mattered.

Shortly after that the Church Ladies headed for the front door with their purses, ready to call it a night. Janet and Victor followed them.

"Thank you so much for singing again," Chris said, taking Lila's hand. "You've turned out to be quite a surprise, Sugar."

Lila blushed. "I love to sing. I just never knew *other* people would like to hear my voice. You're not the only one who's surprised. I used to sing around the house, but then my husband said… Well, never mind."

Chris kissed Lila's hand, and I teared up. It was so touching. My husband had no idea how much this probably meant to Lila. I'd never seen him be so gentle with anyone before.

Taking a deep breath, I also thanked Lila for her performance. "Please feel free to sing with the band anytime you want to. Last time you sang they were almost effusive with their comments about you. You're a welcome visitor."

Jasmine and May each gave Lila a hug.

"You see?" Jasmine said. "You're a wonder. We never knew you could sing."

"Never knew a thing about it," May said, agreeing with Jasmine.

"I was impressed," Victor said. "Say, why don't I follow you ladies home to make sure everything is okay?"

"If you don't mind, Mr. Rogers, I'd like you to stay for a few minutes," Janet said. "I have a couple more questions for you. I think the ladies can make it home safely without an escort."

"Oh, certainly. These ladies are friends with my neighbor. I just thought I was being helpful."

"Oh, you are," Janet replied, "but right now I need your help more than they do."

I raised an eyebrow at Janet. She didn't sound very friendly toward Victor, and I couldn't figure that out. After all, he was the intended victim. I was surprised that she didn't sound more diplomatic.

"Do you want to go back to the lounge?" I asked. "I can make sure there's still a table for you."

"No," Janet replied. "We can sit right here in the entry and talk." She indicated two chairs that were sitting side by side and waited for Victor to seat himself.

Glancing at Chris, I saw that he appeared confused, too.

We hung around the Reservation Desk, hoping we might pick up a word or two while Janet and Victor talked. Their voices were low and we couldn't hear anything. So we watched for body language or any other sign of what was going on.

Victor didn't look happy. In fact, he seemed agitated and frustrated. After about ten minutes he rose from the chair and approached Chris and me.

"Now you know why I didn't want to call the police in the first place," he said.

"Oh? And why is that?" I asked.

He tipped his head in Janet's direction. She was busily writing notes on a small pad of paper. "She doesn't believe that I don't know who's after me."

"Well, it is unusual for someone who's being threatened not to have a clue about it," I said.

"Maybe so, but I don't have any ideas. I wish we'd kept this just between the three of us."

"With Jackson being bumped off, we couldn't do that," Chris said. "The coppers had to involve themselves."

"Yeah, I guess you're right," Victor said, grudgingly agreeing with

Chris. "Well, I'm outta here. I want to get home and make myself safe behind locked doors."

He left and Janet came over to talk to Chris and me.

"You know, there's something that doesn't feel right about that guy. I can't put my finger on it, but there's something odd about this situation. It'll come to me after I study the facts for a while."

Chris rolled his upper lip under, but this time he didn't pull on his earlobe or rock back on his heels. "Well, don't keep us in the dark when you figure it out."

CHAPTER TWENTY-SIX

We picked Mikey up around eleven-thirty on Wednesday night. He was asleep on Constance's couch, and he didn't wake up when Chris carried him out to the car. Constance said he'd conked out as soon as they arrived home. I'd had to practically hog tie the dogs to keep them from waking him up. I sat in the back with them while Mikey slept in the front seat.

On Thursday morning he would have overslept if the dogs hadn't been so excited to see him. I could hear him upstairs, laughing, and it was a good guess that the dogs were climbing all over him and licking his face. Considering their weight, I wouldn't have found it too funny if I was the one they were climbing on.

Chris and Mikey came downstairs together, ready for a homemade breakfast. In celebration of my son's return, I'd prepared his favorite, pancakes with sausage.

"It sure feels good to be home, Mom," he said, forking a piece of sausage. "I feel like I've been gone *forever*."

"I'm glad to have you home, and maybe now things can go back to normal – whatever that is." I walked around the table and gave him a kiss on the cheek.

"Those Church Ladies are kind of nosey, aren't they? I mean, they wanted to know if I have a *girlfriend!* I'm only seven, for crying out loud. Danny and me have plenty to keep us busy without girls."

"I'm sure you do," I replied. "But someday you're going to be a heartbreaker, just like your dad."

Mikey turned to Chris and made a face that said, *eewww*.

Chris laughed. "One of these days you're going to wake up and think that girls aren't so bad – Ace Michael Cross, lady killer."

Mikey turned back to his breakfast and studied his plate. He didn't say anything, but I could see the corners of his lips turn up.

"Speaking of lady killers," Chris said, "I forgot to tell you. Last night Nate and I had a conversation about Lila."

"Lila?"

"Yeah, he was impressed with her singing. He also wanted to know if she's married."

"What'd you tell him?" I asked, smiling.

"I said I thought she was a widow. I also told him that she's mostly tied up with her church friends."

"What did he say to that?"

"He didn't care. He said he was just curious. I got the feeling he might be more than curious."

"Well, what a surprise." Nate was interested in Lila. I smiled, wondering if Lila might like Nate if she met him.

"I can see the wheels turning," Chris said. "Let it go. Let nature take its course."

"Sure," I said, thoughtfully.

We finished breakfast and Chris helped me clear the table while Mikey ran upstairs to retrieve his backpack.

"Come on, Ace," Chris said. "You're going to be late to school if we don't hurry up."

The phone rang and Chris answered it. "Yeah."

I glanced at Mikey. "When you answer the phone, try to say more than *yeah*, okay? Don't follow all of your father's examples."

"Okay." He stood and tapped his foot impatiently. Chris had told him he was going to be late, and yet now his father was on the phone.

"Huh," Chris said to someone at the other end of the line. "Was anything missing?" He listened to the reply. "Let us know if you find out anything. I'm going to be out for a while, but Pamela will be here."

He hung up and before I could ask, he said, "That was Victor. Someone broke into his house while he was at the restaurant last night. It doesn't look like they took anything, but he's still checking. The police told him it was a clean break in. No prints or anything."

"How did they get in?"

"They broke out a window."

"That's odd. If it was the killer, you'd think he would have waited for him and done the deed."

"You'd think," Mikey said.

Oops. Why did I always forget that my son listened to everything I said?

I gave him a hug and told him to have a good day at school. He nodded and the two men in my life left.

I walked outside and spent a little time with Sherlock and Watson, thinking while I threw a ball for them. Janet was right. Something just didn't feel right when I thought about Victor. It seemed like he wasn't really doing anything to help find his potential killer. *That's* what was wrong. Was he really that dense or was there something else behind it? Was he protecting someone? He had to believe that the threat was real after finding out that John Jackson had been murdered. Maybe he was a fatalist – maybe he believed that whatever was going to happen was meant to be.

Victor wasn't a bad guy. He went out of his way to be kind and helpful to his elderly neighbor, Florence. She was such a nice old gal. I was glad she had him to help her out.

I suddenly realized that I was standing with the ball in my hand and that I'd quit throwing it. The realization came when Sherlock barked at me and Watson nudged my behind.

"Quit that," I said, "or I won't throw it at all." Labs can be very pushy when they want to be, and Watson nudged me again.

I heard the phone ringing in the kitchen and threw the ball one last time before leaving the dogs to their own devices. Apparently I hadn't closed the door tightly, because before I could reach the phone Sherlock slid into the wall.

"Idiot," I said, answering the phone. He'd never raced me for the phone before.

"What?" Jasmine asked.

"Sorry, I was talking to the dog. What's up?"

I shooed the dogs back out the door and made sure it was latched.

"The ladies and I are going to drive over to see Florence this morning and we thought you might like to go with us."

"Thanks for thinking of me, but –"

"She feels so lonely sometimes, so we thought we'd stop and buy an angel food cake to take over to her. We'll only stay for an hour or so." She was wheedling, trying to make me feel guilty. How unchristian of her.

I smiled to myself. She was actually being every bit the Christian woman, wanting to help someone in need, even if she was only in need of company.

"When are you leaving?" I asked. Another thought struck me. It would give me a chance to go over and talk to Victor to find out if he knew anymore than when he'd called Chris.

"In about an hour. Is that okay with you?" I had a feeling that if it wasn't okay with me, it wouldn't matter.

"How about if I pick you ladies up? I'll drive." I wasn't sure I trusted Jasmine's driving. It wasn't because of her age, but she and her friends talk so much that I was worried maybe she wouldn't pay enough attention to her driving.

"That works," she said. "Thank you, and God bless you. I know I can come on a bit strong sometimes, Pamela, but Florence is a special little lady. There's just something so trusting and childlike about her that she makes me feel protective."

"And what do you need to protect her from?" I asked.

"Right now, loneliness. She seems to enjoy our visits so much. I promised her that I'd bring her to church with us next Sunday. She was excited, and she's already planning on what to wear, bless her little heart."

We hung up and I called Chris on his cell phone. "What do you want?" His voice came from behind me and I jumped.

"Oh, Bogey Man. You scared ten years off me. I didn't hear you come home. I didn't hear the cell phone ring either."

"I had it on *vibrate*."

"Ah. Well, I was calling to tell you that I'm going over to Florence's with the Church Ladies. Jasmine was telling me how lonely Florence feels, and we're going to try to cheer her up."

Chris put his hands on my cheeks. "You're a good woman, Pamela."

I looked into his eyes. "I wish I could take the credit, but it's Jasmine. She's the good woman."

"So are you. Trust me, Babe."

Although I hadn't heard Chris arrive home, the dogs had. They were scratching at the back door, wanting to come in. Chris walked back through the service porch and opened the door for them. "Come on, you two. Let's go for a walk."

You'd have thought he'd offered them a million dollars each. The squirming and whining were almost unnerving. Their vocabulary was fairly large for dogs, and *walk* was right at the top of their Happy List.

"You're going to take them both? Alone? Don't you want to wait for me to come home?" I asked.

"No, I can handle them. I'll keep them on a short leash."

"Good luck with that," I said, shaking my head. "I'll be gone by the time you come home, but I'll be back in time for us to ride to the restaurant together."

Chris left and I picked up my purse, ready to leave. I smiled to myself, remembering that Nate was interested in Lila. How cute! I decided to pick Lila up first and tell her about Nate without the other ladies listening. Having second thoughts, I decided I'd only tell her about our new lunch chef. I could invite her for lunch and they could meet, and then nature could take its course, as Chris had suggested. I just wanted to give Mother Nature a little nudge.

I picked up the ladies and we headed for Florence's house, stopping on the way to pick up the angel food cake. Lila mentioned that she'd have to be home by one o'clock because she had an appointment that she didn't want to miss.

May bought some frozen strawberries and readymade whipped cream.

"What are you going to do with that?" Lila asked.

"By the time we get to Florence's house the strawberries will be defrosted. I'll mix them with the whipped cream and cut the angel food cake in half. Then I'll put the mixture between the layers and on top. It'll be yummy, believe me."

"It sounds decadent," Jasmine said. "But then, I guess sometimes it's okay to go a little overboard with the sweets."

"Sounds good to me," Lila said. "I can't wait."

"Me, either," I added.

We pulled up in front of Florence's house and I parked.

"I hope she's up," Jasmine said.

"Didn't she know we were coming?" I asked.

"No, we thought we'd surprise her."

"Oh, great. Let's surprise an eighty-something-year-old woman into a heart attack. You should have called her first."

"Pamela, you're being silly. She'll be delighted to see us, bless her little heart."

"I hope you're right," I replied.

With grocery bag in hand, we trooped up to the front door and rang the bell. I could hear noises inside, so at least I knew that Florence wasn't a late sleeper.

The front door opened and Jasmine said, "Surpri…" Her voice trailed off into nothingness.

Victor was standing there and not looking pleased to see us.

CHAPTER TWENTY-SEVEN

"**V**ictor?" I said. "Is everything okay?"

"You took me by surprise. Was Florence expecting you women today?"

"No," May said, "we thought we'd surprise her."

"I guess we surprised someone," Lila said, under her breath.

Jasmine didn't say anything, and that surprised *me*.

"Is Florence here?" I asked, waiting for him to move out of the doorway and let us in.

"Yes. Just a minute." Victor closed the door on us.

Jasmine, not one to stand on formality, turned the handle and opened the door. "Come on, ladies."

We found Florence sitting at the dining table, and Victor was hurriedly picking up some papers and stuffing them in an envelope. I saw the top of the cover page before he could slide in inside. He'd been helping her fill out a Living Will so that if she couldn't speak for herself, the doctors would know what she wanted. I wondered if she was giving Victor Power of Attorney for her health issues.

"Oh, my," Florence said, standing up and grinning. "What a pleasant surprise. Come in, come in. Victor was helping me with some paperwork. My eyesight isn't what it used to be, you know."

"Is there anything we can do to help?" May asked.

"No," Victor said. "We're done here."

Florence smiled up at him.

"I'll put these papers away for you, Flo, and you can visit with your lady friends." Victor had an odd look on his face.

I couldn't help but feel like there was more going on than met the eye.

"This is a personal matter that I'm helping Flo with," he said, by way of explanation. He carried the envelope to a desk in the corner and slid it in a drawer.

I couldn't help but wish I could see what else might be in the envelope.

"I've got to go now, so you can all jibber jabber, or whatever it is you do, and I'll see you later." Victor headed for the front door.

I followed him. "Did you find out anything else about the break-in at your house?" I asked, quietly. One thing I had learned was that he tried to protect Florence from his problems.

"Nothing. There was a twenty dollar bill missing from the top of my dresser, but that's all. The police didn't seem too interested."

"Well, they should be. I'll call Janet and let her know. It seems too coincidental that someone broke into your house the day after that hood was killed."

"Don't bother," he said. "I've talked to my retired cop friend. At least *he* believes the things I tell him, which is more than I can say for your homicide detective. I called him this morning and he said he'd come stay with me for a couple of days. I'll be safe now."

I could see that he'd set his mind on not liking or trusting Janet, so I let it go. I'd probably tell her anyway, but he didn't have to know that.

Victor left and I turned to see that the ladies were in the kitchen, heating water for tea and preparing the angel food cake.

When everything was ready we sat down and enjoyed a delightful dessert, along with our tea. I noticed that Lila kept glancing at her watch, and vowed to make sure she was home in time for her appointment.

Florence seemed very chipper, and it turned out that she was. "I'm so glad you all came over to see me," she said. "What a happy surprise. Gosh, between you women and Victor, I feel so special. What a lovely day this is turning out to be."

"I'm glad to hear that," May said. "We all need lovely days from time to time."

"Yes, we do," Lila agreed. "When I get up in the morning, I thank the Lord for whatever the day brings, good or bad. It helps to say my thank you before I know what's headed my way." She glanced at her watch again.

"That's so *you*," May said. "I may have to follow your example though. That's a great idea, thanking the good Lord ahead of time, no matter what happens."

"So Victor helps you with your paperwork?" I asked.

Three heads turned and looked at me, surprise etched on their faces. I knew I was being abrupt, but I needed information from wherever I could get it. I shrugged at the ladies.

"Oh, yes he does," Florence said. "He helps me with so many things."

I waited, hoping she'd tell me what they'd been working on, but she took a sip of her tea and another bite of cake, letting the subject drop.

This time I shrugged inwardly, knowing in my heart that the subject had just died a quick death.

We spent about an hour and a half with Florence before I said we'd have to be leaving. She'd grown up on a farm and shared some of her stories with us, including the time a bull chased her into the barn, and the time her brother had built a small homemade roller coaster. It hadn't been too safe and her father made her brother tear it down. It had certainly been a different life than I'd experienced.

I had things to do before heading for the restaurant. One thing about the business we'd embarked on was that you generally didn't have a lot of time to yourself. We were fortunate because our employees were so capable and helped us more than their job descriptions called for, and I appreciated every one of them.

When the ladies were settled in the car, and all seatbelts were fastened, I pulled away from the curb. We'd gone about two and a half blocks when I glanced in my rearview mirror and saw that Victor was following us. I pulled over, thinking he wanted to talk to us, but he drove on by and waved at us. He must have been out running errands. However, seeing him was a good reminder that I should keep my eyes open. Jackson's partner was still out there, and there was no guarantee that he wouldn't be looking for Addie.

After dropping the ladies off, I arrived home to find Chris sitting at the kitchen table with a leash in each hand. He looked upset.

"What's wrong?" I asked, having a momentary feeling of panic because he held the leashes but I didn't see any dogs.

"Nothing."

"Where are the dogs?"

"In the backyard."

"Come on," I pushed, "what's wrong?"

"Everything. Nothing." He sighed. "I took the dogs for their walk." He stopped talking, and I felt a glimmer of a chuckle coming on. I had a feeling that this was going to be a funny story. I tried to keep the mirth out of my voice.

"And?"

"Watson wanted to stop and sniff a boulder out in front of Mr. Parks' yard. Sherlock decided he wanted to sniff the mail box post on the other side of the driveway. For a minute I thought they were going to tear me into two pieces."

"Oh, I'm sorry, Sweetie," I said, commiserating with him. I knew how strong the dogs were.

"That's not the end of it."

"It's not?"

"No. Then they decided to trade places, and I got tangled up in their leashes. I fell down before I could stop them." He held out his hand, which was scratched and bleeding. "Then Mr. Parks came out to see if he could help me."

"Uh oh."

"Uh oh is right. He's got to be at least ninety years old, and the last thing I needed was for the dogs to knock him down. Can you imagine if he broke his hip?"

"So what did you do?" I asked.

"I waved him off, and I think I might have made him mad. He said some things under his breath about not being too old to help out a neighbor. I tried to explain, but he kept walking and waved his hand at me behind his back."

A bubble of laughter was working its way up, but I fought it.

"Well, next time we'll both walk the dogs."

"There's more," Chris said. "When we got home the phone was ringing. Sherlock tried to race me for it, but he still had his leash on and this time we both slid into the wall."

I turned and looked at the wall, making sure there weren't any holes in it.

"Miss All was calling. You know, Mikey's teacher."

"What did she want?" The bubble was closer to bursting, but at the same time I had a sinking feeling.

"It seems that she overheard Mikey telling the other kids that you and I are after a hit man. Of course, the other kids wanted to know what a hit man is. He explained – in graphic detail."

I sat down in the chair opposite Chris.

"She wants us to have a talk with him. She gets a kick out of the forties slang he uses, and says the other kids have started using it, too. And she enjoys the stories he tells about our lives and our cases, but this was too much for her."

One of the dogs scratched at the back door, and my bubble finally burst. I began laughing, and the uncharitable look that Chris gave me made me laugh even harder.

"It's not funny, Pamela." He sounded indignant.

"No," I said, through tears of laughter. "It really isn't. But that story was just what I needed to unwind."

"We've got to talk to Ace, but we'll have to wait until tomorrow morning, during breakfast. He needs to learn what he can talk about and when to keep his mouth shut," Chris said.

"A good lesson for all of us. By the way, Chris, when we arrived at Florence's house, Victor was there. I think he's involved in her personal affairs, like with a Living Will. He seemed uncomfortable when we walked in and he shoved it in a drawer."

"That's something I hadn't thought about," Chris said. "Does she have any family?"

"She mentioned that she has nieces and nephews, but she says they don't come around. Why? What are you thinking?"

"I wonder if there's any reason that her family might want to get rid of Victor. Maybe those are the toes he's stepping on."

"I can't imagine why he'd be on a family hit list. She's just a little old lady taking life day by day. It's not like she's wealthy or anything. No, I don't think that's it, but I do think something is going on."

"Now if we can just figure out what that something is."

Chris finally let go of the dogs' leashes, and they fell to the floor.

CHAPTER TWENTY-EIGHT

Things were relatively quiet at the restaurant on Thursday night. We had a decent crowd, and there were no dramas, thankfully. No birthday parties that ended in tragedy and no bad guys peeking through the doorway. We'd left the dogs at home this time, so I didn't have to worry about them. Mikey was safe in his own bed, with Constance staying at our house for the evening. All was right with the world.

Nate came in again and had dinner. Once more he said he wanted to get a feel for the place. He said he did his best cooking when he felt comfortable in a restaurant. At one point I heard him telling the people at the next table that we'd be opening for lunch before long. They were delighted, and I also heard him tell them that they were going to truly enjoy the new chef's offerings, which made me chuckle to myself. I made a mental note to start advertising the new hours as soon as possible.

Around eight o'clock something happened that surprised me. A small woman approached the Reservation Desk and stood, staring at me. Glancing up, I smiled. I blinked and took a closer look.

"Lila?" I hadn't recognized her.

She clamped her lips tightly together and turned in a circle so I could view the whole package, waiting to see if I approved or not. Her hair had been dyed a medium blonde and was styled into a soft and curly look. She was wearing just a small amount of makeup. Her dress was a lighter blue silky number with a full skirt. It wasn't a forties style, but it suited her. And her usual tennis shoes had been replaced by sandals in a contrasting shade of blue.

"You look wonderful," I said. "Absolutely beautiful!" I was as close to speechless as I could come without clamming up completely. "So your appointment was at the beauty shop."

She finally nodded and smiled. "What do you think about the new me?"

Chris had walked up behind her and was listening to our conversation.

He placed his hands on her shoulders and turned her around. "Who's the glamour puss? Lila? You're one heck of a dish this evening. What's the occasion?"

She pointed toward the lounge. "I have things to do tonight. I decided to take Jasmine and May's advice and create a new me. After all, if I'm going to be singing here once in a while, I don't want to look dowdy." She touched her cheeks. "I even went to a department store and had a makeup makeover."

I walked out from behind the desk and gave her as much of a hug as I could without crushing her. She hugged me back and with a small wave of her hand, headed for the lounge.

I left Chris at the Reservation Desk and followed her. She headed straight for the stage, and after checking to make sure who she was, one of the band members took her hand and helped her up. I could see that he was probably telling her how great she looked, and she tipped her head and smiled shyly.

Someone tapped my shoulder and said, "Excuse me." I turned around to find Nate waiting for me to move so he could walk through to the lounge.

I turned and hurried back to Chris.

"It looks like Lila is going to sing again," I said.

"Looks like it."

"And as soon as Nate saw her, he hightailed it into the lounge."

"Good for him."

"Is that all you have to say? Looks like it and good for him?"

"What do you want me to say? Calling all cars, calling all cars, there's a little old man in the lounge who appears to have a crush on a little old lady who's turned out to be a senior babe."

Pursing my lips, I decided I'd just ignore my husband for the moment. I started making the rounds among the customers, asking if they were enjoying their meals and inquiring if they needed anything. Many of our patrons returned at least once a week, and a few stopped me to chat.

I enjoyed my job and I enjoyed our customers. What a way to make a living – doing something I liked.

Lila began singing and I stopped to listen. She sang three forties songs, and seemed so happy. The look on her face was priceless. It appeared that when she was singing, she completely forgot about her shyness and lack of self-confidence. I was sure that her new look didn't hurt any. After the third song, she took a break.

"Lila, you're really something," I said, approaching the stage. "I had no idea you'd be back so soon. And the customers absolutely love you."

She beamed. Her cheeks were rosy and healthy looking. I didn't think it was due to the makeup she wore. "One of the band members called me this morning and asked if I could come in. The lady that usually sings with them is sick, and they said they'd pay me. How could I refuse? The Lord is supplying my needs. I need a new water heater and the timing for this gig is perfect."

Gig? Lila had called her performance a gig. And she had a new look. Would life ever be the same again?

Looking up, I saw Nate approaching us. He appeared to be on a mission.

"Pamela, would you introduce me to your friend?"

After introducing Nate and Lila, I suggested they sit together while she was on her break. He took her arm and guided her to a table in the corner where they could hear each other talk.

With the biggest *I-told-you-so* grin I could muster, I walked out and met Chris by the front door. "Give you one guess what two senior citizens are sitting together in the lounge."

Chris looked at me out of the corner of his eye. "You're in your glory, aren't you?"

"Yes," I said, feeling victorious.

"Well, Peaches, I hope it works out. For their sake, not for yours."

"Chris, you're sounding a little cranky. Care to share anything?"

"The economy." He glanced around the restaurant. "We're doing well right now, but the economy is getting worse all the time. I can't help but wonder how long we can keep our heads above water. I'm really hoping that opening for lunch will help."

"It doesn't seem like business is down," I said. "We're doing okay."

"Yeah, but for how long? I see businesses going under all over town. And opening for lunch means we'll be hiring more staff. We'll need two more waitresses, another sous chef, and then there's Nate."

"We provide something unique, and that's going to help. *Bogey Nights* is somewhere that people can come to in order to forget their everyday lives. Think in terms of reciprocity. I send goods to the food bank as often as possible. You get back what you give. And, if need be, we'll cut a few corners and lower our prices."

"You're quite the little optimist."

"We'll make it. If we don't, then we'll move on with fond memories of what was."

"I love you, Pamela."

Before he could say anything else a young couple approached the desk. "We wanted to stop and tell you what a nice time we've had this evening. This is our third date, and this place helped to make it especially fun." The woman appeared to be around twenty-five or so.

I glanced at Chris. He'd moved into his Bogey persona. "Well, kids, I don't wanna give you the bum's rush, but if this is your third date you'd better get moving. There's a whole dance floor waiting for you in the lounge. Go cut a rug. The first round is on us." He curled his lip under, rocked back on his heels and pulled on his earlobe. He was giving the couple the full treatment.

"Oh, neither of us drinks," the young woman said, looking at him as though he'd lost his marbles. Apparently she didn't know who Humphrey Bogart was.

"Iced tea it is," I replied, quickly. "Now go and enjoy the music."

They glanced at each other, the woman nodded, and off they went, holding hands and looking into each other's eyes.

"Ah, young love," I said.

Chris snorted and turned back to the reservation book.

I heard Lila start singing again and headed for the lounge to tell Daniel, the bartender, about free drinks for the young couple. With that done, I walked out to the kitchen to see how Luis was doing. He'd already started cleaning up the things he figured he wouldn't need for the rest of the shift.

After a little time went by, I peeked around the doorway of the lounge. The young couple sat, still hand in hand, talking like they'd known each other forever. I wondered if they'd ever get around to dancing.

Lila was watching Nate while she sang, delight lighting up her face.

What a night this was turning out to be. And I'd thought it was going to be quiet. Shows how much I know. I made the rounds of the restaurant again.

The band stopped playing. Checking my watch, I saw that it was nine-thirty. They always stopped playing half an hour before closing time, and we closed at ten o'clock on weeknights. On weekends we stayed open until eleven-thirty. I was tired and ready to go home. Chris had the look of someone wanting to sleep, too.

"Not much longer," I said.

Chris nodded. While he covered the Reservation Desk, I began collecting receipts to see how we'd done. Not bad, from what I could see. I took them back and deposited them on my desk. Thinking I heard a noise outside the back door, I opened it and took a look around. I saw a latecomer pull into the parking lot, but it was really too late for dinner. Chris would tactfully turn them away.

Closing the door and locking it, I walked through the kitchen and headed toward Chris.

That's when the lights went out.

I heard someone curse, and a woman screamed. I froze, waiting for my eyes to adjust to the dark.

CHAPTER TWENTY-NINE

Chris kept a flashlight behind the desk and I saw the light come on after only a couple of seconds.

"Who screamed?" I called out.

"I did," a woman's voice said, sounding embarrassed. "Sorry. I was bending over to pick up my napkin and hit my head on the table. Scared myself half to death."

"Everybody stay where you are," Chris said, "and we'll bring you candles."

I'd already started looking for the box we kept the candles in and found it right where it should have been. George began passing out glass globes with candles in them and Susan followed behind, lighting them.

"Chris," I said, looking out the front door, "no one else's lights are out. What do you think is going on?"

"I don't know. I'll go check the fuse box. You stay here and make sure the customers are okay."

Flashlight in hand, he headed for the rear of the restaurant. The fuse box was located outside the back door to my office.

I stopped at one of the closest tables. "Everything okay here?"

"It's actually kind of romantic," a woman answered. Her husband grunted in response.

I smiled. "If you need anything, please let us know."

"We're fine," she replied, patting her husband's hand.

He tipped his head and studied her. "You look a lot younger in candlelight."

I cringed, thinking he was about to catch it.

"So do you, dear," she said good-naturedly. "And I can't see how bald you are."

They both laughed and I knew everything was okay.

The lights didn't come back on while I made the rounds, and Chris didn't return. I was beginning to worry. After checking at a couple more tables, I decided I'd better go look for him.

"George, will you and Susan cover things while I go see what's keeping Chris?"

"Sure," he said, signaling for Susan to join him. I pulled a second flashlight out of the Reception Desk drawer while they were huddled together in the dining area.

Passing the doorway to the lounge, I saw that Daniel had pulled candles out from under the bar for the patrons. Things were going smoothly considering that it was a moonless night and it was black as pitch without the lights – or so I thought.

Arriving in the kitchen I found Chef Luis and Phillip, the sous chef, helping Chris sit down.

"What happened?" I said, rushing over to my husband.

"I don't know," Luis replied. "I heard a noise and went out back to check it out. I found Chris lying on the ground and heard a car pulling out of the parking lot."

"Chris? Are you okay?" I asked. "What happened?"

"Give me a minute," he replied, sounding angry and rubbing the back of his head.

I turned to Luis, but he shrugged his shoulders. Turning, he pulled a towel out of a drawer and handed it to Chris.

Checking the back of Chris's head I saw blood, and asked Luis to moisten the towel. While I waited impatiently for Chris to say something, I dabbed at his head. He winced and pulled the towel out of my hand to look at it.

"Son of a –"

"What *happened*?" I asked, no longer able to hold my tongue.

"I went out back to check the fuse box, but before I could open it someone hit me on the head – hard – and I fell down on my knees. I couldn't even defend myself. All I could do was wait for my head to clear. Whoever it was really rang my bell. It took a couple of minutes to get my bearings back."

"Did he say anything?"

"No. It was a hit and run."

"Luis, you said you heard a car leaving?" I asked.

"Yes. It sounded like they were in a hurry, too."

"I heard a noise not long before the lights went out," I said, "and when I went out back to check it out, there was a car pulling into the parking lot."

"Do you remember what kind of car?" Chris asked.

"Not really. I wasn't paying that much attention. Luis, did you see the car?"

"No, I just heard it, and then I found Chris on the ground. I decided it was more important to check on him than to look for the car."

"Of course," I said. "I think we'd better head for the hospital, Bogey Man. You need to have yourself checked out."

"I'm fine – just pissed off."

"Honey, you could have a concussion or something."

"I said, I'm *fine!* Let it go."

While we argued about whether or not to take a trip to the hospital, Phillip headed outside. Within moments the lights came back on.

"Thanks, Phillip," I said, when he returned.

"Yeah," he said. "Someone had to do it."

"What's going on in here?"

I turned at the sound of Lila's voice.

"Someone attacked Chris, and now I'm trying to talk him into going to the hospital. He doesn't want to go."

Lila closed her eyes and said, "Lord, I pray that you'll keep Chris and Pamela safe, and that Chris will quit being pig-headed and let Pamela drive him to the hospital."

I stopped what I was doing and folded my hands in prayer. "Yes, Lord," I said.

"Father," Lila continued, "I ask in Jesus' name that you heal Chris's wound if she can't talk him into the trip. And –"

"Thank you, Lila," Chris said, "I'm ready to go to the hospital. You two can stop praying now."

I smiled at this woman I'd come to admire so much.

"Thank you, Lord! You work so *fast* sometimes. Amen." Lila was grinning like the Cheshire cat.

I saw that Nate had followed Lila into the kitchen. He stood, watching her thoughtfully, before he smiled and said a loud, "*Amen!*" It appeared that he was fine with Lila's Christianity.

She smiled, looking pleased with Nate's reaction.

"Now let's all go to the hospital," Lila said.

"Oh, no," Chris said. "There's no *all* in this equation. Pamela and I will go and you can help close the place up. Deal?"

"Deal," Lila and Nate replied in unison.

"George knows what to do," I said. "Would you please go talk to him? You can tell him what happened."

Lila nodded and took Nate's hand, leading him out of the kitchen.

"What a night this has turned out to be," Luis said.

"You can say that again," I replied, trying to help Chris stand up.

"I'm not a cripple, Cookie, and I only said I'd go to the hospital so Lila would quit talking to God."

"Whatever it takes." I said a silent thank you before letting go of Chris's arm.

***

I'd used the cell phone to call Constance on our way to the hospital, suggesting she spend the night in the guest room instead of driving home. I had no idea what time we'd be rolling in. She was concerned about Chris and said she'd stay as long as we needed her.

I also called the police. After all, Chris had been attacked. They said they'd meet us at the hospital.

Chris needed a couple of stitches, and the doctor shaved a small spot on his head. My husband was not happy, and the headache he had made his mood even worse. It was more difficult than dealing with an injured child. He'd whined about his injury, and he'd whined about the numbness where the doctor had stitched him up. He even complained because he didn't like the questions the coppers had asked him. He'd whined about a headache, and he'd whined about my driving after we left the hospital. I bit my tongue as long as I could, and even then tried to make nice since I knew he was in pain.

I'd tactfully told him that he should lean back and sleep until we reached the house. He started to grumble about me being bossy.

"Now!" I said, authority punctuating my word. "You're driving me crazy, Chris, so lean back and sleep or prepare yourself for all out warfare."

His eyes widened in surprise when he looked at me, just before he dropped his head forward. "I can't lean back. My head hurts too much."

"Do it any way you want to, but leave me alone while I drive home."

"Yes, Ma'am."

"Ya big baby," I said, under my breath.

"I heard that."

Neither one of us slept well that night and yet I woke up feeling somewhat refreshed, surprising myself.

Chris had finally gone to sleep, so I left him alone while I went down to have my first cup of coffee and talk to Constance. I could hear her moving around in the kitchen.

First things first, so I fed the dogs. Constance had already taken Mikey to school, and instead of going home she'd come back to see if we needed anything. She already had the coffee brewing.

"You're too good to me," I said. "I don't know why you hang around with me. It seems like I'm always asking for favors."

"You are, but that's okay. I've asked you for plenty of favors over the years, so it all evens out."

Constance and I were both widows, each having lost our husbands to cancer. Mikey's father had been young when we lost him. We'd bonded when I moved in next door to her. It was a welcome friendship, and I'd do anything I could for her. She was probably about fifteen years older than me, but our friendship knew no age limits.

"So tell me what happened last night. You were kind of vague on the phone. I tried to wait up for you two, but I just couldn't keep my eyes open."

"Well, first the lights went out in the restaurant, and when Chris went to check the fuse box, someone attacked him. That's about the gist of it. Chris didn't want to go to the hospital, but Lila started praying for him. I think it kind of freaked him out. Anyway, he had three stitches in his noggin, but he doesn't have a concussion."

Constance started to laugh, covering her mouth so she wouldn't wake Chris. "Gotta love that Lila. She gets things done."

"That she does."

"Do you have any idea who attacked Chris?" Constance asked.

"No. And nobody saw a thing. Luis heard a car leaving, and I'd seen someone pull into the parking lot not long before the lights went out, but I wasn't paying attention to the car. All I could think of was that it was too late for anyone to be coming in for dinner."

"Do you think it had something to do with the case you're working on for the Church Ladies?"

"I wasn't robbed, so that had to be it," Chris said, startling both of us. "Maybe it was a warning of sorts."

Constance was grinning, and I turned around to look at Chris. He was wearing his bathrobe, slippers and a fedora. I started to laugh.

"Aren't you a sight this morning? What are you dressed up for?" I couldn't help myself. What an outfit.

"I'm trying to hide my bald patch, and I couldn't find my baseball cap."

Constance coughed politely, hiding her grin behind her hand. "Are you okay, Chris?"

"Been better."

"Your bald patch isn't all that big," I said. "I think you'll live."

"How about a little sympathy here," he said, dragging himself over to the table and sitting down. "I could use a cup of java, too."

Constance stood up and headed for the coffee pot.

"Thank you," Chris said, when she placed a mug in front of him.

"Can I see your head?" she asked.

Chris took off his hat and she leaned in to take a good look.

"I wouldn't wear a hat, if I were you. You've got a good war story to tell with that injury. Although, I guess I'd wear it to work. The customers probably wouldn't want to see your stitches."

Chris took a sip of his coffee. "This had to be the work of John Jackson's partner. Who else would have cold-cocked me like that? I know we're in someone's way. No one else has a beef with me that I know about. If he hadn't made me hear the birdies singin', I would have taken him out."

"I know you would have, Sweetie," I said. "And I'm sorry you heard the birdies sing, but you couldn't have known that someone would deliberately shut the lights off." I had a feeling that Chris thought his manhood was in question, and I wanted him to know it wasn't.

"Was he really unconscious?" Constance asked. "Did the doctor check for a concussion?"

"He wasn't knocked cold, but I'm sure he heard some bells ringing, at the very least."

"What I can't understand," Chris said, "is why this guy is playing games instead of just doing what he was paid to do. Why hasn't he gone after Victor yet?"

"We won't know the answer to that until we find Jackson's partner," I replied.

CHAPTER THIRTY

Before Constance left I asked her what she'd told Mikey about spending the night at our house. She said she'd been relatively honest with him. "I told him that his dad had hit his head and needed to see a doctor, but that he was okay. I told him it wasn't anything to worry about, and he seemed fine with that explanation."

"Thank you again, Constance. I just don't know what I'd do without you."

"Hopefully you'll never have to find out."

Chris rested for most of the day, which was unusual in itself because he was a fairly high energy man. He did, however, seem to like being waited on. I made him tea and toast, and served him in the living room. He asked if I could bring him a napkin. He wanted juice, and I brought him juice. Then he wanted more tea, but on second thought decided he wanted coffee. No, coffee might make his headache worse. Would I please bring him milk instead? As I was returning to the kitchen, he called out reminding me that he needed a napkin. I took him two. He said he was ready for a sandwich, saying that the toast hadn't been enough food. I made him a peanut butter and jelly sandwich. I'd just reentered the kitchen when he asked if we had a bell that he could ring if he needed anything. I clenched my fists and felt my back muscles tighten, and held my hands by my side.

"*No!*" I snapped at him. He was surprised at my sharp answer and I took advantage of the quiet moment and walked out the back door.

I played with the dogs and dusted the house before Mikey came home from school. Danny's mother had picked the two boys up after school and dropped Mikey off. We shared school duty from time to time.

"Hey, Dad!" he yelled, bursting through the front door. "How's your head?"

Chris groaned, still fighting a headache. "Fine. Would you please lower your voice?"

"Okay," Mikey whispered. "How's your head? Can I see it?"

Chris sat up and turned so our son could see his stitches.

"Cool!" Mikey said, examining the doctor's handy work. "Does it hurt?"

"Only when you yell, Ace. Or when I move. Or breath."

I rolled my eyes. How could I not?

Mikey finally put his backpack down and ran out to see the dogs, after showing very little pity for his father. Chris seemed insulted by Mikey's lack of sympathy.

"He's seven. What did you expect?" I asked. "At the most, he may want to take a picture of your head for posterity."

I was seeing a side of Chris that I'd never seen before, although he hadn't been sick or injured since the day we were married.

"Where did he go?" Chris asked.

"To see the dogs."

"Oh." He sounded disappointed that the dogs were receiving what should have been *his* attention.

I heard the back door open, and then the clicking of toenails on the kitchen floor. Knowing what to expect, thanks to lots of experience, I ran over and stopped the dogs in the kitchen before they could run into the living room and jump up on Chris. I held my hands up, palms facing the dogs. They knew this was the signal to *stop*. Surprisingly, they did. Sherlock and Watson didn't always listen to me.

"Mikey," I said, loudly, "get the treats. I don't know how long they're going to mind."

Mikey came in from the service porch with a container full of doggie cookies and handed them to me.

"Good babies," I said, calmly. "Now *stay*." Sherlock wagged his tail, mopping the floor with it, and Watson sat very still, concentrating on the container. They knew what was coming. I handed each of them a treat. Chewing it up, they dribbled crumbs all over the floor.

"Now you two have to remain calm. Chris doesn't need you jumping all over him. Got that?" Anyone listening would have thought they could understand me – and sometimes they seemed to. When I mentioned Chris's name, they both turned to look at him.

"Mikey, go stand by your father, just in case they ignore me."

My son straightened his back, enjoying being the one sent to save Chris. He put his hands up as I had, with his palms facing the dogs. "You two mutts had better not hurt my dad, or you'll be in deep doo doo."

"Mikey!" I said.

"I just said doo doo. That's not a bad thing to say."

"Well…"

"Would everyone please go away and let me get some rest before I have to leave for work?" Chris sounded pathetic, and Mikey fell for it.

"It's okay, Dad. I'll take the dogs outside."

Chris patted Mikey's shoulder. "You're a good son."

"Big fat baby," I mumbled, leaving the room.

"I can still hear you," Chris called after me. "I'd like to hear what you'd sound like if someone had hit *you* over the head."

I wouldn't be whining nearly as much as you are, I thought to myself. No point in stirring things up by speaking my thoughts. I always thought men were supposed to be so manly – strong and silent. I sighed and continued into the kitchen.

Mikey put the dogs outside, handing them each another cookie, and then sat down at the table. He was ready for an afternoon snack – something to hold him over until dinner.

"What would we do without those dog treats?" I asked. "I hate to bribe them to be good, but sometimes it's necessary."

Mikey leaned on the table. "How about a people cookie? We got any of those?"

I handed him a couple of crackers and a small glass of milk. "Do you think this will hold you until dinner?"

"Thank you, and yes. Am I staying home or going to Constance's house tonight?"

"I think you'll go over to her house. She spent the night here last night, so she's probably ready for some stay-at-home time. Okay?"

"Okay. She's got some good games at her house, and she got them just for me."

"That's our Constance," I replied. "You know she loves you like a grandson."

Mikey smiled and ate the rest of his crackers.

Leaving him at the kitchen table with a comic book, I walked out to check on Chris. "Are you feeling any better?" I'd calmed down and realized that I was being too hard on him.

"I am. I'm sorry I've been snapping at you, Cupcake. Headaches really put me under. Pain and I are like water and oil. We don't mix well. Besides,

I'm ticked off that someone got the drop on me. I shoulda heard him coming."

I sat down on the couch next to him, realizing that we'd finally come to the real cause for the complaining. He was embarrassed that he hadn't been able to protect himself. "That's okay, Bogey Man. And I'm sorry for snapping back at you. It was uncalled for, because I know you don't feel well. And, obviously this guy planned it out. You wouldn't have heard him coming."

"I sure wish I'd gotten a look at the goon. Unless the coppers come up with a fingerprint or something, I don't know how anyone's going to figure out who Jackson's partner is."

"Maybe we can ask Addie for a better description. There must be something that would identify him. Saying that he's just plain average doesn't help at all." I thought for a moment. "I could call Donna again and pick her brain."

"Donna?"

"You know, the waitress. The one who's coming to work for us? Oh! That reminds me. I've got to start some hype about *Bogey Nights* being open for lunch."

Leaving Chris on the couch, I returned to the kitchen and phoned Sharon Stone, a reporter and sometimes friend. I hadn't liked her initially, but after she hooked up with Davie, Chris's best friend, I got to know her better. She wasn't all bad, after all.

After promising me that she'd put an article in the newspaper, she asked how things were going for Chris and me.

"Oh, just fine. You know us. Work, work, work. Never a moment to ourselves." I pointedly avoided telling her about Victor because this woman liked nothing more than to insinuate herself into our lives. She was always looking for a good story, trying to move up the ladder at work.

After we hung up I called a sign company and ordered a banner announcing the new hours and lunch.

I felt like I'd done all I could, at least where *Bogey Nights* was concerned.

Picking up the receiver again, I dialed Jasmine's number. It was time to talk to Addie and see if we could get a better description of Jackson's partner.

Jasmine answered, and after blessing me and asking if we'd made any progress, she put Addie on the phone.

"Addie," I said, "do you remember anything about the second man who was at that diner? *Anything* would help."

"Like what?" she asked.

"How tall was he?"

"About average. Maybe as tall as Chris." She paused for a moment. "No, just a shade shorter."

"How about his hair color?" I asked.

"Hmm. Kind of a lighter color, like a light brown. Well, not really brown, but not blond either."

"Age?" I asked.

"Oh, I couldn't tell you that. He wasn't young, but I've never been good at guessing people's ages."

"Eye color?"

"I never saw his eyes. I'm sorry, Pamela, but I just got a brief look at him. I only know what the man with the mustache looked like because of him coming to my house and me hiding out in his camper."

"Speaking of that, how are you feeling?" I asked.

"Oh, fair to middlin'," she replied. "I really got in over my head, and it's taken something away from me. I just don't feel as energetic as I used to. I know it's only been a few days since all of this happened, but it feels like it's been a year. I'm afraid to go out of the house anymore."

"Well, we'll take care of that for you. I don't want you to feel like a prisoner in Jasmine's house. I have a feeling that it won't be long and we'll have this figured out. In the meantime, feel free to come to the restaurant with the other ladies. You'll be safe there." I almost bit my tongue when I remembered that Chris was lying on the couch with a headache and stitches. The last thing he needed was the Church Ladies coming to see us.

"Really? You'd like me to come back to the restaurant?" Addie asked.

"Yes, but let's not rush it," I said quickly. "You do need a couple of days to recover. After all, you went through quite an ordeal."

"Yes, I did. I can't tell my daughter about it, so I called and told her that Jasmine was ill and I was staying here in order to take care of her."

"Good thinking," I said.

"Do you think there's any chance that the second man could still find me?"

"No," I said, hopefully. "I can't think of any way that this man could find you."

CHAPTER THIRTY-ONE

Before I could dig the hole I was in any deeper, Jasmine thankfully took the phone from Addie so she could talk to me.

"Well, God bless her, have you seen Lila? She had a makeover and I can't wait to see her."

"Yes, I saw Lila. She came in and sang at the restaurant again last night. You didn't know that?"

"She mentioned that she was going to see you and Chris last night, but she didn't say that she was going to sing. I haven't talked to her today. I'll be seeing her this evening though. How does she look?"

"Wonderful," I replied. "She's changed her hair color and she's wearing a little makeup. And she was dressed up. She was really pretty when she got rid of the tennis shoes and all that grey."

"I hope we did the right thing in talking her into the changes," Jasmine said. "I wouldn't want her personality to change. At least, not much. I would like to see her come out of her shell though. I pray about her, you know."

"I think your prayers may have been answered. She had a great time last night, and she even…" I let my voice trail off. It wasn't my place to tell Jasmine about Lila meeting Nate.

"She even what, dear?"

"Oh, nothing. She just had a good time. She can tell you about it when you see her."

"Well, I know that singing in a bar isn't exactly the Christian thing to do, but it's not like she's doing something wrong. And she really is enjoying singing. Of course, we've visited your cocktail lounge, and I didn't see anyone getting drunk. I think it actually might be good for her. And she'll be singing again at church this Sunday." Jasmine didn't sound like she was being judgmental about the lounge as much as she was being cautious.

I explained to Jasmine that it was time to get ready for work, and we hung up. I didn't want to blab about Lila and Nate. It really *wasn't* my place.

Being Friday, I dressed up more than I had during the beginning of the week. This time I wore an ankle length darker green thirties style evening gown. That era was big on feminine evening wear. Dresses had become molded to the body and fell into a vertical drape, clinging subtly to the body. Sexy was in. My gown was a couture silk lace/tulle dress. The bodice was a layer of very fine lace over a sleeveless dress, and the skirt consisted of a number of layers of the same fine lace, falling gracefully from about the bottom of my hips over each other and to the floor. The back was quite low cut, which I believed was something relatively new in the styles of that time period. I added some low-heeled silver vintage shoes that I'd found at a local dress shop. They'd been using them for a display, and I'd talked them into selling them to me.

Again, I wore my auburn hair in an up hair style. I was still fiddling with a hair pin as I descended the stairs.

Hearing wolf whistles, I stopped and gazed down the stairs. Chris and Mikey were smiling up at me.

"Hey, boys," I said in imitation of Mae West, "why don't ya come up and see me some time?"

"Who's mom trying to talk like?" Mikey asked, turning to Chris.

"An old time actress named Mae West. You'd get a kick out of her, Ace." Chris never took his eyes off of me while he answered Mikey.

"Oh. Was she as pretty as my mom?"

"No, Ace, she wasn't. No one can beat your mother."

Chris had just made up for all the moaning and groaning without even knowing it. I resolved to look around the house for a bell in case the need ever arose again. I thought I might have one in with the Christmas decorations.

We drove Mikey over to Constance's house and arrived at the restaurant ready to face whatever the night served up to us. Chris said the throbbing had gone away, but he still had a mild headache. He kept his hat on from the moment we left the house until we reached *Bogey Nights*.

Entering the kitchen, we found Phillip and Chef Luis waiting for us. They wanted to know how Chris was and, of course, they wanted to see the wound – shades of my son emanated from the two men.

I left them talking and walked to my office. We'd left the dogs at home again because, and I couldn't help it, I was afraid they might jump up and tear my dress. The lace was so beautiful that I couldn't have stood it if anything happened to it. I sat down at the desk and worked on the books while Chris took care of setting things up for the evening. Phyllis and Gloria both stuck their heads in to say hello, and I waved at them. George and Susan weren't far behind.

Everything was going so smoothly. We opened for business and we had a good crowd coming in that night. Every table in the place had been reserved, which left a couple of tables in the lounge where late comers could sit and eat. Phyllis, Gloria, Susan and George would have their hands full.

When I was done with the books I headed for the lounge to ask if Lila was coming in again. The regular singer was on stage, so I knew I wouldn't be seeing her. Chris was at the desk greeting some patrons and I walked over to help. He'd put his hat back on. I'd suggested we put a bandage on his head, but he was a firm believer that fresh air would heal his head faster than a covered wound – never mind that his hat covered it.

"Oh, Mrs. Cross, I just love that dress," Mrs. Beard said, as I approached. "Wherever did you find it?"

"Thank you," I replied. "Actually, it came from..." I told her about a vintage dress shop I'd found in town and she turned to her husband with a hopeful expression on her face. He smiled at her and took her elbow, ready to follow Chris to their table. I knew she'd probably visit the shop no later than the next day. She was a sweet woman, and her husband indulged her excessively. He knew a good thing when he saw it, and to him, she was it.

We were busy, but it was a good type of busy. Things were still running smoothly, and after the past few days' events, I counted my blessings.

I honestly thought we were going to get through the evening with no drama. Silly me.

Chris and I were standing at the Reservation Desk talking when the phone rang. Chris picked up the receiver, shaking his head. "And I was worried about business falling off."

I smiled at him.

"*Bogey Nights*," he said, using his Bogey voice, "where the elite come to eat and dance all night long." That was something new. I'd never heard him say that before.

I raised my eyebrows at him and he shrugged in return.

"Oh, hi, Addie. Pamela's right here. Hold on a minute."

He handed the receiver to me.

"Hi, Addie, what's up?" I asked.

"I thought I'd better give you a call because the girls are up to it again," she replied.

"What's going on now?"

"Well, Lila came over this afternoon and told us about last night. By the way, what do you think about the gentleman she met? Is he a nice man?"

"I don't really know him," I replied. "He seems to be, and he's a friend of our chef's. He's also coming to work for us, so we've had a couple of conversations with him."

"Oh." Addie hesitated.

"Is that what you're calling about?" I asked.

"Noooo." She dragged the word out, sounding hesitant to tell me whatever it was she had to say.

"Addie, is something wrong?" She was beginning to worry me.

I could hear her take a deep breath. "The girls drove over to Florence's house."

It was like pulling teeth. "Okay, and is that a problem? What's going on?"

She took another breath. "Lila told us about Chris being attacked last night. We talked about it and decided that if someone was attacking Chris, then maybe something else was going to happen."

I thought about it for a moment. "You mean you think things are about to escalate?"

"That's exactly the word that Jasmine used just before we prayed together. Yes, that's what we think. So the girls drove over to Florence's house to watch out for Victor. They have a feeling that tonight might be *the* night."

"Addie, hold on a minute. Let me tell Chris what's going on." I pushed the Hold button and turned to Chris.

By the time I was done explaining, his eyes were mere slits in his face. "What's the matter with those women? Don't they have any sense? How do they think they're going to protect Victor if something happens?" While he talked he was motioning Phyllis over to the desk.

"Should we drive over there?" I asked.

Phyllis approached us. "Do you need something?" she asked.

"Yeah, can you and Gloria watch things while Pamela and I run an errand? We might not be back before closing."

"Sure," she replied. "And when are you going to change my title to Assistant Manager and give me a raise, Boss?"

I could see by the look on her face that she was teasing him, but we had called on her for help a number of times lately. Maybe a raise wouldn't be a bad idea.

I pushed the Talk button and Addie was back on the line. "Addie," I said, "don't worry. Chris and I are going over there and we'll see what's going on. Being careless seems to be a prerequisite of joining you Church Ladies."

"Beg pardon?" Addie said.

"Nothing, Sweetie, we'll take care of things. Don't you worry."

Chris and I left shortly after that. I vowed to start keeping a spare set of clothing in my office for these unexpected occasions. If anything happened to my dress someone was going to be in deep doo doo, to coin one of my son's phrases.

"Don't those women have a lick of sense?" Chris asked.

"You already asked that," I said.

"You never answered me."

"Oh. The main thing now is that we need to get over there in a hurry. There's no telling what kind of trouble the Church Ladies can get into, or stir up."

When we neared Victor's house, Chris slowed down so we could take a look around and try to figure out what was going on. We could see Jasmine's car parked in Florence's driveway, but there were no lights on in the house.

Chris parked a few houses down and we walked toward Florence's place.

The wind had begun to blow, suddenly and with gusto. Glancing up I saw clouds overhead. I looked down at my dress and sighed. A floor length, fragile lace dress had been the wrong choice for this evening.

Wind, possible rain, and a bunch of Church Ladies might be the demise of my lacey choice.

I turned toward Florence's house and saw the blonde head of Jasmine Thorpe pop up from behind her car. By this time Chris was standing next to me. I put my hand on his arm and pointed.

"There's Jasmine," I said, quietly, moving as close to his ear as I could. "I wonder where the others are."

CHAPTER THIRTY-TWO

It didn't take long to find out where the other Church Ladies were. Lila stepped out from behind the car. The wind made her short dark blonde hair stand on end and whipped her gray shapeless old-lady dress around her knees. She'd reverted back to her old style for the evening. Her white tennis shoes stood out in the light from the streetlamp.

May pulled a rubber band out of her pocket and pushed back her long, thick salt and pepper hair, and forming a ponytail, she banded it. "This darned wind is blowing my hair in my eyes."

So much for being sneaky. We were a few houses away and I could clearly hear what she said.

"Shhhh," Jasmine warned. I saw her put her index finger to her lips.

There was a mature mesquite tree with drooping branches at the front of Florence's yard, and the ladies headed for the tree. Watching them, I could see that they thought it would offer cover from prying eyes.

Chris took a step forward, but I kept him from approaching them. "Let's wait for a minute and see what they're up to," I suggested.

There was a flash of lightning, followed in a moment by rumbling thunder.

The ladies now stood behind the tree, trying to watch Victor's house through the limbs. The wind blew a branch and it slapped May in the face. She slapped it back. So much for fear.

There was a light on in Victor's house and I could see his silhouette through the window.

"Let's get back in the car," I said. "We can watch out for them without them knowing we're here."

"Why shouldn't we let them know we're here?" Chris asked, impatiently.

"They're trying to do their part. We should let them be unless we see things getting out of hand. This is probably the most excitement they've ever had."

I figured Chris probably thought I was nuts, and I was absolutely sure he thought the Church Ladies were crazy, but he complied, more or less. "We can't get back in the car or the dome lights will come on."

"So we'll stand behind it."

We moved quietly to the rear of the black jeep. It was so dark out that I was sure they wouldn't see us.

There was more lightning and thunder, and Chris stepped from behind the car. "We have to get them out of there," he said. "Standing under that tree is the worst place they could be right now with all this lightning."

"I hadn't thought of that. You're right."

The wind blew harder. I pulled up the skirt of my dress so it wouldn't drag on the ground and ran toward the ladies.

"Well, we wondered when you two would join us," Jasmine said. "Were you going to hide behind your car all night?"

"Get away from this tree," Chris ordered, pulling on Jasmine's arm. "Are you nuts or something?"

Jasmine turned large and surprised eyes toward Chris.

"We're in the middle of a storm, and you're standing under a tree," he said. "Do you want to be hit by lightning?"

"Oh," she cried out, jumping back.

The other ladies followed suit, and the lights came on in Florence's house.

"*What's going on out there?*" Florence hollered, not sounding at all timid. "*What are you people doing? Get out of my yard.*"

"*It's us,*" Jasmine yelled. "*Can we come in?*"

"*Jasmine? Is that you?*"

We all trudged toward the porch and the front door. Florence opened it and stepped back, waiting for us to enter.

"What a fiasco *this* turned out to be," May said.

"Total chaos," Lila commented.

"Hardly worth the effort," added Jasmine.

We walked into Florence's house and she closed the door behind us. "What are you folks up to?" she asked again, this time sounding suspicious.

"I think it's time we come clean with her," I said. "Someone has threatened to harm Victor, and the ladies were trying to keep an eye on him."

"Oh, that," Florence said, sounding like this was old news. "He told me about it. He said you think someone is out to hurt him, but he assured me it's not true. He thought you might end up saying something to me, and he didn't want me to be shocked."

He hadn't wanted to worry his elderly neighbor. Maybe he wasn't so bad. He'd been helping her with her paperwork, and he tried to watch out for her. He hadn't wanted Florence to worry. He ran errands for her, and took her to doctors' appointments. Could it actually be her family who was after him? Had he overstepped his bounds that much? Could her family be as crazy as everyone else we'd come into contact with so far? My feelings about Victor kept flipping one way and then flopping the other way.

I glanced at Chris and I could see that the wheels were turning. I wondered if he was thinking the same things I was.

Before we could give it anymore thought, we heard a car engine followed by a loud crash from across the street. Chris ran to the door.

"Stay here," he said. "I'll be back." He ran out the door and stopped beside the mesquite tree to scope things out before heading to Victor's house. He moved away quickly when there was another bolt of lightning in the sky. We watched him through the window.

"What was that noise?" Florence asked.

"I don't know. Chris is going to find out. It sounded like it came from Victor's house," I said.

"Oh, well Victor isn't home. This is his bowling night." Florence pulled her robe tighter around her. "Are you sure you people should be poking around in his business?"

"We honestly believe he might be in danger," I replied. "He doesn't believe us, but I'd rather err on the side of caution than let something happen to him."

"My, my. I haven't heard that expression in a long time – err on the side of caution. Well, I suppose you're right. I wouldn't like to see anything happen to him. Do what you think is best, but the only person I can think of who doesn't like him is my nephew."

She didn't seem to grasp the full weight of the situation. Victor had convinced her that he was okay and not in trouble, and she was going to take his word for it. And now we knew that she had a nephew who didn't like Victor. Finally! A suspect. I'd have to be careful with my questions.

"A nephew? Why doesn't he like… What's your nephew's name?"

"Wade. Wade Smiley. He's a good man, just not very trusting."

That name was familiar. Where had I heard it before? I'd have to ask Chris if he recognized it.

"Okay, so why doesn't Wade like Victor?"

"He believes Victor has tried to take his place in my life, but Wade doesn't come over here that often anyway. And I do need someone to help me. Wade had his chance, and he didn't help. He always used his job as an excuse. And Victor has become like a son to me. He's always Johnny-on-the-spot when I need him."

Okay, so there was plenty of reason for jealousy. But there had to be more to it than that.

My thoughts were interrupted by Chris's return. The wind had blown his hat off and he carried it in his hand. Pulling his cell phone out of his pocket, he opened it.

"Who're you calling?" I asked.

"What happened over there?" Jasmine asked.

"Is there trouble?" May inquired.

"What?" Lila kept it to one word.

"Someone threw something through Victor's window, or maybe they shot it out. I don't know, but I'm calling the police. It doesn't look like Victor is home."

"He's not," I said. "It's his bowling night."

"Uh huh." Chris walked out on the porch with the phone to talk to the coppers.

"What happened to your husband's head?" Florence asked.

"Someone hit him last night," I replied.

"Do you mean he was in an automobile accident?"

"No, Ma'am, I mean someone snuck up behind him and struck him on the back of the head." I'd decided it was time to come clean with Florence. She was in danger, too, just from being in the proximity of Victor. She needed to open her eyes and see what was really going on before she ended up hurt – or worse. She'd seemed like a feeble old woman, but I was seeing a different side to her tonight. Maybe we'd awakened her and she was cranky. No matter what the reason was, I had a feeling she could handle whatever we threw at her.

I heard a car engine and peeked out the window. Victor was pulling into his driveway, and Chris was walking across the street to meet him. The wind was howling and I saw Chris trying to keep his hat on his head. It looked like a losing battle to me.

Turning around, I saw Florence take a look at her clock. "Well, Victor is a bit later than usual tonight. If someone really threw something through his window, it's probably a good thing. He doesn't need things that upset him in his life. He told me so."

Good grief! This woman just didn't get it. Victor had enough stress for four men with someone trying to kill him. I rolled my eyes. Of course! Tonight was the night. Someone thought they'd shoot at his house and kill him. It would look like a drive-by random killing. Wait a minute. I'd seen Victor sitting in front of his window.

"I'm thoroughly confused," I said, to no one in particular.

"About what, Dear?" Lila asked.

"About who was sitting inside of Victor's house."

"Oh, that's what we thought at first, too," Jasmine said. "But from our vantage point we could see that it was something sitting on the table in front of the window, although it did resemble a person if you didn't look closely."

Apparently the killer hadn't looked very closely.

"Would you all like some tea?" Florence asked, not sounding the least bit flustered.

CHAPTER THIRTY-THREE

hris returned from talking to Victor and said we should be leaving. "His copper friend is on his way over, and it's about to start raining. It looks ugly out there, and I know you don't want to ruin your glad rags. We'd better hit the bricks."

Turning to the Church Ladies, I raised my eyebrows at them. "Would you like us to follow you home? You don't want to be driving by yourself in the rain."

"Oh, no. We'll just wait until it stops. We'll have some tea with Florence," Jasmine said. She turned a look on the other ladies that I couldn't read, but I had a feeling she was up to something.

As we pulled away from the curb, a police cruiser parked in front of Victor's house. He met them on the porch and they followed him inside.

And the rain came – in buckets, or so it seemed. It poured so hard that we had to pull over and wait until it let up before we headed home, which felt like an hour but was probably two minutes.

"Chris, does the name Wade Smiley sound familiar?"

"Yeah, why?"

"Who is he? I know I've heard the name somewhere."

"He's the mall copper. Why do you ask, Cupcake?"

"Uh oh. I think we have a connection, although I'm not real clear on it. Wade Smiley is Florence's nephew, and he doesn't like Victor."

Chris took a quick look at me and turned back to the road. "Now ain't that something? Think about it. Smiley had access to Jackson at the mall. That could be why Jackson kept showing up there. It would have been a convenient meeting place. Maybe *Smiley* hired Jackson to bump Victor off. And maybe Jackson tried to double cross Smiley. I know mall coppers don't carry gats, but that doesn't mean Smiley doesn't have one. This opens up all sorts of new possibilities."

"Doesn't it though? And another interesting fact. Florence believes everything that Victor tells her. He told her about someone trying to hurt him, but he said it wasn't true. Is he trying to spare her or is there something else going on? Could he suspect her nephew? And you're right, Smiley could have a gun."

Chris turned and glanced at me again. "There's just one thing, and you're going to think I've got bats in the belfry, but I don't think it's Smiley."

"Why *not*?" I asked. It all made perfect sense to me.

"Because I like him. My gut says he didn't know Jackson. I've got him pegged as more of a cream puff than a hard case. He really seemed clueless about what was going on and why."

"Your gut's been wrong before, Bogey Man. This makes too much sense to me, even if it doesn't to you. How many times have you heard the neighbors interviewed on TV after a crime and they say that the killer was such a good person, always there to help anyone who needed it? They're shocked that he's committed a crime of *any* type."

"Good point, but all the same, I'd need some strong proof." Chris was being stubborn about Wade Smiley, and that was unusual. He was generally ready to listen to all sides of a situation.

I didn't want to burst his bubble, but this wasn't the time for him to dig his heels in. "Chris, think about it. There hasn't been anyone else that's made a good suspect. In fact, there hasn't *been* anyone else involved in this."

"Pamela, I can't help the way I feel. I just don't see it."

"Okay, I guess we'll have to agree to disagree and look for some evidence to prove which one of us is right."

"And how do you think we're going to find that kind of evidence?"

"We'll follow Wade for a few days. We'll see where he goes and what he does, and we'll see if he goes anywhere near Victor, other than to visit his aunt. But from what I understand, he very rarely stops to see her."

Chris and I didn't talk about it anymore, each of us lost in our own thoughts.

"I think… Never mind," I said. I didn't want to voice suppositions, just facts.

We drove past the restaurant and saw that it had been closed for the night. Nothing looked out of order, so we drove over to Constance's house and picked Mikey up. As usual, he slept in the car all the way home. Chris carried him up to his bed and tucked him in before going outside to check on the dogs. They were huddled under the table on the patio, waiting out the storm. Chris brought them in and left them on the back porch.

We were both tired and headed straight for the bedroom. I took off my lace dress and gently hung it in the closet, saying a thank you that it hadn't been damaged. It was only a dress, but it was important to me.

***

We'd had a long and tiring week, and it felt good to sleep in. Mikey finally came in and woke us up.

"I fed the dogs and cleaned up their stuff out in the yard. Are you going to fix breakfast this morning or can I go ahead and have cereal?"

Bleary-eyed, I glanced up at him from under the covers. "Give me a few minutes and I'll get up."

Chris climbed out of bed. "You stay here and rest, Babe. Ace and I will make breakfast for you for a change. Is that okay with you, kid?" He looked Mikey in the eye, sending a message.

"Sure, Dad. That'll be fun. You just stay right here, Mom. We'll take care of you this morning."

"Bless you," I said, turning over and closing my eyes.

Forty-five minutes later Sherlock and Watson bounded in and jumped up on the bed, waking me up completely. "Stop slobbering on me," I said, pushing Sherlock away. Watson immediately took his place and licked my cheek. I sat up and pushed her away, too.

Forcing myself to stand up, I made my way to the closet and fished out a shirt and a pair of jeans. I had to do a little jig while I dressed because Watson kept trying to lick my feet.

"Would you please stop that?" I said, once again pushing her away.

"Mom," Mikey called, from the bottom of the stairs. "Come and get it."

I trudged down the stairs feeling like my head was full of cobwebs. One look at the kitchen and my head cleared – a little.

"I'm shocked," I said, smiling. "You haven't burned the house down and the kitchen is relatively clean. How did you manage that?"

"Organization," Mikey said. I knew that he'd gotten that word from Chris. My husband liked organization with everything right where it should be.

"Oh, I see." I gave him a hug. "And what are we having for breakfast?"

"Bacon and eggs, and toast and grits," Chris replied.

Chris and Mikey set all the plates on the table and told me to help myself. I did. I hadn't realized how hungry I was until I saw the food in front of me.

"So, Mom," Mikey said, after eating a few bites. "Me and dad have been talking about your situation, and we've got some ideas."

"My situation?" Uh oh, this didn't sound good.

"Yeah, that you don't trust dad's judgment. He thinks the bad guy didn't do it, and you think he did."

"If he didn't do it, or isn't planning on doing it, then how can he be the bad guy?" I took a bite of eggs.

Mikey frowned. "You know what I mean. He's a *possible* bad guy."

"Ah, I see. So you and your father have been discussing our current case?" I turned a meaningful glance in Chris's direction.

"Mikey's mind isn't as cluttered as ours are," he said. "Without going into too much detail, I laid out some of the facts for him. I wanted to get his take on things."

"Okay, and what do you think, Son?" I asked.

He sat up straight, knowing that his opinion mattered to us, and his face was as serious as I'd ever seen it. "I think that this all has to do with the old lady that lives by Victor. It seems like everything leads back to her, at least from what my dad told me. But, Mom, I would definitely trust dad's ideas about the mall copper."

He folded his left arm across his lower chest and rested his right elbow on that hand, with his right hand up to his mouth. He looked at the ceiling and appeared very contemplative, and as worldly as any seven-year-old can.

"Is there more?" I asked.

"Yes, I think your idea about following the copper is a good one. Can I come along?"

"No," I said. "The last thing I want is to put you in danger, and since we don't really know what's going on, it could come from anywhere."

"Aww, Mom. Let me come."

"Nope," Chris said. "Your mother is right. And it's too late to follow him today anyway."

Before the discussion could go any further, the doorbell rang. Mikey and the dogs ran for the door, and before my son opened it I heard him tell the dogs to *sit* and *stay*. He waited until they were calm before opening the door.

"Oh, hi," Mikey said, sweetly. "My mother is in the kitchen. I know she'll be happy to see you." He was speaking louder than necessary.

Chris and I looked at each other, not knowing what to expect.

The Church Ladies trooped into the kitchen with the dogs following behind them. I should have known.

"God bless you and good morning," Jasmine said, sounding almost too cheerful.

"Well, God bless you, too," I said. "What's got you ladies out and about this morning?"

"Oh, we've got things to tell you," Lila said.

"Interesting stuff," May explained.

"Things that might surprise you," Jasmine added.

"Have a seat, ladies," Chris said, pulling out chairs and removing dirty plates from the table. "Give me a minute and I'll bring you some Joe."

"I'll talk while you take care of the coffee," Jasmine said. She looked like she was about to burst. Her information was important.

"What's going on?" I asked.

"We stayed and talked to Florence last night, as you know. After the police left Victor's house he came over to see what was going on. It was out of the ordinary for Florence to be up that late. He was kind of rude to us, saying that we should let Florence get her rest."

"Well," May said, picking up the story, "Florence didn't like that. She told him that we are her friends and we can come over any time we want to."

"He gave us all a dirty look," Lila said, "and then he left. I think he was upset with Florence. She was upset, too, and said it wasn't any of his business whom she had over or when they were there. She seemed to think he was overstepping his bounds."

"She became very talkative after that," Jasmine said. "We learned a number of things, and I... Actually, it was all four of us who came to some conclusions."

"All four of you?" Chris asked. "You mean that Florence had some ideas?"

"No. I'm talking about Addie. We talked everything over this morning, and we've decided that this whole thing with Victor has to do with Florence."

"Told you so, Mom." We all turned to find Mikey standing in the doorway to the kitchen.

"Why don't you put the dogs outside?" I asked. "I don't want them bothering the ladies."

"Oh, they're fine," Lila said. "I'm getting used to them. They make me feel kind of safe."

Watson sat down directly in front of Lila, which made her smile. "See? They know I'm not so afraid anymore."

"What did your son mean when he said he'd told you so?" May asked.

"Yes, what was that about?" Jasmine's curiosity showed on her face.

Lila glanced up but didn't say anything. She was too busy petting Watson, and Sherlock had sidled over expecting to receive some of the affection.

"We've been discussing Victor and Florence this morning. Chris asked Mikey for his opinion and he believes that this is all about Florence."

CHAPTER THIRTY-FOUR

"We think Mikey is right," Jasmine said. "We really did learn a lot about Florence last night. For instance, Florence has money, but she says no one knows that, except maybe her nephew. On top of the life insurance and retirement funds from her husband, her aunt left her a very large sum of money many years ago."

"She and her husband started buying rental properties when they were still relatively young," May added, "and Florence started selling them off not long after her husband died, God rest his soul. She didn't want the responsibility anymore. Florence is a lot more savvy than anyone gives her credit for."

Lila held her hand in the air like a school child. "She and her husband bought her house when they were newly married. When they moved into a newer and bigger house, they rented out the one she's living in now. That's what made them start thinking about buying up rental properties. After her husband died, she moved back into the old house because it held so many good memories."

"You ladies are pretty savvy yourselves," Chris said. "How did you get her to spill the beans?"

"It was just girl talk, plus she wasn't very happy with Victor for being rude to us," Jasmine said. "And there's more."

"What else did you find out?" I asked.

"We mentioned Victor's retired policeman friend," Lila said.

May had one eye half closed, looking very suspicious. "Florence said she hasn't seen anyone visit Victor except for us. So what does this policeman do? Sneak in the back window?"

"So now we have even more possibilities," I said. "Florence's nephew obviously knows she has money, and he probably figures Victor is after it. He wants to get rid of his competition. That money should rightfully be his in his opinion."

"What about the retired copper, Mom?" Mike asked. "How come Victor made him up?"

I turned to my son. "I have a feeling that Victor knows something about the money, and when there's money involved, people do all kinds of stupid things. He probably figured he could handle it on his own, and maybe he hoped we'd butt out."

"I get that," Mikey said.

"Chris, what do you think?" I asked.

"I think I'm going to talk to Smiley. I still don't believe it's him, but he's the only suspect we've got."

"No, Chris, that could be dangerous. After all, he's already killed once." What was my husband thinking? "I'm going to call and talk to Janet. She's working on Jackson's murder. I'll ask if there's any indication that the killer could have been Wade Smiley."

"You do that, Sweetie, but in the meantime I'm going to call Smiley and set up a meeting with him."

Jasmine turned to her friends. "Oh my, I think we've caused more trouble instead of helping."

"No, you did the right thing," Chris said. "We needed this information. It explains why this whole thing might be about Florence."

Sherlock and Watson began nudging Lila's hand. She'd been listening to us instead of scratching the dogs.

"Mikey, why don't you take the dogs outside now? Get them a couple of cookies and they'll follow you anywhere."

He smiled and did as I asked. The dogs gave Lila one last look and followed the food.

"They do like their treats," she said.

"That they do," I replied.

"Why don't you ladies come to the restaurant for dinner tonight, and Lila, you don't even have to sing. We'll plan on a late dinner, if you don't mind, and that way Chris and Mikey and I can join you."

Lila grinned at me.

"We should know more by then, and at this point I'll feel better having everyone where I can see them. We'll talk after the restaurant closes."

"You mean I get to come, too?" Mikey asked.

"You bet, Ace," Chris replied. "We can set you up in the office if you get sleepy. That couch is pretty comfortable. I've used it a few times myself when we were working late. And we'll bring the dogs along to keep you company. I know how bored you are sometimes at the restaurant."

Jasmine held her hand out toward Lila. "What about your date with Nate?"

Lila appeared dismayed and thoughtful at the same time, and I wondered if she'd forgotten about the date. Inside, my heart did a little tap dance to know that these two people were going to continue seeing each other. I waited, wondering what kind of a decision she'd make.

"Nate can join us," she said. "I'd like my friends to meet him, and this is social so it will be comfortable for all of us."

Jasmine and May turned to their friend with expressions I couldn't read. I found myself holding my breath. Would these women be accepting, or would they feel that Nate was an interloper, ruining their Church Lady group? The two women smiled at the same time, almost as though they'd planned it.

"We can't wait to meet the man who it appears has stolen our Lila's heart," Jasmine said.

"Ditto," May added. "He must be a good man, knowing how picky you would be when it comes to men."

I released my breath and contemplated what good and loving women these ladies were.

Chris and Mikey had silently crept out of the kitchen, not wanting to be a part of this budding romance. My mind's eye could see Chris shaking his head and rolling his eyes at our son. I chuckled.

"What's funny?" Jasmine asked.

"Nothing. I'm just happy," I said.

"Oh, that's so very Christian," May said. "Feeling joy on someone else's behalf is such a good feeling."

"Well, bless your heart," Jasmine added.

Lila simply sat and grinned at all of us.

The ladies left, saying they wanted to go shopping for some vintage dresses. They wanted Addie to go with them and asked if it would be safe.

I assured them that going to the vintage dress shop would likely be about as safe of a trip as they could take.

I tried to call Janet, but she was out of the office. I left her a message, including Wade's relationship to Victor's neighbor, and asked her to call me back.

Chris's headache had disappeared so he and Mikey did a little cleanup in the backyard. I putzed around the house until it was time to change clothes. Remembering that I wanted to keep some casual clothes at the restaurant, I pulled a t-shirt and an extra pair of jeans out of the drawer, and then I added a pair of socks and tennis shoes to the pile.

Chris came upstairs and changed into his suit before going to Mikey's room to help him pick something out. I waited until he was out of the room to change clothes.

There was only one other dress that I liked as much as the lacey one, and I decided I'd wear it because this felt like an occasion with everyone coming to the restaurant.

I'd found an old pattern and paid Susan to make it for me. It was reminiscent of the thirties styles. In a midnight blue satin, it fell gently to the floor while hugging my figure in all the right places, and it had puffed lace and satin sleeves. The back was extremely low, and it fit perfectly since it had been custom-made.

I wore my hair down, letting it fall in soft waves, with a right-hand part and the front brushed to the side.

Chris and Mikey hadn't seen the dress yet and I wondered what their reaction would be. I felt like an auburn-haired bombshell in it.

Coming down the stairs, I could hear Chris and Mikey talking in the kitchen. I tried to make a dramatic entrance into the room, coming around the corner with a flair, but the dogs had other ideas and ran to meet me, which caused me to trip over my own feet. I caught myself by grabbing the door jam.

"No," I said, sternly. "Don't come near me. I don't want any dog hair or slobber on this number. Keep away!" I held my hands up in the *stop* command. My dopey dogs stopped short and sat and grinned at me. Of course, I grabbed two cookies and bent over to hand them out, telling the dogs what good babies they were.

I stood up and finally paid attention to Chris and Mikey.

"You're a vision, Angel," Chris said. "That number could have been made for you."

"It was," I replied, smiling. "Susan made it for me."

"Remind me to thank her." Chris walked up to me and gave me the once over, very clearly telling me how much he appreciated what he was seeing.

"Don't forget that Mikey's in the room," I whispered.

"Oh. Yeah." Chris stepped back.

"You look great, Mom! I didn't know you had it in you."

I raised my eyebrows. Mikey didn't always understand the things he said, he just knew that what he was saying *might* fit the occasion.

"Okay, let's get going. We've got plenty of people to feed tonight." I picked up a silver satin clutch bag I'd bought to go with the dress and headed for the door. "You boys get the dogs settled in the car before I come out. I really don't want them to ruin this dress."

I'd hoped that Janet would call me back before we left, but I didn't hear from her.

We took the green Chevy to the restaurant. Chris thought it was appropriate for the way we looked. I really did get a kick out of him and his vintage car, suit, fedora and everything else he could work into the scheme of vintage things.

***

It turned out to be a perfect evening. Chef Luis and Phillip outdid themselves and everyone raved about the food. For some unknown reason the music sounded even sweeter than usual. People danced and enjoyed themselves.

Jasmine, May and Addie arrived at about eight-thirty, and Lila walked in with Nate shortly after I'd seated the ladies. Chris walked them back to the table, returning with the comment that poor Nate looked like he was headed to a hanging.

I checked on everyone after about fifteen minutes, and it appeared that he'd made quite an impression on the Church Ladies already. They were chatting and smiling, and he seemed to be enjoying himself. Apparently the hanging had been cancelled.

Mikey helped out wherever he could, and finally went outside to see the dogs. I had to call him in for dinner when Chris and I took a break to sit with our friends. Luis had given him a snack earlier to hold him over.

I was so pleased with Chef Luis and Phillip that after dinner I made a point of sticking my head in the kitchen to tell them how wonderful I thought they were. Everyone had ordered a different dish, and each had been cooked to perfection.

Mikey retired to my office with the dogs, ready to lie down on the couch. They were good company for him.

The restaurant finally closed and the staff went home. I looked around at my friends knowing that it was time to get down to business. I'd never heard back from Janet, and I didn't know if Chris had heard back from Wade Smiley or not. I hadn't had a chance to ask him about it.

"Why don't we go talk in the kitchen," I suggested. "Luis said he left some dessert for us." I felt like our group was close enough and casual enough that we didn't have to keep things on a formal level.

We were headed for the kitchen when a loud knock came from the front door of the restaurant.

"I'll get rid of whoever it is and catch up in a minute," Chris said.

I nodded and we continued on our way to the kitchen.

CHAPTER THIRTY-FIVE

Luis had left us a Chocolate Ganache cake. The ganache is basically chocolate mixed with heavy cream which cushions the texture and flavor of the chocolate. It's one of my favorite chocolates.

Before I could start cutting pieces for everyone I heard Chris coming toward the kitchen, and he was talking to someone. I hoped it might be Janet getting back to us, but when I turned around I found Chris and Wade Smiley standing in the doorway – Smiley appeared to be quite angry. My stomach lurched. Had I been right about him?

He looked at each of us in turn. "I am *not* trying to murder Victor Rogers," he said, adamantly. "That guy may be scum, and he might even deserve to die, but I'm not a killer!"

He stepped into the kitchen and I noticed that everyone took a step backward. I was standing behind the counter and didn't move. His anger was almost palpable.

"Chris told you what's going on?" I asked.

"He did, and I'm here to tell you that I've seen a lawyer to try to keep Victor from stealing Aunt Flo's money, and that's about as vicious as I get. And, no, I didn't know John Jackson. Whether you believe me or not, I didn't know him. It was a coincidence that he was murdered in the mall parking lot."

He stopped talking and watched each of us in turn, apparently trying to decide if we believed him or not. I thought about it and realized that I did believe he was telling the truth.

"So, then, who's trying to kill Victor?" I asked of no one in particular.

"That's the million dollar question," Wade said. "I'd like to know the answer to that one myself."

"Want some cake?" I asked, sounding as lame as I felt.

"No. I just wanted to clear the air. Now I'm heading home. I got off work and drove straight over here, hoping you'd still be open. I saw the lights on and knew someone was here."

"I'm sorry, man," Chris said. "We had to know. It was too much when we found out you were related to Florence."

"I guess I understand," he replied. "At least I know that someone is keeping an eye on her. When Victor started kissing up to her she sent me packing. No matter what I said, she took it wrong. That guy has some guts to try to move in on my aunt. Everyone in the family is upset. My sisters are the ones who talked me into going to see an attorney. Aunt Flo won't even talk to them because they tried to tell her that things about Victor didn't seem to add up."

"I'm sorry, too," I said. "I had no idea how bad things are. But it still doesn't answer our burning question. Who wants to kill Victor?"

I felt something touch my leg and I looked down. Mikey had crept out of the office to see what was going on. He was crouched behind the counter.

"Where are the dogs?" I asked.

Standing up, he turned and looked back toward the office. The dogs were sitting in the doorway. They appeared to be on the alert, as though they sensed the tension, but they didn't seem intent on protecting us. It was a small thing, but I decided to trust their judgment. I decided they could just stay where they were for the moment.

"Okay," Wade said, "I'm outta here. I need some sleep before tomorrow's shift."

The Church Ladies had never said a word while we talked, and as Wade left the room I heard Jasmine say, "Ladies, it's time to pray. That young man needs some help. I could hear the tension in his voice, and he's got his hands full with Florence's attitude toward him."

While the ladies prayed I served up the cake. I needed to think. Maybe *I* needed some divine guidance.

Chris had walked out with Wade while I put the cake in the refrigerator. It wouldn't be served again at the restaurant, but I didn't want it sitting out. One of our employees could take it home the next day.

"Oh, for crying out loud," I said, turning to Addie and wondering just when I'd become so clueless. "I should have just asked you. Was that the man you saw with Jackson?"

"No, that wasn't him."

"Uh, Pamela?" Chris stood in the doorway to the kitchen with Wade.

"Yes?"

Someone walked up behind the two men and pushed them into the room. When they moved out of the way I saw Victor standing in the doorway with a gun in his hand. He moved forward and stood next to a cart that held containers of silverware and napkins.

"Victor?" I was incredulous, staring at the gun. "What's going on?"

The ladies began chattering and believe me, they sounded nervous.

"Shut up," Victor ordered. "I don't want to hear a word out of anyone."

My first thought after seeing Victor was of my son. I had to protect him. Frantically, I started looking around for him. He'd ducked back down behind the counter. I motioned for him to stay there.

Addie had moved to my other side. "That's him," she said. "That's the man."

Chris looked at her. "*The* man?" he asked.

She nodded.

"I don't get it," I said. "How can you be the killer when you're supposed to be the victim?"

"I was never the victim. Florence is the one who's going to die. Now shut up!"

How much money did Florence *have?* Was it worth all of this? She must be loaded.

"There's going to be a robbery here tonight. When the robber breaks in, he's going to find all of you here, and there's going to be a blood bath. He'll be able to make eight notches in his gun handle tomorrow."

I mentally counted. There were eight of us. Victor hadn't seen Mikey, which would have made nine. The dogs had moved up and were sitting beside the counter. I motioned for them to stay.

"Oh, yeah, and two dead dogs." Victor didn't miss a thing, except my son. He motioned for Chris and Wade to move over by the rest of us.

"Ladies," Jasmine said, "it's time to pray for this man's soul."

Addie moved away from me and stood by her friends.

They each lowered their head and began praying.

"Shut the hell up," Victor said.

They ignored him and finished their prayer, ending with a request for forgiveness for Victor.

Victor scowled. "It's time. You've made this much harder for me than it had to be. I think it's going to be a pleasure to put a bullet in each one of you."

"Who is this guy?" Nate asked. He was standing at the other end of the counter with a piece of cake sitting in front of him, his fork still held in the air. Of course, he had no idea what was going on. He was new to our little group.

"Your worst nightmare come true," Victor said, turning to look at Nate.

I saw Mikey's hand come up and over the counter. He grabbed a handful of doggie cookies. What was he doing? What if Victor saw him? He squatted down again.

Chris walked over and, taking hold of my shoulders, moved me behind him, trying to protect me.

I heard an odd noise and saw a cookie slide across the floor and land near Victor's feet. Chris reached back and squeezed my arm. I knew he'd seen it, too. I didn't want to give Mikey away by glancing down at him. What was he up to? With my hand at my side, I motioned for him to stop it.

Trying to stall, I asked, "Why does Florence have to die? She thinks of you like a son."

"That she does. In fact, I'm so much like a son to her that she wrote a new will. She's leaving her entire estate to me."

He looked at Wade and sneered. "You're out and I'm in," he said.

"Sometimes you have to draw a line in the sand," Wade said, taking a step forward. "Killing a sweet little old lady who never did anyone any harm is where I draw the line."

"Amen to that," May said, emphatically, grabbing Wade's arm and pulling him back.

Lila stepped forward, fists clenched at her sides. "Just try something, buddy, and see what a bunch of old ladies can do. Well, four old ladies and an old man, and Chris. And Pamela. And Florence's kin. You're outnumbered, Mister."

Victor laughed. "Yeah, I'm really scared."

"What about Jackson?" Chris asked. "Why'd you knock him off?"

"He got greedy. He wanted more than I'd offered him because he found out why I wanted ol' Flo to die."

I saw two more cookies slide across the floor while everyone was talking.

"No more questions. It's time for the robbery to take place. You old ladies want to pray before you go to meet your Maker?"

"You betcha," May said.

"*Shut up!* I didn't mean it." Victor shook his gun at May. He appeared angry, like he hadn't thought the Church Ladies would take him up on his offer.

"Father, you see what's going on here, and you know what's in all of our hearts," Jasmine said. "If this is our time, then take us Home. But if our work here isn't done, then my dear Lord, please do something. Make Victor drop his gun or something, but don't let him wave it at May."

"We're doing your work, Abba Father," May said. "Why just the other day, Lord, we talked to a prostitute and she's coming to church this Sunday. It's a shame we might not be there to greet her, Father, but Your will be done."

"But, Lord," Nate said, joining in, "I just met Lila. Are you sure it's time?" He took a step toward my end of the counter.

"*I said to shut it up!*" Victor yelled. A hint of confusion was beginning to show on his face. Were the ladies getting through to him? I doubted it, but...

Joining in, I said, "Yes, Lord. We're ready when You are."

Chris looked at us like we were *all* nuts. He didn't get it, but one day he would.

Mikey stood up, reaching for the container of doggie cookies on the counter. I tried to push him back down, but he stepped away from me.

"*Mikey!*" I cried, fear gripping me in bands of steel.

"Here, Mister, have a cookie." Mikey threw a doggie treat at Victor. What the heck was he doing?

"Knock it off, kid? *Stop that!* Where'd you come from anyway?"

Mikey shoved the container closer to Chris, who seemed to understand what was going on.

"Yeah," Chris said, tossing a cookie, "have a treat."

I glanced at the dogs and they were practically vibrating. They seemed to sense that something was wrong, but they weren't sure what it was because they kept seeing their doggie cookies flying across the room. Their only contact with Victor had been as a friend. They'd even received a treat at that meeting. I realized that people weren't the only ones who had conflicted feelings. And the light dawned on me, too. *Thank you, Lord*, I thought. *You do come through when I least expect it sometimes.*

"Yes, Victor, have a snack," I said, and threw another doggie cookie.

Jasmine, Lila, May and Florence stopped praying and just watched us.

"Oh, I understand," Lila said, grabbing a treat and throwing it. She handed one to Nate, who threw it at Victor's head.

"Stop throwing things at me or I'm shooting you all right now." Victor was not only confused, but so angry that he was practically frothing at the mouth. He aimed his gun at Chris, who never flinched.

I turned to the dogs. "Want a cookie? Go get it," I said softly.

Victor stood in the middle of several doggie treats. The dogs lunged, hitting him in the knees before he could react, and he hit the floor with a loud thud, cracking his head on the tile and knocking over the cart of silverware in the process. Knives, forks and spoons landed all around and on top of him, with the ones landing on the floor creating a loud clatter. Napkins fluttered through the air. His gun went off, harmlessly shooting a hole in the ceiling.

Have I ever mentioned how fast Labrador retrievers can be? Especially when food's involved? Trust me on this one. They only glanced at Victor while eating their treats as fast as they could.

The front door of the restaurant crashed open. I looked up to see Janet and another detective standing in the doorway with their guns drawn.

CHAPTER THIRTY-SIX

Chris, Wade and Nate descended on Victor like a pack of angry wolves. If Janet hadn't arrived when she did, I don't know what they would have done to him.

The next few minutes were total chaos. The dogs didn't know what to think and since they knew Janet, they went right to her, long tongues hanging out of the sides of their mouths, looking dopey as only a Lab can. After greeting her and doing a nervous doggie dance, they went back to their cookies.

Mikey started to cry, which surprised me because he'd been so brave through the whole fiasco. "I did it, Mom, I saved everyone."

Giving him a bear hug, I said, "That you did, Ace. You really did save everyone."

The tears didn't last long because before he could take another breath the Church Ladies had descended on him with hugs and grandmotherly kisses and God Bless Yous. I clung to his hand during his moment in the sun because… Well, because I loved him and he was smart enough to save us all, but mostly because things could have turned out so very differently. It would have killed me if anything had happened to my precious son.

Janet saw the gun, still held in Victor's hand, and took it from him before he could react.

"What's going on here?" she asked.

Victor tried to stand up and Chris gave him an angry look that caused him to stay where he was. Wade placed his foot on Victor's chest, and with a great effort, Nate sat down on his feet. Nate was no spring chicken, and getting down to floor level was no easy task.

"This is your killer," Chris said. "He's the one who bumped off John Jackson. They were partners."

Before he could say any more, everyone started talking at once.

Janet turned to her partner who already had the cuffs out and was heading for Victor. Janet nodded and her partner cuffed the killer and turned him over to two uniformed coppers who'd just walked in. Janet must have called for backup as soon as she heard the gunshot.

In all the excitement I hadn't even heard the sirens.

"One at a time," Janet said, loudly, waving her hands at us. "I can't understand what's going on if you all talk at once."

Mikey, as brave as he was trying to act, had walked over to me and clung to my hand, standing as close as he could. I patted him on the back and leaned over to say as many soothing words as I could think of, but my mind was in such a dither that it wasn't all that easy.

Chris held his hand up for silence. "I'll fill her in. Why don't you all go out to the tables and relax."

Yeah, like anyone could relax right now.

"I sure could use a glass of wine," Lila said.

"I think we all could," Jasmine replied. "Is it okay, Chris?"

"Sure. We'll be out in a minute. And take Mikey with you." He didn't want our son to hear everything that we were going to tell Janet.

"Do I have to, Dad?"

"Yes, Ace, you do. Some things aren't meant for a boy to hear."

Forcing myself to let go of Mikey's hand, I let Addie take his hand, and he reluctantly followed the ladies and Nate out to the lounge.

I stood with Chris while he told Janet the whole ugly story, from Addie climbing into the camper all the way to Victor showing up at *Bogey Nights* with a gun. Wade had stayed behind when the others left. He had a personal stake in the outcome of Janet's actions.

"So this guy wanted to murder his elderly neighbor for an inheritance. And you're her nephew?" She turned to Wade.

"Yes, I am. Maybe now I can talk some sense into her. I can't believe she fell for this guy's line of crap."

I glanced at the dogs. They were both lying on the floor, licking their paws and acting very contented.

"If it hadn't been for Mikey and the dogs, who knows what might have happened?" I said. "I'm sure Chris would have figured something out, but thanks to Mikey, Chris didn't have to take any wild chances."

"Honestly, Babe, that son of ours is crazy like a fox. *I* never would have thought to use the treats and the dogs to bring that bum down."

"You ain't just whistlin' Dixie." I smiled at my husband in agreement.

"Okay," Janet said. "I'll need to take formal statements from everyone.

This guy's going to be charged with murder, and probably attempted murder, and who knows what else? The D.A. should have a grand time with this one. This guy was after everyone from his neighbor to all of you." She swung her arm around indicating the entire restaurant, apparently figuring that would include all of us.

Janet stopped in the lounge to tell everyone about needing their statements, but said they could come in to the station the next day. By that time it was quite early on a Saturday morning, and our little group looked pretty bedraggled. After all, most of the adults were in their late seventies, and this would have been too much excitement for most people anyway. Mikey had fallen asleep in the booth with his head leaning on Addie's arm.

Nate had taken it upon himself to open a bottle of wine and everyone had a wine glass sitting in front of them.

He was sitting next to Lila. "My dear, you certainly don't lead a boring life. Tonight was the most excitement I've had since I was in the military. Is it always like this?"

Lila put her hand on Nate's arm. "Oh, no. Usually our lives are pretty dull. You just came along at the right time."

The *right* time? I wondered about that.

***

Florence and her family reconciled. The poor woman was shaken to her very core when she found out what Victor had planned for her. I hoped her family could handle what she was going through mentally because she wanted nothing to do with anyone except her family.

Even the Church Ladies were told to stay away. However, knowing Jasmine and the rest of the ladies, I knew they wouldn't let go. They'd wheedle and pray and push until Florence let them back in the fold. I knew in my heart that this would be a good thing. Wade had taken a liking to the women so I was certain he'd be singing their praises, too.

A month went by and *Bogey Nights* had started opening for lunch. Nate was working out very well and our patrons loved his cooking. Between him and Luis, we seemed to be attracting an even bigger crowd. We'd developed a reputation for outstanding cuisine. I suppose the notoriety we received because of Victor didn't hurt either. People have a natural morbid curiosity and they wanted to see the scene of the *almost* crime.

Donna, the waitress we'd hired from the diner, was working out we too. She seemed to enjoy working in the atmosphere that *Bogey Ni* offered. She said that even though she was working, she felt like sh attending a costume party several times a week.

Lila and Nate continued to see each other, and Lila sang at the restaurant one night a week. She also sang at church more often, and Nate had decided he liked her and her lifestyle. He had become a regular at church on Sunday mornings.

The Church Ladies? They continued to pray for anything and everyone, and Chris and I had developed a soft spot in our hearts for them. Although Lila spent time with Nate, she didn't desert her friends.

Constance, Mikey and I took to sitting in the row just behind the Church Ladies on Sunday mornings. We liked being close to them, and Constance even developed more tolerance for their pushy ways.

Addie finally went home and began to lose her fear of leaving the house, thanks to her friends. The Church Ladies wouldn't let her hang onto her fear. They prayed and they nagged and they made sure they took her places.

I had to laugh when Addie's neighbor, Elsie, showed up at church one Sunday. It just happened to be the same Sunday that the prostitute attended, and they struck up a friendship – kind of like grandmother and granddaughter, and they continued to come to church. Each one encouraged the other one.

Mikey is nothing, if not resilient. By the Monday after the incident, he couldn't wait to get to school to tell everyone about it. His teacher, Miss All, called to ask if any of what he said was true. I confirmed his story, and she decided to have him write a paper about what had happened and read it in front of the class, although she insisted he tone it down a bit. I was very surprised that she did that, and even more surprised that Mikey's paper was well-written. Maybe my son had an author buried deep inside of him. Of course, the story was filled with forties slang, which tended to give it a little humor. At my suggestion he played up the dogs' part in the whole thing, and played down the gun.

Chris told me he might consider going to church with me when Lila ˙ɒ again, but although she's been like a little canary, that hasn't ˙d yet.

˙ontinue to pray for him. I told him about their prayers and ˙ɒd.

END

ABOUT THE AUTHOR

Marja was born and raised in Southern California. She worked in both civil and criminal law for 15 years, state transportation for another 17 years, and most recently for a city building department. She has lived and worked in California, Nevada, Oregon, Alaska and Arizona.

McGraw also wrote a weekly column for a small town newspaper in Northern Nevada, and conducted a Writers' Support Group in Northern Arizona. A member of Sisters in Crime (SinC), she was also the Editor for the SinC-Internet Newsletter for a year and a half.

She has appeared on KOLO-TV in Reno, Nevada, and KLBC in Laughlin, Nevada, and various radio talk shows.

Marja says that each of her mysteries contains a little humor, a little romance and A Little Murder! Books include *Bogey Nights,* the first in the Bogey Man Mysteries, and it's soon to be joined by *Bogey's Ace in the Hole. A Well-Kept Family Secret, Bubba's Ghost, Prudy's Back!, The Bogey Man* and *Old Murders Never Die* are all part of the Sandi Webster series.

She and her husband now live in Arizona, where life is *good.*